MOON IN THE WATER

MOON IN THE WATER

STAN GORDON

Five Star • Waterville, Maine

First Edition
First Printing: July 2005

Published in 2005 in conjunction with Tekno Books and Ed Gorman.

Set in 11 pt. Plantin by Liana M. Walker.

Printed in the United States on permanent paper.

Library of Congress Cataloging-in-Publication Data

Gordon, Stan, 1942—
    Moon in the water / Stan Gordon.—1st ed.
      p. cm.
    ISBN 1-59414-118-5(hc : alk. paper)
    1. Lozen—Fiction. 2. Apache women—Fiction.
3. Women shamans—Fiction. 4. Women soldiers—Fiction.
5. Chiricahua women—Fiction. 6. Apache Indians—Wars,
1883–1886—Fiction. 7. Southwestern states—Fiction.
I. Title.
PS3607.O5945M66 2005
813′.6—dc22   2003065570

DEDICATION

This book is dedicated to oppressed people everywhere, who despite their suffering have the courage and spirit to keep on fighting.

ACKNOWLEDGEMENTS

Without the support of my dear friend and mentor Jane Candia Coleman, this book would never have been written. In addition, Adella C. Swift and Sara Buck, elders of the San Carlos Apache Tribe, were a monumental help to me in understanding the ways and traditions of the *In-déh,* The People, as was Herb Stevens, director of the reservation cultural center. I am extremely grateful for my wife Linda, who, in the four years it took me to complete this novel, was willing to play second fiddle to the other woman, Lozen.

AUTHOR'S NOTE

While based on a real person, this book is entirely a work of fiction. Although battle and action scenes are the work of my imagination, many incidents and historical events are true. Chronicled in Apache history are Lozen's Power Of The Blue Hands, and the killing of a longhorn steer with only a knife. I have endeavored to describe Apache culture as it was in the fifty-six years the story takes place. I hope you enjoy reading this high ride adventure of people, places and spiritual insights as much as I did in writing it.

APACHE TERMS
AND TIME FRAMES

Dai-a-dai: Feast of Maidens, the puberty rite

Enju: Good, well done

Indaa: White Eyes, whites

In-déh: The People

Nakaiyé: Mexicans

Nohwik'edandiihi: Enemy

Shichoo: Grandfather

Shimaa: Mother

Shiwóyé: Grandmother

Tchi-hénè: Red Paint People,
                      the Warm Springs Tribe

Usen: God, the Creator, Life Giver

Nantan: Chief

Yudaha: Navajo

Harvests: Years

Moons: Days, nights

PROLOGUE

Indian Territory, North of Santa Fe, 1830

Under the shade of a creosote bush, an Apache baby played with bird bones dangling from the canopy of her cradleboard, and sucked on a tiny gourd pacifier. It was early morning, and nearby, her mother and other women were harvesting broad-leafed yucca plants, dropping the pink fruit into baskets. "Soon, you will have a treat from these stalks here, daughter," Besh-a-taye said to her infant. "Tasty, sweet honey." At the sound of her mother's voice, Lozen kicked out excitedly with her feet.

As the morning lingered on, the women paused from their work to bury a fruit, a rite of renewal for the next year. They prayed, giving thanks for the food to *Gaun,* The Mountain Spirit. Suddenly, the hollow coo of a mourning dove sounded from the cliff above, followed by three more.

At the sentry's warning, Besh-a-taye dropped her fruit, seized the cradleboard and ran to where the horses were tethered. Others were already there, grabbing reins and mounting. "Hurry, hurry," someone whispered. "There is no time to waste."

Besh-a-taye jumped onto her horse's back, hoisted Lozen across her lap, and dug her heels into the pony's sides. She glanced back, caught a glimpse of white men on horseback, women running. She rode faster. There was a gunshot. A scream. More shots. Men yelling. She didn't have to look again to know that her people were being killed and scalped for blood money. As she topped a rocky incline, the cradleboard slipped. Besh-a-taye grabbed for it, but her hands were oily from the fruit, and she couldn't hold on. Her baby inside, it crashed to the ground.

She reined in her pony, vaulted off and ran to where the cradleboard lay on its side against a large boulder. The canopy was ripped to shreds, and she could see fragments of wood scattered about. Heart pounding, she kneeled and, as she carefully turned the *tosche* over, sighed a breath of relief. Lozen was still firmly laced in, and didn't have a scratch. Yet, there was something. Besh-a-taye's eyes went wide—Lozen's hands had turned blue! *Not from the fall,* she thought. *What, then?*

She picked up the gouged cradleboard, slipped her arms through the tump lines attached to the frame and put it onto her back. Her daughter would not fall again. Another yell sounded from behind and she ran to her horse. A hard gallop and she caught up to the others. When they were far away and out of danger, they stopped to rest and water the horses at a stream. Out of the twenty women on the harvest, fifteen had survived. Besh-a-taye took off the cradleboard, took her daughter from the buckskin lining inside and began nursing. In her panic to escape, she had forgotten about the baby's hands. Now, taking the tiny fingers in her own, she was relieved to see they had returned to their usual color.

Another half-day's ride and they entered their village at Ojo

Caliente, the home of the Warm Springs Tribe. Great chiefs, the ancestors of her people, had once lived there. Others would follow. Yet it would be the *shizhaazh'he*, the girl-child she now rocked gently, who would become the most revered of all, for only she would hold the Power Of The Blue Hands.

CHAPTER ONE

LESSONS

Not long after Lozen learned to walk, her father was killed on a raid outside Zacatecas, and her grandfather became Lesson Giver. "Get out there. Run in the cold and snow," he said, pushing her out of the warm tipi. "It will build confidence, strength and endurance. Without them, no Apache can survive." She stumbled and fell, but each day trotted a few more halting steps.

On her third birthday, her grandmother pierced her ears with the needle-like point from a pincushion *Nejapa*. "Do not yowl so loudly, granddaughter, the coyotes will come for you," the elder cautioned, putting small pieces of pinion wood through the tiny lobes.

When Lozen was old enough to understand the Way of the Ancestors, her mother took her down to the stream. After praying to the water, Besh-a-taye scooped up a handful and dashed it on Lozen's face. "When you were only in your second day, I did this to you, then put you in the cold stream.

You wailed, but after the second day, you stopped. You learned to endure, to be strong and quiet. Being silent like the mountain lion keeps an Apache alive, especially when enemies lurk."

Besh-a-taye gestured to the west. "All water is sacred, daughter. Not far from here is a lake. It is where all Apache life began, from Child Of The Water. Our *Tchi-hénè* ancestors were created out of that lake and lifted up onto the land. That is why water must be treated with reverence. Even when you drink from a creek or stream, a prayer is necessary." She gently kissed Lozen's nose. "Always use the water properly, with respect."

Her mother then taught her to braid with wild iris, and the bear and candy grasses that grew in abundance. Lozen especially enjoyed making colorful designs with the purple, white and yellow flowers of the *Dalea dalea,* laying out the silky patterns on dark animal skins. She and her friend Kinsee made dwellings from twigs and pieces of hides, and put their tiny buckskin dolls inside.

The girls loved to dance and, under leafy hats woven from blue aster, stepped to the drumming of their playmates, who beat with sticks on hollow logs. One of their favorite pastimes was to blow into a woody choisya shrub, clapping their hands in delight when it echoed back a fawn's cry. They hunted four-leafed clovers, and Lozen often won the game by being the first to find one.

By the time she was eight, Lozen had lost interest in the-way-of-the-girl-child, and spent her playtime running through dense woods and rolling hills, alongside the creeks that cut blue ribbons across broad grasslands. She longed for the playthings of the boys—willow sticks with pellets stuck on their muddy ends that they whipped at lizards, the small bows and snowberry arrows. Not a day passed that she didn't pester her grandfather.

"I can do what the boys do. Do it better. Teach me."

"Hah! You are a little girl who wants to be a big warrior, wear a tribute feather," he said, tousling her hair. At seventy winters, his arms were still sinewy with muscle, and his chest rose from his belly like a boulder. His left shoulder carried the battle scar of a lance, and he took a sip of horse nettle tea to calm the soreness that had increased with his years.

"I have run to the place where the white stallion lives and back in one moon, *shichoo*."

He had shadowed her on horseback that day, and knew she spoke the truth. When he was a boy, it had taken him two moons, a fact he didn't feel necessary to reveal. "Do it better, eh?" He nodded, and her wide smile brought a twinkle to his eyes.

On a sultry morning, he presented her with a shallow-curved maple bow painted black, and three stick-sharpened arrows with the bark peeled off. "Those birds and squirrels. You have to see them before they see you and run away." He curled his wizened fingers, moved them like a crawling spider. "When you spot game, go slowly, creep like a whisper. Watch for dry leaves and twigs that may crack underfoot. The smallest stones rolling downhill will alert an animal. Tread carefully. Hunt cautiously."

He drew a circle in the earth, and inside that, another. "When I was a boy, I went swimming and left my shirt on the bank. That night I had swollen sores on my chest and back. My mother took me to see Medicine Woman. She looked me over, drew circles like these. She said the sores were round, like a coiled snake, and told us one had rested inside my shirt." He waved his hand. "Snakes are evil; stay away from them. Do not eat the small, wild pigs. Like eagles, they eat snakes."

15

A motionless black hunter stood on a nearby crag, and he gestured at it. "Beware of Crow. Its feathers bring great sickness. Never hunt or touch them, or Owl. If you shoot at him, the vicious and bad will rise from the dead and feast on your blood."

Lozen's first targets were trees, and a rawhide animal her grandmother had made. When she could bunch three arrows dead center, she practiced stealth, crawling along the ground on her stomach and elbows, as her grandfather had shown her. But time after time her prey escaped, and she began to wonder if she would ever get a kill. All the boys her age had succeeded, and even Kinsee had brought home a coati. Angry and frustrated, Lozen was in no mood for her older brother's teasing.

"You have become a good shot at hitting things that can't hear or see you," Victorio said, as they sat with the rest of the family around a cooking fire. "We have no taste for the bark of those trees you kill." She jabbed him in the thigh with one of her arrows, and he yelped, leaping away. Lozen reached for a piece of onion to put into the cooking pot, but her grandfather motioned her away. "That is why the animals flee from you. Never eat onion or the roots of the osha before a hunt; they can smell you, especially the deer."

Lozen ate only fruit and ash bread pulled from the coals, then slept outside so that she wouldn't smell from the cooking smoke inside the tipi. Rising before sunrise, she disturbed an owl, and it blinked at her with a great yellow eye before settling back into its feathers.

By the time the sun peeked over the mountains, Lozen had positioned herself behind a tree near the creek. Stringing her bow, she waited. A fox came to drink and she sighted down her shaft, but a jay shrieked and it darted away. She sighed resignedly and, as she lowered her bow, spotted a gray squirrel on a limb, not ten horses' lengths away. The animal was nibbling on an acorn, and she felled it with her first shot. She cut out the still-beating heart, swallowed it, then uttered the prayer her grandfather had taught her. "*Usen,* I give thanks to this squirrel that gave its life for me. May all my hunts from this day be abundant."

She soon became adept at slaying snowbirds and rabbits with rock and sling, and one day, her grandfather suggested she participate in a sling-training contest that he would judge. "Don't get hit here," he warned, rapping a thick knuckle on her forehead. You cannot fight if your brains are turned to cow dung."

Just after the morning meal, on a flat area covered with stones, the match took place. Her grandfather assigned the teams, splitting the ten participants into evenly divided groups. "If you are slow in battle, you will die," he counseled. "This game here will help make you quick, sharpen your reflexes. Now I will tell you the rules." He held up a piece of wood. "When I drop this, grab up stones and fill your slings, then throw at the other team. Those with the most left standing are the winners."

He let go of the wood and the boys scrambled for rocks, and in their haste to win, threw wildly. A stone whistled past Lozen's ear, another kicked up dirt at her feet. "Are you going to fight, or stand there like an old woman!" a teammate shouted.

Without answering, she whirled her sling. A boy on the opposite team screamed, grabbed his cracked elbow. She whipped another stone and a second boy dropped, clutching his knee. The remaining players stopped, staring in disbelief at the barefoot girl in her squaw dress.

Lozen's grandfather placed his hand on her shoulder. "This team here has won."

17

There were no cheers from her teammates, or the customary back-clapping for one who'd led them to victory. Instead, they joined the others, picked up the wounded and silently dispersed.

Lozen felt like a lame horse, abandoned by the herd. But her grandfather was still there, and she dared not reveal her feelings of hurt and anger. That would show weakness, a trait unacceptable for would-be-warriors, even those at the age of ten. She pushed her feelings deep and, with head held high, turned back towards her tipi. She had won and, for the first time in her life, brought honor and dignity to her family.

Returning home, she was overjoyed at the surprise Besh-a-taye had waiting. There, laid out on her blanket, was a warrior's outfit. Lozen ran and hugged her mother, then pulled off her dress and donned her new trousers and buckskin leggings. "Thank you, *shimaa*," she exclaimed, tucking in a long-sleeved, calico shirt.

"Now, you will stop pestering me, daughter." Lozen's eyes were casting about, and Besh-a-taye read them. "There is no loincloth. That is the mark of a warrior, not a plaything to be worn by a girl."

"But I won the sling game, and . . ."

"This talk is over. No loincloth."

When Lozen awoke the next morning, her mother and grandparents were still under their sleeping robes. She had planned for this moment, and had gone to bed fully dressed in her new clothes. From a rabbit skin pouch, she took a piece of calfskin she had cut the night before, and tucked it into the front of her pants so that it hung down the front. Quiet as a floating feather, she pulled on her moccasins. Her grandfather rustled in his sleep, and she hastened towards the tipi opening, almost knocking over the lance and shield leaning next to it. She pulled back the flap, stooped and emerged into the dawn light.

The sun had just tipped over the mountain peaks, and the pale skins of the tipis were bathed in apricot, giving them a mellow glow. Babies were beginning to cry for their mothers' milk, and tendrils from hundreds of smoke holes trailed towards a sky that would soon turn the color of bluebirds. Lozen could see horses grazing in budding meadows, and beyond them, the misty steam that rose from Smoky Water. The hot, bubbling pools provided soothing and healing minerals, and were a source of replenishment for her tribe.

She gulped in the sweet smell of dewy air and, adjusting the ragged loincloth that hung from her waist, puffed out her chest and strode in the direction of the pools. Someone was coming from the other way and, as he came closer, she could see it was Victorio. Though the air nipped at naked skin, he wore only a breechclout. At twenty, he was lean and tall, with strong arms and finely muscled legs. His shining, wet hair hung straight as a stallion's tail. As sister and brother approached, he glared at her with piercing, dark-set eyes.

"Who are you to wear this?" he shouted, ripping the rough-cut cloth from her waist and throwing it at her feet. "Only men are worthy. You are but a girl-child playing warrior, and an unruly one!"

Lozen's face flushed crimson. She bent, picked up the cloth. Victorio snatched it away, shook it in his closed fist. "I will return this to our mother for you." Lozen hunched her shoulders, stared at the ground. Under her brother's baleful glare, she felt like a tiny bird, its bones being crushed. She began to skulk away. Victorio grabbed her by the back of the neck, pushed her forward. "You think you are a brave, eh? Let's see how brave you are!" He gave her a hard shove in the back and kept it up until they reached his tipi. "Inside, sit by the fire," he ordered.

As Lozen sat cross-legged, Victorio took his knife from a sheath, slit open her sleeve, and tore apart the cloth. He went to his medicine bag, took out a buckskin pouch filled with dried sage, and tapped it over Lozen's bare arm. Picking up a smoldering stick from the embers of the fire, he twirled it slowly until it glowed. For the first time, Lozen noticed the long scar on her brother's forearm.

"When you were only a baby in our mother's arms, I had to do this to prove myself. Are you ready to prove *yourself?*"

Lozen glanced at the stick, the scar, the sage, and back to the stick. She took a deep breath and heart pounding, nodded.

"Cry out or make the slightest sound, and you will fail." He touched the end of the burning wood to the sage.

Smoke rose from Lozen's arm and her skin felt as though the sun had set upon it. Tears welled in her eyes and she bit her lip so hard that blood flowed down her chin. Every fiber in her body wanted to scream out, but she clenched her teeth and sucked back the pain. She could smell the sage, her own burning flesh. At one point, she was sure she was going to stain her pants.

"You did better than I thought," Victorio commended, as the smoke ebbed. "Go down to the stream, keep your arm in there awhile. Find an aloe plant and put some on. It will take many moons, and then the pain will go away." In recognition of her feat, he held up his arm next to her small, trembling one. "You will always carry the mark of courage."

Lozen stood, exited the tipi and ran as fast as she could to the water. She sighed deeply as the coolness soothed the fire on her flesh. Afterwards, she cut open an aloe, squeezing the sticky insides over her charred skin. Her flesh soon blistered, but after several days of treatment, the pain began to lessen.

"You did not cry out, a sign of courage," said Besh-a-taye, as the two of them rolled dried acorn meat and pemmican into balls for winter storage.

"I wanted to; it was very painful."

Her mother rolled out another ball and placed it on a stack in front of her. "Had you cried out, you would never have passed the test. That would have been lots more painful for you."

After helping her mother, Lozen went to the creek that ran east of the village. Heading down an embankment, her eyes caught a sandy shape. Carved by the water, a bear was splayed like a huge skin on the stream bottom. A broad head rested between two forepaws, claws etched by darkened stones. At the end of the snout, a black rock gleamed like a polished nose. The coat was a sparkling bed of white pebbles, elongated and stretched by an easy current. Entranced, Lozen stood awhile, staring. It was warm, yet a chill ran through her and goose bumps appeared on her arms. Although puzzled, she liked how she felt—good all over.

It was a day of a day of awakenings, of a path that led her to Salinas Peak, the spiritual mountain of the *In-déh,* The People. A bald eagle soared and, keeping the underside of the black, ten-foot wingspan in sight, she followed the raptor. When it disappeared behind a crag or the towering oaks and pines, she listened for the "kark, kark, kark" of its harsh cry, and when it emerged again, picked up the sky trail.

The sun began its journey to sleep, and Lozen headed back to camp. She crossed a meadow filled with yellow and purple wildflowers and, as she reached the other side, Victorio appeared from the edge of the timberline. Lozen knew it was past the time when a girl should be out alone, that he had set out to find her.

"Eagle and I were one!" she shouted, running towards

him, gesturing at the sky. "My feet had wings. I saw our camp, the tops of the trees and mountains, wild horses running. There was a mare with a black colt that had a white streak painted here"—she ran her finger down her nose—"the one I want for my pony."

Victorio nodded towards Salinas Peak, its dark shape silhouetted against the fleeting flames of an orange and red sky. "The one-who-seizes-and-carries-away has shared its great power and spirit with you. It is time for you to learn about the Mountain People. We will go in the morning."

The Sacred Place was near the crest of the mountain, and it took them half a day on foot to reach the clearing. Hemmed by tall trees, a stack of neatly piled rocks stood high as Lozen's head, its width three times her length. On the east side were four fist-sized openings. Victorio picked up a handful of leaves and, holding them to each of the stack's corners, prayed.

> In the middle of this Holy Mountain is its heart
> It beats strong, like the drum in my own heart
> Mountain Spirits, keep our game plentiful
> Watch over them
> Watch over me
> I ask you this for long life
> For good luck

He dropped a leaf in each hole, turned to his sister. "I carried these stones here, made this blessing place. Each time you come, bring a new stone. In that way, the Mountain Spirits will get to know you."

Lozen memorized the Blessing Way. She visited the Sacred Place often, and at ritual's end, sat cross-legged, back straight and eyes closed, breathing deeply. During one trancelike state, her keen ears picked up the soft footfalls of padded hunting feet. The padding came closer, slowed, then stopped. Opening her eyes, Lozen gazed into the face of a cougar. There was pain in the slitted, brownish-gold eyes, and the animal was panting heavily. The furry whiteness inside its drooping black moustache was flecked with blood, and crimson dripped down its chin, staining its tawny chest. On a log to its left, three spotted cubs squatted, their blue-gray eyes wide with curiosity.

Lozen stared at the arrow that had pierced their mother's jaw. The barbed head was embedded inside her mouth, and the animal's tongue was raw from constant movement over the V-shaped spike. Lozen knew that, unable to drink or hunt, mother and cubs would die. She would have to remove the arrow. On hands and knees, her heart beating rapidly, she crawled forward.

Except for her flicking tongue, the huge cat remained motionless. Ever so slowly, Lozen placed her hands inside the wounded beast's mouth, gripped the mulberry shaft and, with the animal's hot breath on her face, bore down, trying to break off the arrowhead. The cougar remained still. "Brave, like an Apache," Lozen whispered.

The bloody cavity left scant room to maneuver, and she could feel the razor-sharp fangs scraping her hands, the barbed edge of the arrowhead cutting her flesh. Sweat poured from her brow, her hands and arms ached and she could feel her strength ebbing. Just as she was about to give up, the wood suddenly snapped in half. Lozen took a deep breath, then carefully removed the arrowhead. Grabbing the outside of the shaft near the red-tailed hawk feathers, she pulled it out of the cougar's jaw.

The animal winced and shook its head, checking to see if its jaws were really free. Satisfied, it moved towards the cubs, and after licking each one with a scarlet tongue, turned and gazed at the girl-child. Soft-blinking eyes welcomed her to another world, a world that demanded freedom. The cougar called to her children, and they waddled behind her, melting into the underbrush.

The one-hundred-pound cat revisited often. Thrusting her head under the girl's chin, she would nuzzle and purr softly as Lozen stroked the ears and head. Another time it left a deer, the fur meticulously torn away as she would do for her cubs, to keep them from choking while they fed.

"You have special powers," Besh-a-taye told her daughter, as she skinned the hide and cut up the meat.

Lozen ran her fingers along a scar on the outside of her hand. "Victorio said I held strong medicine powers. I do not know what they mean, how to use them. Sometimes I am afraid."

Besh-a-taye put a hand under her daughter's chin, tilted up her head, looked into her eyes. "The cougar didn't just leave the deer for you; many will share in the feast. The animals know you are one with their spirit, thank you for protecting them. You may someday do the same for your people."

CHAPTER TWO

MUD ON YOUR FEET, WATER IN YOUR MOUTH

The first time she ran in a race, Lozen was pitted against six boys, all bigger and stronger. As was the custom for beginners, Besh-a-taye rubbed mud on her daughter's feet. "To bring you luck, my child."

At the starting line, a husky boy looked the scrawny challenger up and down. "If that mud is going to make you swift, your *shimaa* should have painted your entire body."

"She put on too much," taunted another. "The weight will slow her down!"

"It is said those who shrill like mockingbirds run like turtles," Lozen answered bluntly, then shrunk back as the angry boys closed around her. But people were gathering to watch the race, and the pack broke off, uttering vengeful oaths.

A boisterous gauntlet formed down the center of the village. Elders sat on stools, smoking pipes and talking. Women mended clothing and wove baskets, and giggling children bounced up and down on their fathers' shoulders, while mothers rocked babies in their arms. Some of the friskier children wove in and out of the throng, chasing scampering dogs.

Lozen looked at the old man who sat on a flattened stump next to the starting line. A full head of grayish-white hair framed his dark, crinkled face, and it reminded her of cracked lines in sun-baked clay. She focused on the six-foot lance held in his left hand.

"The drop of the lance is the signal to run," Besh-a-taye had told her. "Be careful. If you go before the tip touches the ground, you will be out of the race."

The boys crowded the edge of the furrowed line in the sand, pushing Lozen towards the rear. Eyes on the lance-holder, the runners became edgier and they tilted forward, rocking on heels and toes. The old man looked up, staring at a hawk that floated in the sky. The boys knew his tricks—only Lozen followed his gaze.

The lance dropped and the boys jumped out, leaving the startled newcomer. Running head-to-head, they covered the ground like jackrabbits, battling each other for the lead. They were only a body length from the finish line, when the mud-footed girl flew past.

No maiden had ever beaten boys in a short footrace before, and yells of surprise burst from the crowd, the women more jubilant than the men. Victorio had been the only warrior to wager on his sister and, grinning fiendishly, collected blankets, tobacco and other spoils from the disgruntled losers.

Lozen glanced at her stunned antagonists. "The mud worked well. Try it next time. You will have a better chance." But no one stood a chance. Time after time, the best anyone could do was to watch her fleeting backside. After several more races, no one wanted to run against her.

"Thank your *shimaa* for your speed," her grandmother

told her. "When you were in your first year of winter, she rubbed a live quail across the bottom of your feet." Lozen's brow furrowed, and the old woman answered by making a back and forth running motion with her fingers. "See how the quail runs swiftly."

Eyes lit with mirth, her husband gestured at their granddaughter. "We will have to find a pony for this one to race."

The next morning, Lozen asked Victorio to meet her on the camp's outskirts. After his sister's encounter with the eagle and cougar, and her recent triumphs, he was curious as to what she had in mind.

"I want to race your pony," she told him.

"When you are ready, Little Sister," he said, patting the neck of his brown and white pinto. She nodded past him towards the end of the meadow. "To the fallen trees there and back."

Victorio looked at the deadfall. "I will give you three gallops' lead."

Lozen shot her brother a look that would have made a bear urinate with fear. "I do not need more steps to beat you!" She smacked the pinto hard on the rump, and it bolted. Lozen's legs churned, her shoulders and arms pumping up and down in a blur. Runner and rider reached the log simultaneously, but Lozen was able to make the turn quicker, and maintained a short lead until the pinto shot past. Back where they'd started, she gasped for air.

Ready to run again, the pony snorted and stamped its hooves. Victorio kept a tight rein and, turning away, headed for his best friend's tipi. Tezye would be impressed that a maiden had nearly outrun Swift As Wind.

A breeze blew up from the valley floor, rustling cottonwood leaves and whisking Lozen's hair into fine, black wisps.

Standing calf-deep in a stream, she pulled a squaw dress from the water, wrung it damp and placed it on a rock to dry. She dipped in a pair of trousers, then began rubbing them clean. The water eddied and bubbled around her, and she could feel smooth stones beneath her feet.

She looked toward the encampment. Morning had raced out of the dawn and the sun was a blinding, yellow ball. Someone was approaching and she squinted, trying to make out the silhouetted figure. The form drew closer, and she recognized the long, purposeful gait, the powerful strides of Tezye. His exploits were legendary, and Lozen had heard them repeated many times over many campfires. Her favorite story was about the time he had run steadily for five moons to warn the village of an approaching war party. Even though the enemy was on horseback, he had beaten them by a full day, and those that weren't killed were driven off.

Suddenly, Tezye was on the bank. Bare-chested, he wore only a breechclout and high-topped moccasins with a knife sheathed into an outside pocket. Whipcord tough, his body was braided sinew, veins sewn together and bound with hard muscle.

"I have seen you run, and your brother has spoken to me about your race with the horse. But you have much to learn. I will train you."

Lozen's jaw dropped and she stood there, holding the dripping trousers. In the entire Apache nation, no one was more respected or renowned a runner than Tezye. And he wanted to teach her!

"I do not have all day to waste, waiting for your answer."

Lozen gulped. "I would be grateful."

"Come back here when you are done with your chores."

Lozen's blood ran with anticipation, and she hurried with her tasks. After finishing the wash and gathering firewood, she found Tezye by the stream. "Take a mouthful of water. Hold it while we run. Each time you spit it out or swallow it, we will come back here, start over." He took a mouthful with her, and they began to run alongside the rock-strewn banks. The creek ran east of the village and, where the last tipi stood, curved in an arc down and past the seven pools of Smoky Water. Lozen made it to the first pool before the water dribbled out of her mouth. Tezye was ahead and to her left, and when he turned around and headed back, she wondered how he knew.

With her second mouthful she puffed out her cheeks, thinking it would enable her to hold the water longer. It climbed up her nose, dripped out her nostrils, and she swallowed it. Time and again they started out, only to return and begin over. The day and Lozen dragged on. But by the time the mountains pulled long shadows from the sun, she was able to hold the water past the pools and into the valley. "I will come for you tomorrow," Tezye said, trotting away.

Lozen didn't want him to come for her tomorrow, or any other day. She had swallowed so much water her distended stomach felt like a boulder, and her sore feet scuffed in the dirt as she walked home.

Besh-a-taye had made a meal of stewed antelope meat and mesquite beans, but for the first time in her life the young girl couldn't eat, and fell asleep as soon as she crawled under her blanket. She was dreaming the dreams of bad omens, water overflowing and washing her away, when a hand on her shoulder shook her awake.

"It is time," whispered Tezye.

Groggy, eyelids still heavy, she struggled to clear the fuzziness from her head. *How can it be time? I have just fallen asleep!* She followed her tormentor, stumbled outside to an early morning moon in the still-darkened sky. They began again, and Lozen's first impulse was to spit the water out and go back to bed. But her desire to achieve held her. By midday she had made it to the base of Sacred Mountain, and the next day didn't swallow the water once.

On the fourth dawn, Tezye was waiting outside her tipi, jiggling something in his hand. He extended it, opening his palm to reveal several smooth stones, gesturing for her to take them. "Put these in your mouth. Hold them long as you can. Same as the water."

"What if I swallow them?"

"Find others to take their place."

Lozen wondered if acorns would be next.

They ran until the sun was halfway to the noonday meal. By now the stones had settled in the bottom of her jaw, and were chafing her gums. As she tried to reposition them with her tongue, she pushed them out. Tezye was at her shoulder. "Grab up two more, keep running."

Lozen stopped and looked at the hard-packed earth. "These rocks here are sharp, and dirty," she protested, her voice half-statement, half-plea.

He cast her a doleful glance. "The path of the warrior is full of knives." He picked up two stones, and popped them in his mouth.

Reluctantly, Lozen followed. Hot from the sun, the rocks burned her tongue and inflamed her raw gums. She thought of the cougar and arrow, wondering if anyone was coming to save her, but knowing better. Pain and rebellion dogged her every step, yet her desire overshadowed them, and she completed the ten-mile journey.

At the stream, she gingerly removed the stones from her mouth. Tezye spit his out like they were seeds. He swept his palm face-down in front of him, turned it over and swept it back. "This lesson is over. At sunup, we begin endurance training." He turned and walked away.

Lozen could feel her anger welling, and she glared after him. There had been no praise for her efforts, no explanation for the lesson. Not even one day's rest! Tears streamed down her cheeks, and she could taste the bitterness of frustration and disappointment. Trying to make sense of it, her brain fumbled for an answer. *I thought the lessons were over. He wants me to quit because I am a girl! He is afraid I will become a better runner than he, and he will lose face.*

She sat heavily, staring out across the water. Sunlight sifted through the treetops, sparkling the stream with liquid stars. Skimming over the water, a great blue heron glided by, and when it uttered a deep harsh croak, Lozen knew it was speaking to her. "Put your worries on my wings. I will carry them away." The blue-gray bird wings lifted into the trees, and Lozen could feel her anger and fear going with them.

She removed her moccasins, prayed to the water, then splashed water on her face and waded into the creek. Bending, she cupped her hands and took a drink. At first the water stung, but its coolness soothed her aching mouth and dry throat, and she took another. As she straightened, she spied a pronghorn antelope upstream, calmly lapping. It raised its head, and Lozen could see the double, white-banded fur necklace that encircled its throat. Once again the Great Spirit, *Usen*, had sent her a sign. Once again she did not know its meaning. Filled with curiosity, she hurried home to relate the day's events.

"I will tell you about Antelope," her mother said, stirring a pot of acorn stew. "First, know this. Those who think they are the only ones to deserve praise do not give it."

"Tezye?"

"All men."

Lozen dipped her finger into the hot gruel, quickly removed it and licked it clean. "What of grandfather?"

Her grandmother Sha-na, who was mending moccasins nearby, answered. "What of him? He is a man, same as the others. Just older and more stubborn."

"You want to know about the legend of Antelope, eh?" asked Besh-a-taye. Lozen nodded, dipped her finger in again.

"Soon after the beginning of The People, Antelope was sent by *Usen* to teach the two-leggeds a lesson in survival. The weather was harsh, prey scarce. They were without clothing and starving. Antelope spoke to them. 'To stay alive, you must take action. Kill me now. Eat my meat to nourish you, use my coat to keep you warm. Waste nothing. Take all my parts and make good use of them. It is part of my birth and my rebirth, as it is yours. I am *Usen*'s gift to you so that you may endure, bear more children and carry on your creation. Act quickly, or you will perish.' "

Sha-na took up the story. "The humans did as they were told. From then on, each time they killed an animal, they knew it was a gift, that they were honoring its spirit. It is the same for us, now."

"The antelope I saw wasn't killed. We are not naked or starving. I don't understand the meaning."

Besh-a-taye ladled three cups of steaming broth to cool. "The one you saw was a sign for you to take action, so that you may gain strength of mind and heart, overcome fear." She tapped her daughter's head with a spoon. "Your head says what your body will or won't do. If you want to reach a place, think how far you have come, not how much of the journey remains. It is a good lesson for all of life."

Sha-na handed Lozen a pair of calf-high moccasins. She had made the bottoms from thick rawhide, lined the insides with tanned, durable deerskin. "These are for you, to help you run."

Lozen's blood stirred with excitement. She would become one with the antelope. Fast. Graceful. With the will and stamina to run forever! She threw her arms around the old woman's neck. "Thank you, *shiwóyé*."

In the morning's first light, teacher and student jogged along a narrow deer trail south of the village. Rabbits burst out of the bushes, white-patched tails bounding up and down. A bobwhite quail darted from the underbrush, quickly followed by chicks on scurrying, paddlewheel feet. Lozen thought the birds with their speckled backs, red-hued breasts and black masks were more colorful than any costumed dancer she'd seen.

The trail played out, leading into a dry, bramble-bound creek. Thorns choked the narrow sides and Lozen winced each time a needlelike tip pricked her arms and legs, catching her flesh with stinging ferocity. She watched Tezye maneuver through the gauntlet without so much as a scratch, and was thankful when the drainage emptied into a wash. No barbs, but filled with rocks and boulders.

"Careful here," he warned. "If you break an ankle, I do not intend to carry you back."

There was no easy ground, and Lozen had to watch every step, while looking ahead and down simultaneously. She ran across a series of egg-shaped rocks, jumped onto and over a boulder, hit the sandy gravel on the other side and kept going. A lizard scooted across her path, and she nimbly sidestepped.

The wash opened into a riverbed, and after the dangerous treading, Lozen was grateful for the wide expanse. Tezye led her to the center, where the sand was deepest, the running hardest. A roadrunner appeared out of nowhere, ran parallel with them, then sped out of sight. The longer they ran, the more Lozen could feel the strain in her tendons and calves from the giving sand. Finally, Tezye headed towards the steep riverbank. Lozen slogged after him, watched him bolt over the top like a young goat. Her legs on fire, she struggled to the lip of the bank. What she saw next made her forget her pain—Tezye was squatting next to a watering hole! She ran to the pond, dropped to her stomach and plunged her head beneath the water. She stayed under as long as her breath would allow, then lifted her head, shaking it like a wet dog.

"This cool water . . ."

Tezye cut her off, tossed her a parfleche. "Eat and be quiet. You learn nothing by talking." Lozen sat up, took some prickly pear from the pouch, and nibbled at the fruit.

"Look around you," Tezye instructed. "Are there moccasin tracks other than ours? Fresh animal and bird tracks say this place is safe, for no human scent has scared them away." He nodded to one side. "The tree here, what do you see?"

Lozen swallowed the last fruit. "Leaves and branches."

Tezye spoke harshly. "You know nothing. Is the trunk thick enough to conceal a man?" He picked up a leaf. "If there are leaves on the ground only in one place, none in any other, someone may be lurking above. Always be aware of your surroundings. Those who rush the bear get eaten by the jaws of disaster." He pulled his knife, drew a circle in the dirt. "Before entering a place, go around it, then close in and make another circle going the other way. Watch for signs: the sun striking metal, a shadow that doesn't belong. That way you will stay alive."

They headed back, crossed the riverbed and went up the wash, and reentered the creek. Lozen winced, as cuts that had crusted over with dried blood were ripped open again by the barbed spikes. Tezye yelled at her from behind. "You are running straight up, into the fire thorns. Loosen your shoulders. Bend your legs. Flow like the

34

wind, turn your body like the stream."

Lozen adapted and changed her stance. A quilled demon sprang before her and she shifted her weight, brushing by. Another attacked and she flew past without so much as a nick.

"*Enju!*" said her teacher.

Grandfather Moon was reaching for the stars when Lozen limped through the flap of her family's tipi. Her legs were logs and she collapsed in a heap. With great effort, she pulled off her new moccasins. They had kept her from getting blisters, but her calves hurt and her shins were bruised from repeated encounters with boulders.

Besh-a-taye scrutinized her daughter's battle-scarred body. "A hungry wildcat tried to eat you, eh? I will boil lizard tail root, wash your cuts so they may heal."

Lozen mumbled her thanks, and fell asleep with the dampness on her skin.

When she got up the next morning and tried to stand, she gasped and almost fell over. Her ankles screamed in pain, and the bottoms of her feet felt as though they'd been pounded with rocks. It was impossible for her to bear any weight, and she crawled to where Besh-a-taye was cutting thin pieces of dried deer meat. Ravenous, Lozen bolted down several strips, then begged for more.

Tezye didn't come that day, or the next, but on the third, showed up outside her tipi with Shonta, a revered warrior. At forty, he was ten years Tezye's senior, and had been his mentor. Tall and hard, every vein in his muscular arms and legs stood out. Lozen thought he looked like a piece of twisted rope.

"I have horse trading in another village," Tezye said. "Shonta will train you until I return."

Still footsore, Lozen limped beside her new teacher, who

led her up a hill in back of the tipi. Shonta gestured towards a cluster of grass some thirty paces away. "Look carefully, there."

Lozen peered hard at the swatch. "There is nothing."

"Get closer to the ground."

She lay on her belly, studied the grass. A forked tongue flicked between the blades. "Snake," she whispered.

"Enemies are like snakes. Watch for that which makes no sound, for it is the most treacherous, little one."

For Lozen, the days folded into seasons, the seasons into a harvest. With Tezye and Shonta, it never got easier. In the desert, they followed irregular patterns between dense prickly pear and barrel cactus to find an opening, a path. They dodged rattlesnakes that blended with oat-brown grasses, jogged through arroyos suffocated with palo verde and mesquite, dogtrotted along washes that led into fortresses of pronged cholla and ocotillo. They ran up lofty bluffs and down ravines, back up again. Dried fruit and grains were eaten on the run, and they only paused to drink from clear streams, or to suck moisture from the flesh of peeled cactus.

The most strenuous training took place on mountains. Before tackling one of the formidable inclines, Shonta told her, "After this, running elsewhere will seem like swimming across a calm lake."

The Bighorn Sheep trail climbed sharply, and by the time they hit the halfway point, Lozen's thigh muscles felt as if they were going to burst through her skin. "This mountain will not defeat me," she kept muttering, pumping her arms and shoulders, using her upper body to help pull her up the grade.

Tezye and Shonta were out of view, and just when Lozen thought she could no longer take another step, she rounded a bend and saw them. She hit the crest of the rimrock, threw her arms around a surprised Tezye, then whooped and danced around Shonta.

Heading down, her eyes drifted over the valley. Near the mountain's base, a herd of grazing horses were dark specks in a field of green, and beyond them, purple sage stretched into an indigo horizon. Lozen felt like a colt that had just discovered its legs were made for running. For the first time in her training, she was enjoying herself. She challenged her teachers, either keeping pace, or surging ahead.

Nothing about her training surprised her anymore, not even the morning Shonta showed up with a cradleboard slung over his back, a bag of rocks laced in. Another rested by his side, and he helped her heft it over her shoulders. "To increase your stamina, your strength, little one." With the weight on their backs, they ran every place they had been before. Lozen was growing stronger, more resilient.

On a day when grasses and flowers were going to seed, and the wind sounded like howling wolves, Tezye sent for Lozen. They met next to the stream that ran by the camp, stood by cottonwood trees with their brown and gold leaves fluttering down. The Ghost Face of Lifeless Winter would soon descend upon them, bringing cold on frosty wings.

"Your lessons are over. I will now tell you their meaning," Tezye said. "The first was patience. Without it, no Apache can survive." He picked up several stones. "You did well, never asked about these, why you had to carry them in your mouth, or the water. In the desert, the one thing that will kill you fastest is thirst. Breathing through your mouth dries your throat, increases that thirst. By holding the water and stones, you learned to breathe only through your nose."

He chucked the stones aside. "You were allowed little rest, and had to resist tiredness, pain, hunger. By accepting them, you became one with them. Now, they cannot defeat you." Tezye took a hawk feather from his hair, and placed it in hers. A smile edged the corners of his stern mouth, and his words sent chills of pride and delight up Lozen's spine. "You have earned this. If someone questions why you wear it, send them to me."

Lozen would think of these times often, for it was Tezye's wisdom that would keep her alive.

CHAPTER THREE

WHITE PAINTED WOMAN

It was the New Life Season, and sparkling droplets dripped from leaves and trees, cutting crooked fingers in the snow. As the sun stayed awake longer, icy channels snaked down the slopes. Otters rolled and played in once-frozen streams; deer, elk and antelope cropped new grass, mother bears hunted for berries and suckled their young.

The time had a special meaning, for Lozen would soon celebrate her puberty rite and pass into womanhood. Sha-na had promised to tell her how the sacred ceremony came to be. Working the last of five deerskins for Lozen's sacred costume, the old woman's eyes shone bright as stars on a clear, cold night. In her sixtieth winter, she was still lean and strong, and bore the proud forbearance of a warrior woman, one who had accompanied her husband in raids and war parties.

"Tell me, *shiwóyé,* about White Painted Woman, the ceremony," Lozen said, as she watched her grandmother scrape the skin with a horse rib covered in rawhide.

"White Painted Woman had power over fertility and long life. Without her, there would be no Chiricahuas, Mescaleros, Mimbrenos or Coyoteros. No Apaches at all. We, the *Tchihéné*, the Red Paint People, would not be here. Neither would the Mountain People, the *Tchok-anen*. Or the *Net'na*, The Enemy People, also called Indian White Man. The *Bedonkohe*, the In Front At The End People, would not exist."

Lozen giggled. "Why do they call them by that name?"

"Do not make fun of others, or be like the mockingbird that respects nothing. It is because of where they live, nearest to the Pima Indian raiding grounds, far to the west. We are many tribes from many places, but one people." Sha-na shifted her weight, bearing down on the skin.

"In the beginning, *Usen*, Giver of Life created *Esdzanadeha*, White Painted Woman. She bore that name because her body and face were painted with a white clay. He sent her to our land to dwell in a cave. Other supernaturals lived there, the evil cannibal Owl Giant who rose out of the darkness and feasted on her children. White Painted Woman prayed to *Usen*, and he told her to go outside. The clouds got dark and heavy. Cold rain pelted her body. The water ran into her, through her, but she remained still."

Sha-na sat back, her butt resting on her calves. With her finger, she drew a jagged line in the air. "Lightning struck her four times, yet she was not injured. The storm passed and the dawn came. That night she had slept with the sun and it now shone peaceful and warm. A colorful rainbow of blue, yellow, red and orange curved across the sky. There was a soft gurgling sound and White Painted Woman looked down to see her newborn son. She named him Killer Of Enemies. Two moons later she bore another infant, Child Of The Water."

"Two moons later?"

"Supernaturals do things humans can't. White Painted Woman wrapped the babies in warm blankets and returned to the cave. The water had washed away her fear and she thought clearly. She tied a line of bones along one side of the cave, then dug a hole under her fire. Whenever Owl Giant beat his wings, the bones would jump and rattle, give warning, and she would quickly hide the children in the warm pit."

Sha-na tapped Lozen's forehead. "In this way of stealth and cunning, she was able to protect her sons until they grew big and strong. One day, Killer Of Enemies traveled to the depths of the cave and killed Owl Giant. The two brothers slew many evil ones—the bull and prairie dog, others who killed with glowing red coals from their eyes."

The elder moved to the other side of the hide and resumed her scraping. It was hot, tedious work, particularly on bent, old knees. For a long time, there was silence. Finally, Lozen could wait no longer. "What happened then?"

"The world was now safe, and from mud, Child Of The Water created the two-leggeds. There was an Indian man and woman. A white man and woman." Sha-na gathered up the deerskin and, to add to its softness, placed it in a mixture of water and cattle brains.

"Child Of The Water made a mountain from the mud. It was full of forests, plants and game. The People were to live upon the wild things. He made another mountain and split it. Tame animals came out. The White Eyes would breed what they would use and eat."

Sha-na pushed down on the robe, "In this way, Child Of The Water determined the habits for all living things. He was also wise, and created separateness. He told The People that a sea would divide them from those not Indian born. They were confused; no water stood between them. The ocean was not of water, but trust. To this day the *Nakaiyé* and *Indaa* do not trust us, attack us wherever we go."

"Mexicans and White Eyes are our enemies."

"They fight for the same reason all people fight. They are afraid of those not like them." She paused, and took a drink from a water-filled cow's bladder. "One day White Painted Woman felt tired and old. She walked towards Father Sun, and saw herself approaching. Two came together as one, and she was a beautiful young woman again. Soon after, she called all the Apaches to gather. White Painted Woman wore an elegant buckskin costume and her face was painted red, her body covered with yellow pollen. The markings stood for blood, life and fertility. She spoke to The People.

"After a maiden passes her first flow, a ceremony will take place. It will be called the *dai-a-dai,* the Feast of Maidens. It will honor the sacredness of bearing new life, and make her suitable for marriage. The girl will wear a costume like mine. Sacred Baskets will be made to hold ritual food. During the ceremony, four runs will take place to honor the four directions of life."

Sha-na stood and began twirling about, her arms over her head. "White Painted Woman said, 'Everything will be blessed and sung over by the medicine man. While he chants, the maiden will dance. The girl will possess my spirit and hold the power to bless, to heal. She will have physical strength and live long, with no crippling of her body. In this way, she will assure prosperity and survival for all. On the last ceremonial night, Crown Dancers will imitate *Gaun,* the mountain spirit.' "

Sha-na stopped dancing. "Child Of The Water spoke. He told The People to build a ceremonial dwelling, to bring food there. He said, 'Grab at it. Play with it. Eat it. It will be a sign of plenty.' " She took the dripping deerskin out of the mixture. "That was the way it began. That is the way it is now and will always be."

The next morning, when the skin had dried, Sha-na took it inside the tipi and scraped it one last time with a sharp piece of lava rock. Folding it in half, she cut a slit in the center for the head and neck. "Try this on, granddaughter."

Lozen's eyes danced. She had never felt anything so soft, and she fingered the robe, pressing it to her skin.

Sha-na smiled. "The deer must have shed its coat just for you. I must still cut the fringes, and your costume must be painted with yellow pollen, beaded and sewn. Shinash-a-too will bless it. His medicine is strong, and his songs will bring good luck for all."

Lozen pulled the skin up over her head. "Who will guide me in my feast?"

"One who had a spiritual contact with White Painted Woman and came to be one with her. Den-me has the right kind of knowledge so that you will have a good ceremony. She will feed you ritual foods, instruct you in womanly ways. You will learn about becoming a good wife and mother. She will push you out for your runs to the Sacred Basket. Listen to her closely, Lozen. She is old and very wise."

Den-me was on her knees, rolling up the bottom of her tipi to let in fresh air, when Lozen poked her head through the door. She motioned the maiden inside, continuing her work. On one section of the tipi, someone had drawn the Apache Creation, and Lozen, in wonder, stared. There was an emblem of a yellow sun, and inside that, the image of a woman in white. Behind, a sacred dwelling rose above her, and below, a child clung to a ribbon of blue water that streamed down from her dress. There was a bonfire and figures of the masked dancers, and in the curves of the circle, animals and birds.

"You brought the ritual feather?"

Lozen turned to see a short, heavyset woman who tilted from side-to-side when she walked, and whose skin was the gray color of the Cloud Ancients. She nodded at Den-me and, taking the eagle feather, motioned with the white tip towards the elderly practitioner. On the fourth pass, Den-me took it. "I will lead you in your ceremony now, watch over and take good care of you. You will live with me until your *dai-a-dai* is over." From the pouch around her neck, Den-me took a piece of white wampum shell. "For your costume. Though there is no blood kinship between us, from this day on we will treat each other as mother and daughter, exchange presents throughout life."

For two weeks before the start of the ceremony, the camp hummed with excitement. On horseback and afoot, guests and neighboring tribes poured into the village with their families. Near where the ceremony would be held, tipis and brush-covered wickiups began to spring up. A flat section of ground to the east was left for the Sacred Dwelling.

Lozen's uncle Nana, a venerated leader, had invited all the great chiefs. None would refuse such a request, for it would show disrespect to the Warm Springs clan.

Standing by her tipi with Besh-a-taye, Lozen watched as the chiefs arrived on prancing stallions. Juh of the *Nednhi* traveled from his Blue Mountain stronghold in the Sierra Madres, while brightly-clad Mangas Coloradas of the Coppermine Apaches came from the south. Lozen had never seen an Indian that big. "He is as large as Salinas Peak and colorful as an oriole," she whispered to her mother.

"He is respected and revered among Apaches and enemies alike. His raids against the Mexicans are as many as he is hands tall."

A dignified man passed on a white stallion, and Besh-a-taye nodded at him in recognition. Eyes smiling, Cochise returned the greeting. Tall and muscular, his straight hair hung like an obsidian waterfall over wide shoulders, and his entire body was pepper-marked from buckshot. Lozen looked into his handsome face with its straight nose and round eyes.

"He is Mangas' son-in-law," said Besh-a-taye. "Mangas is wise. He knows how to choose husbands to build his tribe's strength, to increase its territory and ensure the future of his people. Another of his daughters is married to a Navajo chief, the third to a neighboring band of our own people."

"He would not marry *me* off in that way!"

Besh-a-taye ignored her. "The *Bedonkohes* come. That short one there is called Geronimo, with his wife, Alope. He is fast becoming a brave warrior, his reputation grows."

Loco, an older cousin of Victorio's, rode into camp alone. A stocky man with a round face and disfigured left eye, he was the gruffest of the chiefs and had a quick temper.

"Ever since he killed that bear, he has taken on its nature," Besh-a-taye told Lozen. "It scarred his eye, gave him a limp. Now he growls and walks like one, takes out his anger on his wives and slaves. Sometimes he acts crazy."

"Is that why he is called Loco?"

"Some say so. Others think it is because he trusts the pale ones."

"He wears the bear claw necklace."

"It is his right. It would be dangerous medicine for him, if he had not won the battle against *shosh*."

"If he growls too much, it may someday strangle him," answered Lozen.

"Your understanding of human nature goes far beyond your thirteen harvests, daughter."

On the first day of the ceremony, Lozen bathed before

dawn and, as she faced the rising sun, Den-me put pollen on her head, face and the bridge of her nose, praying all the while. With a swatch of gama grass she brushed her disciple's hair, then dressed her from the ground up. First the right beaded moccasin with upturned toes, then the left. Skirt, robe and other adornments followed. Lozen was now White Painted Woman, and would be so-called until the *dai-a-dai* ended.

Lozen tingled with excitement. "I feel like I can walk on clouds."

"Go only where you are told. Stay in the sacred tipi most of the time during the ceremony, and the four days after," instructed Den-me, wagging a crooked finger. "Only then can you can take off your clothes and bathe." She placed a piece of sweet yucca fruit in White Painted Woman's mouth. "So you will have a good appetite throughout life. You will eat many good things, but do not eat too much, or you will look like those cows the Comanche call women."

She touched the tube attached to Lozen's robe. "Drink only from this hollowed-out wood. Don't let your lips touch water, for if your skin gets wet, it will rain. Don't look at the sky. A storm will come and you will ruin the peoples' good times." Den-me tugged lightly at the yucca stick hanging on Lozen's left side.

"Do you know what this is for?"

"I must not scratch myself. I may only use this stick."

"Try not to use it too much. You will look foolish, like a dog with fleas." She cast Lozen a sobering glance. "Keep a pleasant way about you. That way the trait will last all your life. Do not talk, laugh or smile too much, or your face will wrinkle and you will become old before your time."

"I will do as you say, *shimaa*."

"Not all Apache girls are as obedient as you. Some have to

be constantly scolded, others beaten. I had one who would not listen. She cursed and was angry. She is now a beautiful woman, yet still has a bad mouth and mean temper. No man wants her."

"I am not sure I want to be married. No man impresses me."

"Mmph. In time, my daughter."

While Lozen was being dressed, the ceremonial tipi was being erected. Shinash-a-too sprinkled pollen on each of the stripped spruce poles, and tied sage, snakeweed and eagle feathers to the boughs at the tops. Victorio, Nana and two other male relatives slid the four poles into pre-dug holes, then raised them with long ropes until they came to a peak.

Lozen could hear Shinash-a-too begin a dwelling song. She delighted in the words, the shaking sound of his rattle made from the hooves of four different animals.

Killer Of Enemies and White Painted Woman made the songs
The songs of the dwelling this way
For long life stands the blue stallion

The same verse was repeated three more times, each with a different-colored stallion. Yellow. White. Black.

More songs were chanted, and from a dozen cooking huts, women carried bowls and baskets laden with food, placing them in front of the tipi. From every corner of the village, people streamed to the feast. Women hurried to bring their men food, warriors discussed their last raids, elders told stories to curious children. When all had eaten their fill, they formed a wide semicircle around the open-air, ceremonial tipi.

Led by Den-me, Lozen walked to the sacred tipi. Head held high, her eyes sparkled with the sacred spirit of White

Painted Woman. Murmurs of approval rippled through the crowd.

Washed in yucca root suds, Lozen's hair gleamed like a raven's black wings, tinged chestnut by the sun. Around her neck, a braided necklace with patterns of white-winged doves lay against her creamy buckskin robe, and she wore earrings of white, turquoise and black. On her forehead was a rainbow abalone shell; on her feet beaded moccasins with upturned toes. Designs of the morning star, crescent moon, arcs for the rainbow and circles for the sun were beaded into her costume, and the tuft of a black-tailed doe hung from the back of her dress. Above it, a snow-white eagle feather dangled from a wampum shell. "So you will live a long life, until your hair turns the color of the feather," Den-me told her.

Lozen carried another symbol for longevity, a cane made by Shinash-a-too. The medicine man had painted it with yellow pollen, and fastened two golden eagle feathers and two orange oriole feathers at the top. "The eagle will protect you against illness," he explained. "Mind these others well. The oriole keeps to its own business and behaves. It is a happy bird with a good disposition."

Den-me placed buckskin on the spruce needle floor of the dwelling, and Lozen kneeled before a coiled, unicorn plant basket filled with sacred objects. Yellow tule pollen was applied over her painted clay-red face, and to her back and shoulders. "Pollen for purity, to re-create White Painted Woman's fertilization by the sun," her teacher said.

With Den-me dancing beside her, Lozen rocked back and forth on her knees, imitating the posture of White Painted Woman's first menstruation. When she finished, she stood and began welcoming the long line filing into the tipi. As each Apache entered, Lozen blessed them. Two parents brought in an unruly boy, and at their request, Lozen took some pollen and hit him lightly on the mouth four times.

"There!" said his mother, looking into his smeared face. "Now you won't talk evil anymore, and will be good."

A rickety old man with a crooked arm shuffled forward. Praying, Lozen gently massaged the bent limb with pollen. Suddenly, the elder whooped, and cocked his arm up and down. "She healed me!"

Burdened with the Face Of The Unfaithful, a young woman approached. Her stub of a nose told that she had been with another man. As punishment, her husband had marked her betrayal with his knife. "Make me pretty again, so that a man will want me," the woman pleaded.

Lozen placed her hand over the woman's heart. "*Usen* only sees what is in here. You are already beautiful."

The blessing line ended, and Den-me placed Lozen face-down on the buckskin, massaging her from head to foot. "I am molding you so you will be supple as a sapling, grow straight as the oak. So you will become a fine woman with good morals."

Den-me instructed Lozen to rise, and outlined her footprints with pollen. "You are ready to take the four runs around the Sacred Basket. Do it well and your life will be surrounded by beauty, good health. All will know your fitness, your strength." She gently pushed Lozen out of the tipi. "Always start with your right foot."

The first of four chants began, and Lozen trotted forward, followed by Den-me and Besh-a-taye. As she circled the basket, she became the owner of the first stage of life a girl would pass through—puberty. Adolescence, womanhood and maturity rounded out the next three, and she completed these on her own. After each run, the basket was placed farther away, and in a different direction. On the fourth run, the distance had more than doubled from the first.

This would be her last time, and Lozen wanted it to be her best. Eagle made her soar with grace; Antelope stretched her limbs, applying its swiftness. She reached the basket and, making the turn around it, shrilled a high-pitched cry to honor White Painted Woman. The crowd cheered, Sha-na along with them, "No one has ever run so swift, or been as nimble as my granddaughter!"

Lozen returned to the ceremonial tipi and stood on the buckskin. Cattail pollen was sprinkled over her head and shoulders by Shinash-a-too. Then, holding the Sacred Basket above her head, he emptied the candy, kernels of corn and fruit. "White Painted Woman has given us food, good crops, enough for the future. This makes it so."

The words had barely left his mouth, when the waiting children scrambled for the treats. Lozen remembered what her mother had told her. "Always be giving, share what you have with others. Once you have no use for something, give it to someone else. That is our way."

Lozen picked up the buckskin, shook it, then threw it to the east. Hunting would be good, deer meat plentiful. From a nearby pile, she took three blankets, casting each in a different direction. She would always be warm now, and her camp would be clean.

The puberty rite was over, although the celebration would continue for three more days. Inside the tipi, Lozen sat with Den-me, Besh-a-taye and Sha-na around a small fire.

"I feel her!" Lozen exclaimed. "I feel White Painted Woman within me." Her voice dropped. "Yet, while I am joyous, my heart is sad."

The words her grandmother spoke were as soft as the wings of a moth. "We share your feelings, granddaughter. Here, in this place and time, you are White Painted Woman. You have drawn The People into you, and we are as one with your happiness, the divinity you hold. Your healing powers are a special gift from *Usen*. Use them wisely, never for your own interests."

Besh-a-taye touched Lozen's cheek. "You are not filled with sadness, but reverence and gratitude for your heritage, your people, your life. Your heart knows it is a special time of peace, of healing. It is not our way to look back, to dwell on the past. But it is important we remember it, where we came from."

Lozen swallowed hard and tears misted her eyes. She knew from that day forward her people meant more to her than anything on earth.

That night was the beginning of a great celebration. Just after sundown, ten hooded Crown Dancers appeared from a hill nearby. Led by Shinash-a-too, each carried two long sticks painted with jagged streaks of blue lightning. Impersonating the supernaturals, they filed into the ceremonial grounds and gathered around a huge bonfire.

Another joined them, Long Nose, the clown. Covered in white paint, he wore only moccasins and a loincloth. In one hand he carried an eagle feather, in the other, a short club. His mask of scraped rawhide had angular ears and a big, strange-looking nose. Lozen thought he looked like a cross between a wild pig with a stretched snout and a mule with tall ears. He carried on with wild antics, teasing the dancers, making the people laugh.

The upper bodies of the dancers were painted in charcoal and clay, mixed with yucca juice for color. Narrow bands of black, white, yellow and blue streaked their arms and chests. There were branching lines for cactus, zigzags for lightning. One dancer had yellow snakes on his back; another, white arrowheads. Others carried pointed stars, triangles and sawtooth designs on their skin. Fringed skirts were held in place by wide, yellow sashes around their waists. They high-stepped to the drumming, the eagle feathers tied to their elbows dancing with them.

But it was their headdresses that drew the most attention. Each dancer wore a black-hooded mask attached to a wide, U-shaped yucca frame. Wood earrings with sharpened ends hung from both sides and at the top, prong-shaped horns jutted high into the air.

The Crown Dancers made their way throughout the camp, and where there was sickness or trouble they chanted, motioning with their hands for the evil spirits to be gone, blowing them away with forceful breaths. They disappeared into the darkness, then burst forth and trotted around the great bonfire. Women's cries and prayers greeted them, and the men sounded "hoo-hoo-hoo" calls, urging others to sing.

Melodies erupted from the crowd. Drumming and chanting swelled. The tall headdresses swayed back and forth, painted antlers bobbing up and down in the firelight. The best performers were rewarded with throaty approval.

When the moon reached half its sleep in the sky, the sacred dancers retired. Men and women formed circles around the drummers, and began dancing around them. The women sang and laughed, about no one in particular. "She married a man with big buttocks," they shrilled. "Now she spends all her time mending pants."

Late into the night, the round dancing ended and face-to-face dancing started. It was the favorite among the women, for now they could choose a partner. If a man refused, he would be looked down upon, and have little chance with women in the future.

"I met your father in this way," Besh-a-taye told Lozen, as they watched couples pair up. "He didn't like me at first.

Even in camp he stayed away. But then there was a *dai-a-dai,*
like yours. I kept poking him, pulling on his clothes. The
more he ignored me, the more I poked. It was fun! He danced
with me each night until daybreak. Right then we fell in love.
These are the words he sang.

> *I see that girl*
> *My heart becomes full of joy*
> *My own sweetheart I see*
> *Then I stay this way.*

Lozen smiled, kissed her mother softly and, with Den-me,
returned to the elder's tipi. She desperately wanted to crawl
out of her costume and bathe, but dared not disobey. It
would bring disrespect to her family. Lozen glanced at her
mentor who was curled up on her blanket, snoring. She remembered her warning, "Do not go around too much." But
Lozen needed to be alone, away from the closeness of the tipi,
the noise and crowds. She would run on silent feet, and in the
dark, no one would see or hear her. Not wanting to dirty her
moccasins, she removed them and stepped outside.

The air hung heavy with the sweet smell of honeysuckle.
Like a racehorse, Lozen stretched her legs. The noise of the
singers, dancers and drummers ebbed, and soon she was at
the camp's outskirts. She dropped into a gully, feeling the
cool sand beneath her feet. Suddenly, a claw of fear scraped
her spine. Something, someone, was very close! Was it a
demon? She should never have left the tipi! Had Owl Giant
returned to feast on her for being unruly? Like an antelope
chased by a puma, she sprinted out of the gulch. The terror
was still there, moving with her, silently matching her frenetic
pace.

Trying to glimpse her tormentor, she cut sharply to her

left. If it was Owl Giant, she dared not look into the evil one's eyes, or she would die. Then she saw it, and stopped so abruptly that she almost backed over herself. Looking from the ground to the bright moon, she scoffed at her foolish fears, and made a solemn oath that her own shadow would never frighten her again.

CHAPTER FOUR

TO BE A WARRIOR

At an early age, Lozen had been taught horsemanship. She knew how to mount by catching hold of a horse's mane, digging her toes into its foreleg and swinging up onto its back. Shonta showed her how to kneel on a moving pony's back and, reaching up with a club, knock a flying turkey out of the air. She became proficient at chasing zigzagging rabbits on her galloping pony, leaning down and killing them with a single blow from her hunting stick. Now, in her fifteenth year, she was learning more skills.

Mounting a horse from the rear at a dead run wasn't as easy as it looked, and she bounced off the old mare's rump, landing hard on her own. The horse cast a woeful look back over its shoulder at her, and when it watered the earth with a whitish-yellow stream, Lozen scurried to get out of the way.

"You want to be known as Horse Butt Woman, ay?" chided Shonta, shaking his head. "We have been at this all morning and you're no better than when we started." He positioned himself well behind the tethered horse. "You are jumping too soon. I will show you again." Sprinting like a gunshot, he vaulted over the pony's hindquarters and landed on its back. Sliding off, he patted its withers. "This is your target. Focus here."

Stinging from his rebuke, Lozen's brooding eyes switched from Shonta to the mare's neck. Gathering herself, she ran full tilt and completed a smooth leap onto its back.

"You do better when you're angry, little one."

"It's not hard with you around."

Shonta rubbed the mare's ears. "Anger is a dark pass where clear thinking cannot travel. If you let your emotions have their way, you will always be defeated." He turned away. "Keep practicing until I come back."

By the time he returned, Lozen had managed several successful jumps. She patted the pony's back. "See here, Shonta. I have not fallen once. This pony did not defeat me."

"Hah! The horse is older than the ancients and can barely move. When the enemy chases you, you will have to mount on the run." He dismounted from his mustang, placed his hand on the two-year-old's rump. "This here pony. When he runs, go right after him. Mount in the same way you did before." He slapped the pony. Running after it, Lozen leapt too soon, and landed flat on her face.

"From Horse Butt Woman to She Lies With Dirt. You are determined to change your name, aya?"

Lozen picked herself up. "Show me."

"Some things are to be learned on your own, for you may not always have someone to teach you. Get the horse, go again until you can do it right."

Lozen constantly found herself on the ground, watching the black tail of the mustang as it trotted away. While her only reward was a chafed nose and bruised chest, she was learning to judge her distances and measure her leaps. Late in the day, she completed her first successful mount.

"Now you can keep the name your parents gave you," Shonta joked. "Go to your brother now; he has something to tell you."

Lozen found Victorio outside his tipi, where he was brushing down his stallion. He tickled it behind its ears, blew gently into its nostrils. "Remember when I got this here horse? He was wilder than the wind, tried to kick my teeth out."

"Aya. You left him tied up, and when he was thirsty and starved led him to the creek, then to graze. With a bulging stomach of water and grass, he couldn't run or buck. You climbed upon him with no trouble."

"It is a better way than the whites and Mexicans, who use saddles and spurs, rob a horse of its spirit." Taking the rope that was looped over the stallion's muzzle, Victorio began leading it away. Lozen walked beside him. Under a sky swirled plum and yellow, they headed for the creek.

"It has been decided that you will go on the Four Raids of the Sturdy. If you pass all the tests, you will be allowed to train for the warpath."

Lozen shivered with excitement. "It is a great honor, brother."

They came to a field, and the ground became a bed of soft grass. Birds lifted ahead of them, and when they passed, settled again.

"Two moons ago the council met. I told them you had won many contests over the young men of the tribe, that you were worthy of consideration. Tezye and Shonta stood on your side. Still . . ." he waved his hand, ". . . it took much convincing. Loco and others were opposed, for no maiden has ever been allowed to go. We argued all night. Right before dawn, Nana spoke up for you. It was his voice that turned the count in your favor."

"I will thank him."

They came to the stream, sat on a mossy bank. Victorio let the horse loose and it wandered away and began to drink. "There is a condition, a test you must pass, or you will not be allowed to go. No woman has ever done this. If you succeed, it will increase your worth with the council, show them my words were not puffs of smoke on the wind." He then explained what was expected of her.

"What brave would agree to wrestle a woman, brother?"

A slight smile crossed Victorio's lips. "There are many ways to trap a bear, Little Sister. The ambush is already being set." He didn't tell her that her opponent, Kayate, had already been chosen, and that Shonta and Tezye had been baiting him, feeding him lies.

"She says if you are as clumsy as you are ugly, it will be easy to defeat you," Shonta told Kayate.

"Her name for you is, He Loses To Girls," Tezye chimed in. "She says you are weak in bow competition, and run like a dying horse."

"I will crush her into cactus juice!" Kayate shouted, opening and closing his thick fists.

Tezye put his hand on the boy's broad shoulder, followed by Shonta on the other side. Their voices were as stern as their looks. Underneath, they smiled. "She is a woman who does not know her place," said one. "You are the best one to show her," affirmed the other.

The news that Kayate would wrestle a maiden ran through the camp like wildfire, and by match time a large throng had gathered. Hooting and cheering, they formed a circle around the combatants in the village center. The same age as Lozen, Kayate was a head taller and outweighed her by many baskets of fruit. Dressed only in a loincloth, his arms and shoulder muscles bulged, and his bare chest stood out like a bluff. Lozen wore a long-sleeved shirt, trousers and a red bandanna. Like her opponent, she was barefoot.

They put their hands on each other's waists, waiting for the loud cry from Tezye that would signal them to begin. Eyes locked, they slowly moved in a circle. Grinning like a fox, Kayate squeezed Lozen's waist. "You have good hips, a firm body. It is a shame I will have to throw it to the ground, bruise you."

"You have no respect for women, you are always eyeing them," Lozen hissed. "I remember the time I danced with you. You had your hands on me then too, wanted me to go right out and fool around like those Navajo girls. You have missed all your lessons in manners."

Kayate's face turned dark. "I'm not fooling around now. You think you are as good as the men, that you belong with us because you can run and shoot arrows. I will teach *you* some manners!"

Lozen took her hands from his waist, tapped his forehead with her fingers. "Your head is as thick as the rest of you; you can't teach what you don't know." Just then the cry to begin rang out, and she realized she had made a crucial mistake— by taking her hands away, she had left herself open to attack. Before she could recover and jump away, Kayate grabbed her in a bear hug, lifting her off her feet. Nose-to-nose with his prize, he toted her around the circle, bouncing her up and down in his arms.

"See this bag of wind here. I will make her obey like an Apache woman, throw her around where and when I want." The crowd whooped and laughed.

Her brain a mass of confusion, Lozen was fast losing confidence. *I have made a bad mistake, and have no chance of winning. My family will think I'm a disgrace, cast me out. There will be no warrior training for me, for I have brought dishonor to my uncle and brother.* Desperate, she pushed down hard on Kayate's arms, trying to pry them apart. It was like trying to escape from a piece of wet rawhide that had tightened in the sun. The spectators jeered.

"Kayate, see how far you can fling her!"

"Careful she does not bite your head off."

"It is too swelled; no one has a mouth that big!" yelled Lozen's friend, Kinsee. Her taunt got everyone laughing.

Kayate swung Lozen around one way, then the other, pulling her to him in a crushing grip.

"Slower than a dead horse? Too weak to pull a bow, eh?" he said, mimicking what the warriors had told him.

Lozen's back felt as though it was about to break, and her breath was going out of her, when she spied her grandfather standing in the crowd. His words sounded in her head. "When your mind tells you that you're trapped, your body follows. To free yourself, concentrate on your enemy's weakness, not his strength. Use cunning."

Suddenly, Lozen realized that although she was held in a bear's grip, her arms were free! She stopped struggling, spread her arms wide, curled her fingers inwards and slammed her palms against Kayate's ears. Taken by surprise, he whipsawed her from side to side. She hit him again. Reeling, cursing, he tried to hurl his captive, when for the third time, the thunder struck. He dropped her and cupped his hands over his ears. Lozen threw her right leg behind his, hammered an open palm upwards into his chin and, with her other hand, yanked down on his hair. Flipped off his feet, Kayate landed on his butt.

The match over, the men turned away while the women flashed happy smiles. *"Houw, houw!"* they yipped, surrounding the winner, congratulating her.

Lozen was a mound of joy, her face a flower that had just tasted the sun. She felt light-hearted, almost giddy. *I have passed the council's test. I'm going to be trained as a warrior!* She looked at Kayate on the ground, his hands still clasped to his ears. *For a bag of wind, I blew you away pretty good,* she thought.

It was a blistering night, the air so dry it could have set itself on fire. Under a faint moon, eight warriors guided their horses between clumps of prickly pear and stunted mesquite. When the ground became naked, the pace increased to a rhythmic lope. Running behind them, Lozen and the other novices tried to keep up with the rigorous ebb and flow. It had been that way for two moons, the party stopping only once to drink and water the horses.

"We will wean them away from the comforts of Ojo Caliente, of our village," Victorio said to Shonta and Tezye, as the three men rode abreast. "Those who pass this first test will go on the Four Raids of the Sturdy, and be marked as warriors."

Shonta waved his arm. "They are like green peelings skinned from nuts. That one, Kinsee, has not proven herself."

Tezye spoke. "She sits on a horse well and is good with weapons. Only Lozen can outrun her. She is worthy of the challenge."

"She is the granddaughter of Breeds Horses, one who has a place of honor next to Mangas. The girl was allowed to go at his request. I granted it out of respect," Victorio answered. Uneasiness flitted across his eyes, and he changed the subject.

"Those diggers of yellow metal cross the land like insects drawn to a dead horse. They seek riches far to the west where the big lake full of salt lives. It is only a matter of time before they find their way to our homeland. Soldiers will come to protect them, cattle-raisers to feed them. The game will be driven away. It will be difficult to feed our people."

Tezye gestured at the runners. "Our plan for these young ones is a good one then. Those who endure will become stronger, help us stand against the invaders."

The moon vanished in a web of clouds. Victorio reined in, dismounting next to a massive agave. "We will camp here." Close behind, the novices breathed a collective sigh of relief, and sprawled on the ground. "Not you," he commanded, motioning into the darkness. "Go, *dotkah*. You will be given until dawn. Then, we will imitate the enemy and come looking for you. Hide well. Those found last will be chosen for the Four Raids. Leave your knives, run alone."

Dismayed, exhausted to her core, Lozen struggled to her feet. As each of her companions disappeared into the blackness, she headed towards a string of low hills, the black humps barely visible against the inky horizon. Only the yipping wail of a coyote broke the vast stillness.

Lozen ran parallel to the rolling mounds, then headed into them. She looked for an expanse of rocky ground, or a series of boulders where she could leap from one to another to hide her tracks. But the ragtag hills were as bare as the desert floor.

Night flowed into morning, into midday. The heat rose up in shimmering ribbons, the land shifting back and forth in front of her eyes. She counted in her head the last day she had eaten. Today would be three. Thirst clawed at her throat, hunger at her belly. Her face streaked with dust and sweat, her hair a bramble patch; she searched for a spot of green, a tree or bush that would indicate water. There was only a clump of bear grass the color of her buckskin moccasins. As she approached, a black-tailed jackrabbit bounded forth.

"Kee-err! Kee-ee-err!" Legs and talons extended, a hawk swooped, narrowly missing the hare that shot into a hole. Keeping a watchful eye on the hole, she took in her surroundings. Nearby, an ocotillo defended with curved, flesh-nipping thorns. Lozen knew her answer to catching the rabbit lay in the plant. But how would she do it? A childhood lesson came back to her.

"Go to that small tree over there. Strike it. Fight it. It will make you strong," Tezye commanded. Lozen pounded the tree until her hands were sore. "My nowigans will break," she complained.

"The tree cannot kill you. Lack of strength and endurance will."

She attacked the tree again, but the pain shot into her arms, coursed into her shoulders and neck like a knife slicing veins. "I cannot," she whined.

"Your eyes are too close to your bladder. You cry too much." He motioned with his hand. "Break the branch that hangs overhead, then you will be finished for today."

It took Lozen three tries before she jumped high enough to grab the limb. She tried to pull down, use her weight to break it, but her hands still throbbed and she had to let go. "We will be here until I grow too old to fight," she said dejectedly.

"Like the oak, you have other limbs."

He was telling her something, but what? She walked around the tree, studied it. Suddenly, she hoisted herself up onto the branch. Straddling the wood, she inched along to the end and, wrapping her strong legs around it, swung upside-down. Extending her arms, she grabbed a bush directly

*underneath and, using it as an anchor, pulled down hard
with her legs. The branch snapped, bouncing off her head as
she fell to the ground.*

*Tezye laughed. "You found a new way to use your head.
Often it is better to think before you act."*

Lozen now studied the ocotillo. Removing a calf-high
moccasin, she placed the open side over the long, thorny end
of a stalk. It took her several tries of hard tugging on the moccasin, but finally a sharp crack split the stillness and the stalk
broke loose. With a stone, she hacked off the bottom spikes.
Holding the shaven end, she thrust her catch-stick into the
burrow, poking and turning until it caught fur. She twisted
harder, pulled out her prey and slit its throat with the knife-
like edge of the stone. Using the tool again, she cut ragged
patches of meat from the belly. As she ate, she turned in a
circle, scanning the bleak landscape. The only movement was
a funnel of sand eddying skyward.

A sudden realization gripped her! The rabbit's blood
could be hidden with sand and she could gather the chipped
thorns, but there would be no concealing the broken stalk,
and there was nothing to wipe her tracks clean. The warriors
would see her signs. Catch her!

She held the animal at arm's length. Her eyes shifted from
it to the stalk and back again. Rubbing the pelt clean in the
dirt, she impaled it on the thorns. She undid her headband,
tied one end to the bare part of the stalk, then looped the
other through the back of her tunic sash and knotted it. With
the hanging pole attached to her waist, she ran thirty paces
and stopped. Her natural movement had caused the rabbit-
and-ocotillo broom to sway slightly from side to side,
blending her tracks into the sand. Inspecting her handiwork,
she broke into a satisfied grin.

She moved away quickly, wanting to place as much distance between herself and the remaining telltale signs as possible. The afternoon sun beat her with savage determination, and she struck out for a speck of mountains, barely visible at the end of the far-reaching plain. She wished she knew the words to shorten the day, make the night come. She remembered the story of an Apache chief who had done it long ago. His warriors were on their way to set an ambush, but the light stayed too long and they would have been spotted. The chief sang and the darkness came.

She shrugged off the heat and ran. By the time she reached the base of the mountain, the sun had dropped a full quarter in the sky. Not yet intent on setting, it notched itself between two peaks. Deepening shadows offered welcome relief, but Lozen steered away.

"Shade is where the enemy and wild animals will look for you," Tezye had taught her. "They know their prey will go there to escape the heat and sun. Even when it's a hot day, stay clear. Hide in tall grass, thick bushes. If you are wearing bright colors, remove them. Be one with your surroundings."

Lozen made for a high treeline. She wondered if anyone was following, and searched for a vantage point. After a series of severe switchbacks, two boulders appeared, a tall clump of grass tucked between them. She kneeled, parting the reed-like stems. Below, a brown, lifeless expanse greeted her. Only the molten ball moved, dropping slightly. She would wait. And watch. When night came, it would bring cover and she could search for water, a place to sleep.

Shadows began to lengthen, taking on irregular, looming shapes. She blinked heavily. Dark spots floated in front of her, and her chin dropped to her chest. Suddenly, a noise jarred her awake and, when she opened her eyes, she saw a shredded pelt at her feet. "If I were the enemy, *you* would be strung over the end of the stick."

At the sound of the voice, Lozen wheeled. Behind and above her, Tezye was squatting on his haunches, holding the reins of his horse. "It was a good trick, using the rabbit as a track-hider." He lifted his head towards the sky where three vultures wagon-wheeled in a downward spiral. "Buzzard sees many things. Next time bury the remains of your prey so it does not point out your path." He slid onto his horse and, with an outstretched arm, helped Lozen climb up behind him. He turned his horse into the high, rocky fastness.

"Be alert, even when you are asleep," he said over his shoulder. "The breeze changing directions, insects or birds stopping their calls, then starting again, or an animal calling when it shouldn't. Even a slight change in your body heat can mean danger."

"What if these things are natural? Must I always be wary?"

"Only if you want to stay alive."

A short time later Lozen stood in a blue-green drinking pool. She plunged her head underneath, lifted it and shook her hair vigorously, enjoying the waterfall of silver pellets. "It is a good place here."

Tezye looked past her. "What I tell now, you must know and practice. You must be cautious of many things. Forget once and you may die. Build fires only in safe places, where smoke cannot be seen from high cliffs. At night, keep the flames low, or they will throw your shadow, give you away." He leaned against the trunk of an oak. "Always sit with your back protected. It's too easy for bullets and arrows to find their way there." He waved his hand. "Go find a concealed place away from the water. We will eat there and sleep, return in the morning."

Upstream, where the tress grew thick and the water turned into a trickle, Lozen found a small cave among the rocks. She crawled inside, and was soon sleeping the sleep of the dead. When she awoke, it was dawn. Tezye was sitting cross-legged outside the entrance. He threw her a parfleche filled with grains. "Eat. Then we will go."

It was a long ride back, but by twilight, they spotted cooking fires. As they entered camp, Kinsee ran forward, greeting Lozen as she slid off the back of Tezye's pony. "You have won! No one else was able to hide that long, to outdistance the warriors. Even Kayate was found before you."

"What of you?"

Kinsee bowed her head. "I was the first."

Lozen reached for her friend's hand. "You will not go, then."

Kinsee nodded, and then raised her head. Her eyes sparkled and her face beamed like a new sun. Gripping Lozen's hand tightly, she was barely able to contain her whisper. "I am with child."

Lozen whooped. "That one, Kanda-zi, you have been sleeping with, better marry you."

"My parents have been very strict and watched me carefully since my feast. It was not easy for us to get together."

"Easy enough, I think." Both girls laughed.

"We were at many dances and I always chose him as a partner, so my parents knew someday we might marry. His family spoke to mine and it was arranged. Kanda-zi took two fine horses to my father and many blankets. He has agreed."

Lozen drew her close, hugged her. "I am happy for you, wife and mother-to-be."

"And I, you, warrior-to-be."

CHAPTER FIVE

BLUE HANDS—THE POWER

A herd of buffalo rumbled across a milk gray sky, thundering over the village. Thumb-sized drops splattered the ground into wet pockets, then turned into pummeling sheets. Urging the descent, the Great Spirit responded with claps of crackling applause.

Inside Victorio's tipi, Lozen sat cross-legged with the six remaining novices. They paid little attention to the storm, the lightning arrows of the Thunder People. Every eye keyed on their chief. There was no smile on his lips, no lightness in his face, as he gazed down upon them. Coal black eyes punctuated each sentence with dead earnestness.

"Kinsee will not continue. The rest of you will go on the raids." The novices exchanged approving glances. "Do not become too full of yourselves," Victorio warned. "There is still much to know. You must learn the rules, how to conduct yourselves to become good warriors. If you do not behave properly, or do what is expected of you, it will be your nature throughout life. You will fail, get others killed, or die your-self." He paused to let his meaning register.

"When you return from a raid, if you have sex many times you will always be lustful and have loose morals." He cast a baleful eye at Kayate. "You will talk about women with no re-spect." Victorio patted his stomach. "Between raids, eat only as much as you need. If you take more, you will become like the pig and never be satisfied." His voice became sterner, and he snapped his fist to his heart. "If you are weak here—you will fail. When you are afraid, walk through your fears to learn courage. A good warrior must follow instructions and be counted upon." He gestured at the spoils lining the tipi's walls. "Warriors enjoy many things. Blankets. Weapons. Horses. There will be gifts for your wives and children, your relatives and the elders. Your people will honor you; your en-emies respect you. When you go to the bow shaman to learn the ways of raiding . . ." A quizzical expression crossed his face and he shifted his gaze, following the others who were staring at Lozen. Arms stretched in front of her, palms up, her hands had turned blue.

Not knowing what was happening to her, she stammered, "The, the enemy. Three are close!"

A shout came from outside and Victorio reached for his lance. The others jumped to their feet, following him as he exited the tipi. In the dying drizzle, a breech-clouted boy came running from the edge of the timberline, jerking his thumb over his shoulder at something they couldn't see. "*Nakaiyé!* Tezye and Shonta have captured three!" Re-peating his message, he raced through the village.

On mud-splattered horses, the warriors entered the camp, pulling the prisoners behind them. Tethered around their necks with ropes, hands bound in front of them, the Mexican soldiers stumbled along the sodden ground. Their bright red-

and-white uniforms had turned into dirty rags, and their skin was raw from being dragged. The villagers formed a gauntlet, and as the prisoners passed, shook their fists, yelled and spit on them.

His eyes dark and sad, Shonta turned his horse towards a squaw. She read his leaden face, then threw her hands up and began to wail.

Tezye dismounted in front of Victorio. "We found her husband Taka at the Mexicans' camp. There were many soldiers. From a bluff, we could see what they had done to him. His head was sticking on a post; they had scalped him and cut off his ears for the bounty their government pays." He snarled at the captives. "These here were scouting when we ambushed them."

A shriek stabbed the air and the squaw rushed forward, smashing one of the soldiers in the head with a war club. He fell to his knees, blood spurting from his wound. "You will pay for my husband's death!" With a savage swipe, she whacked another prisoner in the ribs. He groaned and doubled over, drew his elbows to his sides. Raising her arm to punish the third man, the squaw suddenly went limp, and dropping the club, began to sob. Two women came forward, led her away.

Victorio took his sister's arm and held it aloft. "This one here has strong medicine!" he boomed. "When the *Nakaiyé* were near, her hands told us and became the color of a clear sky. We will now know when the enemy comes. *Usen* has given her a gift no one else holds, the Power Of The Blue Hands!" Eyebrows went up, lips pursed, and a mixed murmur of awe and curiosity ran through the Apaches.

Lozen stared at her fingers. The tingling sensation was gone and they had returned to their normal color. *What was that? What just happened to me?* Victorio interrupted her thoughts. "Little Sister, get your pony and go with the women, follow what they do. It is time you learned how to punish our enemies."

One of the soldiers caught Victorio's last sentence. "I beg of you, *noshkaa!*" he pleaded, his voice jumping like a jackrabbit. "We had nothing to do with your warrior's death. It was the officers; we are just lowly soldiers!"

Jaw muscles tight as a hunter's bowstring, Victorio trained his eyes on the man. He kept his voice resolute, almost friendly. "Some of us speak Spanish, but you speak Apache. Talk in our tongue then, so all can understand. Taka was a brave warrior, not a foolish one. Why did he enter your camp?"

"Your warrior was seen on a ridge overlooking our bivouac. An officer carrying a white flag of truce rode out to meet him. Because I speak Apache, I was ordered to accompany him."

"What did you tell him?"

The soldier stiffened and his coffee-brown face turned sallow. "*Madre de Dios,* only what I was ordered! That we would trade him a new rifle for the blanket he carried and give him gifts for his family." He looked at his comrades, his words squeezed into a thimble. "He came back with us and was admiring the rifle when my captain shot him in the back. I, we, didn't know what he was going to do."

"What does your captain look like?"

The prisoner lifted his bound wrists and ran a thumb down his cheek. "He has a scar here, and a big moustache, bigger than mine."

"Release them, they are not the ones," Victorio demanded. At the order, angry voices of surprise and indignation rippled through the crowd. The soldier glanced about nervously. "We're free?" As Shonta cut his bonds, he re-

71

peated his words to his companions. *"Compadres, estamos libre."*

Shonta sliced the last rope. "Horses are waiting at the edge of the village."

The soldiers made for the treeline; the gauntlet closed in. The crowd cursed, hit them with clubs, tripped and kicked them. Finally, the soldiers spotted the horses. *"Andale, amigos!"* shouted their spokesman, urging the others to hurry.

As they passed the last cluster of tipis, high-pitched war cries rang out, and a dozen women on horseback converged on the bewildered men. Jabbing with spears, they closed in a circle. Twisting and turning, the captives held up their hands, trying to fend off the attacks that came from every direction. A needle-sharp point drove through the eye of the Apache-speaker, coring out the socket and splitting his cheekbone to the bottom of his jaw. A second man dropped to his knees, made the sign of the cross on his chest and began to pray. A downward thrust from behind skewered his neck and he fell over, his hands still clenched together.

Not yet sure of herself, Lozen held back. A woman with a dripping lance pumped it up and down over her head, ruby drops spattering her hair and shoulders. "Stick them, kill them!" screamed Taka's widow. Kicking her feet into her pony's ribs, lance braced at her side, Lozen surged into the circle of death.

The last-standing prisoner, a bull of a man, bellowed and rushed her horse. He was missing a thumb and his shoulder bled from a bone-deep gash. Lozen hesitated, and in that split instant he swiped her thrust aside, grabbed the weapon and ripped it from her hands. Pulling back in a throwing motion, he was aiming it straight at her when Besh-a-taye's lance rammed into his stomach. He took a few staggering steps, then toppled forward, the weight of his body driving the spear through his core. The women, silent, broke and headed away.

Her head hanging, Lozen moved at a funereal pace in the opposite direction. Besh-a-taye pulled up next to her. "Do not be so sad, daughter. It was another lesson."

Lozen's shame wriggled through her like a river of snakes. "I let the others down; someone could have been killed."

"What did you learn from it?"

Lozen shrugged.

"In battle, never hesitate or question what must be done. Forget once, and it may be your last time." She touched Lozen's arm. "Do you know why we took revenge on three Mexicans when they killed only one Apache, only Taka?"

Lozen shook her head.

"That is how many of them it takes to kill one warrior." She turned her horse. "Come."

They headed back through the village. Puffs of white smoke lifted against a clearing blue sky, and the sun brushed Lozen's face with a warm glow. Noisy children ran around and around their plodding horses, women gazed from tipi doorways, elders and warriors raised their pipes in acknowledgement.

Coming to Victorio's tipi, the women dismounted. Seated on a log nearby, he was replacing the broken tip of a lance, binding a bayonet to the sotol stalk with cow's hide. Without looking up, he waved a strip at Lozen. "The people speak well of you, honor your Power Of The Blue Hands."

Lozen squatted, arms folded over her knees. The ground held a special fascination. "The power did not help me kill the Mexicans. My hands turning blue has no meaning, serves no purpose."

Besh-a-taye took Lozen's fingers, nodded towards the heavens. "See Eagle there. It owns the sky. All birds and many animals fear it. Its beak is sharp as a lance and its claws can pierce a deer's lungs. I have seen it take a fawn on the fly, lift it to its mountain nest to feed its young. Yet with all that power and strength, it needs the breeze to guide its wings, to hold it in the sky. It trusts its instincts that it will not fail. You must do the same with your gift."

She turned her attention to Victorio. "You are a brave and cunning chief and know many things. But just as your sister, you made a mistake. She was unskilled with infighting, the way of the lance, and was not ready for the circle of death."

His voice low and respectful, Victorio answered. "The enemy was unarmed and we were many. I saw no danger."

"*THAT* was your mistake, my son."

Victorio grabbed two blunted lances, and thrust them at his sister. "Take these. Meet me where the sunflowers grow tall. I will come when I am finished here."

Lozen rocked back and forth on her heels. "I am no longer worthy of training."

"Warriors have no time for foolish pride and self-pity. Do as you're told!"

Lozen's face turned crimson. Holding a pole in each hand, she walked to the south end of the village, kicking stones as she went. She climbed a hillock, and on the other side, came to a field of canary flowers. Green-black bees bumbled from petal to petal, their droning filling her ears. She took a breath, inhaling as if she were trying to drink in the air and sunshine. Just as she was beginning to settle down from the scolding, Victorio's voice intruded, and he burst through a cluster of tall plants.

"In four moons you will go on your first raid. You must be ready." He took one of the poles from her hand. "There are many ways to use these. Watch, and learn." Gripping his staff underhand, he jabbed the air. "Stick the enemy in this way. A fast runner can go from one to another, strike many." Lozen imitated his actions.

Switching to an overhand grip, Victorio poised the lance above his head and struck it into the dirt. "This way you can kill quickly, through the skull or into the back. Throw your lance only if you have another weapon or there is no other way. Without a knife or bow, you are defenseless."

Staff at the ready, he began to circle his sister. "Try and stick me." Lozen stabbed vigorously, but he deftly batted away her attempt, the tip of his stalk bouncing painfully off her chest. "Am I that small a target, you can't hit me? Concentrate, you are letting the fox steal your mind."

Fuming at the taunting and her own inadequacy, Lozen advanced her attack. With every ounce of strength in her, she rushed forward, thrusting at her tormentor's belly. Victorio didn't sidestep. He barely moved. When the end of the stalk was a hand away, he merely shifted his weight from his front to his back foot. Thus rooted, he turned his torso slightly, grabbing the lance as it brushed by. With the full force of her frustration and body behind it, Lozen fell flat. Victorio prodded her in the rear with his lance. "Again."

The day lingered on, and Lozen's butt and torso were bruised tender from Victorio's prodding and strikes. When he left to relieve himself, she welcomed the break.

Until now, not even a gnat of a breeze had stirred. Eyes closed, she stood in the hush of the stillness and prayed.

A current of cool air wrapped itself around her body, twirling gently. Nothing else moved. Not the lightest petal, not the wisps on the willows. A draft flowed through the passageway of her spirit. Once again she was White Painted Woman. Reborn. Refreshed. A sweeping shadow darkened her momentary blindness and she opened her eyes to the sky.

Eagle. Floating. Swooping. The Great Spirit had answered.

Victorio, his business finished, returned. The two took up their sparring positions. "Thrust, Little Sister."

There was a flash in Lozen's eyes, a rise in her voice. "I await *you,* my brother."

"You are not bruised enough, eh?" His staff sped towards her midsection, but his target wasn't there, and he was struck with a hard shock of wood that hammered his sternum. Lozen mocked him. "Again, brother."

Staffs held in front of them, they eyed each other like wolves sizing up prey. Lozen shifted nimbly from foot-to-foot, the end of her pole circling at chest height to catch his slightest dodge. He went right, then left. The tip moved closer. Seeking an opening, Victorio feinted above her ear, then at her groin. Her pole whistled and he gasped from a hit to his stomach and doubled over. The flat of Lozen's lance was coming down on his back when, at the last second, he reached up and caught it. They tugged on their respective ends good-naturedly.

Victorio straightened. "I have taught you well."

"Your training and patience are teaching me to be a good fighter."

That night, as Lozen helped her grandmother braid agave fibers into rope, she related the afternoon's events.

"You have learned two important lessons, Lozen. The first was how to use the lance properly. The second . . ." stretching the fibers between her hands, she pulled them taut, ". . . was how to bait a man's pride. Both will be useful."

The following morning by the bow shaman's tipi, Lozen sat shoulder-to-shoulder with the other novices, listening to instructions from the venerated medicine man. A skullcap with a blue mountain and red horizon sat snugly on his head. Fitted over that was a band of wolf fur crested with antelope horns. His white bone necklace provided stark contrast to his plum shirt.

Still wiry at sixty, Knows No Wounds was respected for both his strong war medicine and reputation as a tenacious fighter. Armed with only a spear and shield, he would wade into the midst of the enemy, killing them without incurring a scratch. He had also become wealthy from many successful raids, and owned the finest string of ponies in camp. The apprentices listened as he lectured on the ways of the raid.

"When you speak, you must say things differently. It is called 'the beginners way to talk.' If you want to talk about Owl, say, 'he-who-wanders-about-at-night.' No matter how funny you think something is, don't smile or joke around. The warriors will not take it as lightly as you, and you will be punished."

Kayate nudged Lozen. "I will do everything in my power to make you laugh."

"With your face, it shouldn't be too hard." Their eyes met and Lozen couldn't contain the smile that split her face, for even the most evil mask never had such a scowl!

The shaman fixed them with a steely look, then swept his gaze over the others, "Once you leave this village, you will be watched as the lion watches the deer." He waved the leather quirt attached to his wrist. "Only take water from the drinking tube that will be attached to your side. If water touches your lips, you will grow ugly fur on your face like the White Eyes and Mexicans. No woman will come near you, for they do not like the roughness of javelina against their skin."

Lozen jabbed Kayate. "I will do everything in *my* power to help you grow hair on your face." Knows No Wounds shot her a scolding glance with his eyes.

"I will tell you more things now. Be the first ones up in the morning and the last to eat, drink or sleep. You will always be given the toughest parts of meat. If you go down by the fire, don't warm your food. Eat it cold, or you will always have bad luck with horses. To keep your strength and still be able to run, take food lightly like the quail."

"What *else* must we do?" asked Kayate.

"Observe the warriors, learn from them, serve them. If you go to sleep before they do, it shows disrespect. Sleep only when given permission. To help you stay awake, you will lie on a rock at night." The shaman waited a slow drumbeat. "A terrible storm will come upon the village if you bathe before returning from the raids." Pinching his nose between thumb and forefinger, he focused on Kayate with accusatory eyes. "Which should not be a problem for you."

The novices broke into belly-splitting laughter. Embarrassed, Kayate pushed and shoved them, but succeeded in only increasing their mirth. Smiling like a fox, Knows No Wounds waited until they calmed, then turned serious once more.

"Fail to follow the rules and your feet will blister, your body will become sore. You will limp and walk like a bent old woman. Everyone will know you cheated." He beckoned with his quirt for them to rise. "On each of the raids, each of you will be known as Child Of The Water. Do as I say and the warriors will respect and honor you. Go now and pray." Watching them disperse, he called after them softly. "Sleep well tonight warrior cubs; it will be your last chance for many moons."

Finding a secluded spot on a grassy slope, Lozen tried to pray. It was impossible. The Four Raids were something she had trained for, suffered for and desperately wanted, and she

78

was just too excited. Her feet took a path back to the village and the sun warmed her back. She could see a shiny spider web stretched across the end of a hollow log, and farther on, a whitetail buck fed on acorns, its velvety antlers stripped and shredded from rubbing against branches. Rutting time was near.

A strange creature with an armor-like shell, peg-like teeth and stumpy legs crossed her path. It was not an animal she was familiar with. Her mother would know. Hurrying on, Lozen found her inside their tipi. Meat was curing on a rack by the fire, and stew boiled in a pot. Her grandfather sat quietly nearby, smoking his pipe and wrapping a piece of rawhide around the stone head of a war club.

"The animal you have described is called an armadillo," said Besh-a-taye, as she mended a moccasin. "It wears its shield on its back and no enemy can penetrate there. It has traveled a long way from México to share its power with you. If its medicine is strong, you will always be protected from harm."

Lozen's grandfather held up his palm. "Lozen, did you see the cross of ashes painted on the bow shaman's hand?"

Lozen nodded.

"He gets his power from the Morning Star."

"I have heard Loco speak of power from the gun."

"Stay away from Loco. He has a mean streak in him like them bears. He is not fond of girls who want to be warriors. Loco doesn't have the Power, but Geronimo does. Once he stood on a hill in plain view of three soldiers. Two shot at him and missed. The other one's gun jammed and Geronimo killed them all. The supernaturals fixed it for him."

Besh-a-taye set the moccasin aside. "The medicine that Geronimo and Knows No Wounds carry is known as 'enemies-against-power.' Only those highly skilled in raiding and battle are worthy of the gift given by the gods."

"You honor your family, Lozen," her grandfather said proudly. "No other woman has ever gone on the Four Raids. Not even from the beginning, from the days of the ancients."

"What of my *shimaa* here?"

"She served your father well, rode and fought bravely next to his side. Yet she was never trained as a warrior. You are the first."

Besh-a-taye stirred the pot of stew. "Eat heartily now. Tomorrow will be a long one."

Dawn welcomed the raiders with a haze of pale blue ice. Pockets of steam blew out of their ponies' nostrils, hanging in the air like frosted clouds. Lozen shivered, not from the cold, but with anticipation. Like the puberty rite, the first raid was a festive and special occasion, and the entire tribe had come to pay tribute.

A boy with a buckskin ball tucked under his arm approached her with his mother. "Ever since you smacked him with pollen during your *dai-a-dai,* your feast, he has behaved in the right way," she said, putting her hand on her son's head and smiling. "Now it is your turn for good fortune. We women, we will pray for you very hard!"

Lozen nodded graciously. The *gorosi,* the songs of well-wishing floated across the camp.

"Let your path be an easy one," her family sang.

"This pollen is to protect you," murmured the crowd, as Knows No Wounds striped the novices' faces yellow.

Kinsee led a loud group in singing. "Do not think about anger, war or death. Only horses and cattle should roam in your head. Enjoy your journey and feel good!"

Bows and quivers slung across their backs, knives tucked into waistbands, the plunderers mounted their ponies. A few of the braves carried guns. With the exception of loincloths yet to be earned, the novices were dressed as the warriors— pants tucked into high-topped moccasins, long-sleeved shirts and headbands. Running alongside the procession, children waved and shouted, while dogs with feverish tails joined them.

The first rays of the sun fingered the peaks, and Lozen's face glowed like the reddish-brown mesas in the distance. She rode tall and straight, her heart singing. She touched her arm, felt the sage scar under her sleeve from five harvests ago. It seemed like a hundred.

The band passed through the valley, through forests blanketed in deep green. While the novices were ordered to silence, the braves joked and laughed, boasting about the raids and the spoils they would capture. The afternoon sun baked hot, then reversed quickly as twilight fell. From the timberline, a scout came galloping towards them, reining in hard next to Victorio. Tezye, Shonta and Loco joined them. Hunched against the cold, blankets pulled around their shoulders, the men huddled, listening to the scout's report.

The *Nakaiyé* that killed Taka had broken camp and were moving south, back to México. With over one hundred fifty men, plus horses, wagons and livestock, the troops would need a lot of water to sustain them. Only one place within forty miles held enough, and they would have to pass through a narrow canyon to get there.

"We will be waiting," Victorio said, his voice as biting as the air. The raiding party immediately reverted into one of war.

To help shield them from the wind that came up, and to keep their fires burning, the band made camp in a hollow created by a high ring of boulders. Knows No Wounds gathered the novices. "You are still warrior cubs and cannot join in the fierce dance of war. Gather up wood for the bonfire; then you can join in the chanting."

Soon a red and orange blaze was leaping into the fast-falling blackness. Four warriors entered from the east and marched around the bonfire. After they made one full circle, Victorio and five others melded with them.

Lozen had stretched and tied goatskins over two empty water gourds, and she and Kayate drummed a rhythmic pattern with long sticks. Torsos arching up and down, their feet stepping to the beat, the twirling warriors danced with the flames, throwing shapeless shadows across the rocks. Two braves aimed breechloaders into the sky but did not fire. Others pumped bows, arrows, lances and war clubs above their heads. Some filled their mouths with bullets, or chanted.

"Wah! Wah!" they sang softly. "This is the way I'm going out. This is the way I am going to fight!"

After the ceremony ended, Lozen went to Victorio. "Why do you sing fierce songs so quietly?" she asked. "Why did no one shoot their guns?"

"If you make noise during a war dance, you will do the same in battle and draw fire." He bedded down under a thick robe. "Tomorrow we will take death to our enemy. We will be quiet then, too."

CHAPTER SIX

THE WORM

The Mexican troops wove down the narrow valley like a long, crimson worm. They swore at their heavy, stifling uniforms, the bright cardinal-red colors that made them easy targets. Grumbling incessantly about the generals who made the rules and the *pendejo* officers who carried them out, they found little solace in the fact that they were not among the majority of troops fighting and dying in the losing war with *Los Estados Unidos.*

To meet the American invasion, General Antonio Lopez de Santa Ana had emptied every one of his country's presidios and garrisons of its fighting forces. With no soldiers to defend, nothing could stop the Apaches from raiding and plundering. Those who didn't resist lived. For the foolhardy, defense was a graveyard act.

Suffering major losses in men, cattle and horses, México's richest ranchers and noblemen demanded something to be done. To assuage them, the general promised to send a contingent of experienced, battle-hardened men to control the marauders. In truth, all those soldiers were committed in the war against the Yankees. Yet, Santa Ana had to show the *ricos* some results. Therefore, he issued only one edict to his contingent of Apache-hunting troops, many of whom he had released from prison—find and kill *Indios,* bring him their scalps and ears.

The Apaches knew of the one-legged leader's orders, and would have relished the opportunity to even out all his limbs. Under his genocidal urging and influence, the Scalping Bounty Law of 1835 had been established in Sonora. Since that time, no Apache of any age or gender was safe from the greedy slaughterers unleashed across the territories.

The soldiers' most recent campaign proved to be an abysmal failure. In eleven months, they had only managed to kill a dozen Apaches, mostly women and children. Their last effort netted a single brave baited into camp that they'd scalped and beheaded. To add to his woes, the captain would have to explain the loss of three soldiers, who disappeared as if some desert devil welled up out of the ground and snatched them, leaving only a cover of sand.

Trying to think of a plausible excuse for his ineptness, he fingered the scar that ran from cheekbone to chin. Something or someone had to save him from Santa Ana's wrath and a demotion, or worse, a firing squad! He glanced at his tall lieutenant. A good man who followed orders and did as he was told. But he was also very young and not too smart. The captain's mood brightened. His scapegoat was riding just ahead.

As the column reached the canyon's guts, a bundle came hurtling down from the ridge above, showering the men nearest the wall with rocks and dirt. Another dropped heavily at the rear, while a third thudded directly in front of the officers' rearing horses. A sergeant barked an order and the men quickly slid off their skittish mounts. Smoothbore muskets pointing skywards, they took a bead on the high, empty rims.

The lieutenant unsnapped his leather holster and yanked out his pistol. Dismounting, he headed for what looked like a piece of red baggage, its sides torn into fragments. As he got closer, the ragged strips became part of the distorted shape, creating a lump of crumpled crimson.

Not knowing what to expect, he put a boot on its side and pulled it towards him, gun pointing down. Slowly, the lump rolled over. The lieutenant's arms dropped to his sides and his breath sucked in to his backbone. He stood numbed, the pistol hanging limply from his trigger finger. Carved out above a piece of white exposed bone, the decayed cave of a blue-black socket stared up at him. The belly was gutted and a pair of hacked ears was tied around the neck with a cord of intestines. The entire body looked like it had been dropped into a pit of blades. The gun dropped to the ground and he began screaming, the canyon echoing his horror.

The captain shouted at the top of his lungs. *"Que es?"* Another voice came rattling from behind and, turning in his saddle, the officer thought he heard his sergeant yelling something about missing soldiers. But his lieutenant's tormented cries curled down the canyon like prongs of barbed wire screeching against rock walls, making discernment impossible.

Abruptly, the screams stopped. Trying to stem the acid curdle welling up inside him, the lieutenant grabbed his throat. He dropped to his knees and in ponderous heaves, retched.

At the sound of the choking, his exasperated superior swiveled back. He pointed at the corpse, his voice scorching. *"Que caramba!* What the *hell* is going on!"

Eyes tearing from the eruption inside him, the officer

stood on wobbly legs, answering in a stuttering rasp. "I think, I think, maybe it's Private Morales, but, but I can't be. . . ." An arrow burst through his forehead and he dropped face-down into his own vomit.

Like a misdirected whirlwind, the captain whipped from side to side in his stirrups, searching the canyon walls for the source of death. The sergeant galloped up next to him. A savvy soldier, he knew the longer they hesitated, the less their chances for survival, and had his troops ready to ride. He nodded at the fallen officer. "*Vamanos, Capitán.* Or we will all die that way!"

"Follow my lead, Sergeant!" Pistol raised high, he motioned forward. Three arrows hissed from hidden ghosts, striking his chest in a neat semicircle. As he slumped onto his horse's neck, the sergeant grabbed the fallen reins and, leading the horse, set a hard gallop. The trailing soldiers passed their three dead *compañeros,* the officer lying in his own blood and muck, their leader who had since fallen under his mount.

Lozen and the novices had followed Victorio's orders perfectly, pushing the bodies off the cliff in the steepest part of the canyon. Making use of the chaos below, three braves slipped like lizards behind craggy outcroppings just beyond the column's front. Experienced fighters and unparalleled bowmen, they knew exactly what to do and when to do it, tactics and strategy having been planned the night before. Since the soldiers far outnumbered Victorio's small band of ten warriors, a full-scale attack was out of the question. They'd kill only the scar-faced one and the other officer, and then disappear.

Watching the troops beeline out of the canyon, Lozen thought about Taka. His widow and family would be happy to hear he'd been avenged.

CHAPTER SEVEN

FIRST KILL

For the next year, the Apaches ranged back and forth from the San Mateo and Black Range Mountains of New Mexico, to south of the border and west into Arizona. They raided missions and small towns, such as Ciudad Juarez, and then continued into the bigger cities of Sonora and Chihuahua. Each time the pillagers returned, the village enjoyed a bounty of blankets, clothing, bayonets and steel for weapons, saddles and bridles, cattle and horses.

Some raids were as short as a week. One of these netted two Mexican girls taken to be slaves. They would be treated well, and no man would be allowed to take advantage of them. Another excursion lasted seventy days and took the band hundreds of miles to the Gulf of California.

"The sky and sea are as one," said Lozen when she saw the limitless expanse. "The top of the water moves up and down like hills with blue and white backs."

The slender warrior woman had more than proven herself

worthy of every assigned task. If each novice collected an armful of wood for the evening fire, or brush for the warming circle, she gathered three. It was not uncommon to see her trudging into camp laden with water pouches for man and beast. She welcomed sentry duty, often standing back-to-back watches. The more arduous the work, the more she applied herself.

When the band finally returned to Ojo Caliente, the sun was the color of a blood pool, and as it set, the moon rose in a pale red glow, then turned silver. After sleeping for a full day, Lozen went to Shinash-a-too's tipi. Sitting cross-legged and facing one another, she presented him with several abalone shells collected from the beach. In turn, the shaman would gift them to those he had cured, to ward off further illness.

"I have something for you." He reached behind him, brought forth a buckskin war cap adorned with feathers. "These wing feathers from the hummingbird will make you fast, so no one can see or catch you. The eagle's will give you power, let you see far so you can spot the enemy. The whites and Mexicans will be frightened of these speckled ones, same as the quail that darts out from nowhere and scares you."

Lozen took the cap, thanked him, then ran to show her mother. She found her outside their tipi, sorting a large pile of acorns and pinion nuts. "That's a good war cap with strong medicine," Besh-a-taye said. "But it can't help me sort these nuts here." Lozen put the cap aside and sat next to her mother.

"The warriors' respect grows for you, and you have made Victorio proud. His decision that you be trained is honored by your actions. Now you will be allowed to smoke, and make your own decisions. You will go on the next raid or war party as a warrior."

Lozen stuffed a handful of acorns into a parfleche of badger fur. "I wish only to serve my brother and people. I dedicate my life to this."

"An honorable thing. But a woman with no man is like a stream without water. Kayate is strong, brave. He will own many horses and cattle someday. His parents have spoken to our family about taking you for his wife."

Lozen's eyes blazed and she could have cracked an acorn shell with her teeth. "Kayate? That overgrown bear thinks every woman wants to share his tipi!" A long silence passed as the winter store was packed into bags. Besh-a-taye waited until the coals of anger cooled. "You have a temper like your brother," she said evenly, "and sometimes do not keep your head."

"Taka was not angry when he lost his head."

"Taka's greed caused him to be unwise. If you do not think before you speak or act, you may find the same ending."

Lozen lowered her voice and bowed her head. "I did not mean to answer with the snapping jaws of the hungry wolf, or be disrespectful."

"Mm. Your brother turned down Kayate's offer of many fine horses."

Lozen let out a sigh of relief. "I do not need or want a man. None warms my heart."

Besh-a-taye let a handful of pinions rest in her palm. "Like these, your thoughts are hard. Someday a man will soften you."

"I have not even killed one yet," came the hard-edged answer. She held up two fingers. "In this many moons we go on the next raid."

Teasing wrinkles formed around her mother's narrowing eyes. "Two days, eh? Be careful then; with all those warriors along, you don't want to shoot your future husband by mistake."

Feeding on dangling mesquite bean pods, a doe raised her head towards the sound of approaching horses. For a few moments she stood galvanized, a clump of dry husks between her teeth. Satisfied there was no immediate danger, she continued chewing. The oncoming riders stopped on an adjacent bluff.

Lozen wore a calico vest over a long-sleeved tan shirt. From her waist, a wide loincloth hung to her knees, trailing between leggings that tucked into calf-high moccasins. A buckskin belt held sheath and knife, while a bow and an arrow-filled quiver slanted across her shoulders and back. Since this was a raiding party, she had forfeited her new war cap for a red headband. Except for smooth, soft skin, the warrior woman looked like any other brave.

Below the ridge, stands of trees fell away into a flatland, the harsh brown timberline melding into easy grasslands of oatmeal and green. Protected by the soaring boundary of a towering mountain peak, a log cabin sat nestled at the rear of a pasture. Nearby, rough-hewn lumber was stacked next to the beginnings of a new barn, and beyond that forty fat cattle grazed, their bodies outlined like canvased wagons against a slow-setting sun. A dozen horses milled in a corral and, tied to one of the posts, a mongrel yelped and barked ferociously, lunging against the rope circling its neck. Accustomed to the yapping, the horses paid it no attention.

"Leave the breeding stallion," ordered Victorio. "That way we can return next year, gather the new crop of his offspring. We are only after horses and cattle. Do not attack unless threatened."

The dog was barking alarmingly now, and Victorio spoke to Lozen. She dismounted and, like a skein of wind-whipped smoke, disappeared in the direction of the homestead. A short time passed. The yapping stopped.

From the corner of the woodpile, Lozen had a clear view of the cabin. The door opened a crack and she could hear hurried and raised voices, one a man's, another a woman's. The door swung open and Lozen could see a woman grasping her man's arm, pleading in a loud voice. He pulled free, said something and pointed outside. A small girl appeared, hugged her father's tent-sized overalls. The man patted her on the head, gave his woman a quick kiss on the cheek and, ducking under the doorjamb, stepped out. The heavy log door creaked and slammed shut behind him.

On one knee, bow up and arrow nocked in the string, Lozen stared at a body as big as a tipi. Red hair hung from his chin; massive hands held a long rifle. A gunbelt was slung over one shoulder. He looked towards the corral, and a scowl crossed his weatherbeaten face. Only one stallion and two mares remained. Apaches were driving the rest of the horses and the cattle into the hills.

Yelling, his huge feet pounding like horses' hooves, he began to run. He tripped over a lump and, falling heavily on his chest, sprawled in the dirt, gunbelt flying. Staring at his arrowed dog, he muttered under his breath, then jumped to his feet. Notching the rifle stock into his shoulder, he steadied the barrel on the top rail of the corral and threw down a bead on one of the trailing Indians.

An arrow slammed into his ear and ripped a bloody wound, twisting him around. In rapid succession, two more hammered into his chest. He fell over the rail and hung there, an enormous propped-up scarecrow, rifle hanging from his lifeless trigger finger.

Lozen turned and ran to join her band.

CHAPTER EIGHT

GRAY WOLF

Pursued by a dozen cavalry, a lone Indian galloped across a shaft of canyon floor. He lost them around a bend, and turned into one of the wide seams that cracked the granite walls. Twisting and turning his mount, he climbed through the rocky defiles. The shale-ridden trail was steep and, with its continuing switchbacks, he had to move carefully. One mistake and he could fall over the edge to his death. He came to a spot with a clear view of the trail below. The soldiers were snaking upwards.

He wasn't the only one watching. From their lookout in the palisades above, two warriors were taking in the chase. "I have not seen an Indian like him before. He is a stranger here," said Tezye.

"He distances himself from the soldiers," answered Kayate.

"Umph. Like a treed cougar, he makes his own trap. The track he follows ends at the edge of a cliff."

"The Pony Soldiers will catch him then."

"He is an Indian; they are the enemy. We will help him."

Kayate nodded with his chin. "There are too many soldiers to fight."

"When you are outnumbered, use your head, not your hands." Tezye gestured towards a spur of boulders halfway down the bluff. "Go to that herd of large rocks. When you get there, you will be between the soldiers and the hunted one. Let out a war cry, show yourself quickly between the boulders. After they spot you, run away. Take off your headband and shirt, let yourself be seen again, utter another cry. Shoot an arrow or two. In that way they will think there are many warriors and turn from the chase."

"What of you?"

"Your deception will give me time to reach the chased one, lead him to safety."

Without a word, Kayate slipped off his horse and slanted down off the escarpment. It wasn't long until he reached the boulders. He examined the hiding place. It was a perfect spot. The narrow path below him held a dangerous turn—the Pony Soldiers would have to move like bunched snails. Secreting himself so that he could see, he waited until the soldiers reached him. After the fourth one had passed, he let out a shrill war cry, disappeared among the rocks and trees, then showed himself and was gone.

Taken by surprise, the soldiers responded as though they'd hit a stone wall. Trying to contain their skittish mounts, the men struggled to maneuver in the thin gap. Curses and oaths mingled with the jostling of saddles and harried hooves. Another high-pitched whoop ripped the air. Then, from a different direction, several arrows fell.

Above, the Indian watched his pursuers struggle to contain their horses, then continued upwards. Rounding the next bend, he halted abruptly. Near the edge of a cliff, a lone brave sat on his horse. Hands and weapon operating as one, the long shaft of the Indian's flintlock came up, pointing at the warrior's chest. The brave made no attempt to reach for his own weapon, but instead turned away. He rode along the rimrock, and then down into a jagged crease. The outsider followed.

Two days later, the same breech-clouted boy that had brought the message about the captured Mexicans now carried news about a stranger. The village teemed with curiosity, and as Tezye and Kayate entered camp with the brave, chattering women and playful children surrounded them or fell in beside their mounts. Eyeing the stranger with distrust, elders and warriors stood mutely by.

Taller than his escorts, the outsider sat straight and dignified on his horse. Two strands of braided black hair draped over powerfully-built shoulders, and a single white eagle feather adorned the back of his head. He wore wood-scalloped red earrings and a sheathed knife hung from his neck. The tip came to just above his waist, pointing to a blue loincloth. Hooked into a dark green belt was a long-handled tomahawk. An ammunition bag held by a strap of beaver fur looped diagonally over his shoulder and chest.

The Indian's arms and chest looked like they had been carved from stone, the angular torso narrowing to a slim, hard waist. Under taut copper skin, lean thighs rippled with sinewy muscle and long legs stretched into reddish-brown moccasins. His nose was aquiline, his lips thin. From the warrior's ears, painted black lines arched across high cheekbones down to the bottom of a sharp jaw.

Standing with several other women, Lozen didn't realize she was gawking until Kinsee poked her. "Your jaws are open so wide you must be catching insects for dinner."

"Will you invite him to your tipi before he dismounts?" chirped another woman.

The only sound that reached Lozen was that of her beating heart. Ignoring the taunts, she ran to get ahead of the riders, to be near her brother when they reached him. She wanted to hear everything, to know everything about this man, the mere sight of whom sent tingles coursing through her veins.

"This one here, we found him running from the soldiers in the Canyon of the Ancients," explained Tezye. "He knows our language, says a Lipan Apache gave him shelter during a fierce storm. He learned it there."

Victorio stood with arms folded across his chest. His voice held a suspicious tone, and his deepset eyes held no hint of friendliness. "You are not one of us, or any Indian we have ever seen. What is your tribe?"

The warrior's voice was as deep as his chest. "I am called Gray Wolf. My clan is the Seneca and I am their chief. I come from the Nation of the Long House far to the east." He gestured at Tezye and Kayate. "If not for your warriors and my own swift pony, I would be captured or dead. I am thankful to the great chief Victorio, and the two that saved my life."

"You come from a place no one here has ever been to, or heard of. Why are you here?"

"At one time my people were strong and healthy and lived to be old. We made much wampum from furs hunted and sold. We traded and bought wisely and acquired many pieces of land, raised fruitful crops. All others respected us as a nation of wealth and power. Then many whites came and took our land. They killed the game for themselves and trampled our crops." He paused and, when he continued, his voice swelled. "When we tried to protect what was ours, they sent soldiers and drove us from our homes. Our long houses sat naked and bare.

"The White Eyes dogged us like a wolf pack on the trail of the wounded moose. Wherever we went, the soldiers followed to kill or capture us. They put us in places called reservations, places we did not know called Allegheny and Cattaraugus. We escaped, but they always caught and returned us." Palms up, he stretched his arms in front of him. "Like the Apache, we are a free nation and do not want to live under the rule of another. The council decided a new land far away could be the answer. I have come to seek that land."

Victorio unfolded his arms. "We share a common blood, a common enemy. You are welcome here."

The Seneca took his Kentucky long rifle from a sheath that hung from his horse. Holding it chest-high with both hands, he handed it to the Apache leader.

Victorio examined the ornate brass patchwork set in the side of the maple stock. He threw the flintlock to his shoulder and sighted it to the sky. "It's a good gun with a straight barrel."

"It is yours."

Victorio lowered the rifle. "One of our braves was murdered by Mexicans, and his widow and children have left here to live with her sister. Their lodge is yours. Kayate will show you. We will water and feed your horse. Someone will bring you food."

Her eyes glued to Gray Wolf, Lozen watched until he and Kayate were out of sight. Butterflies fluttered in her stomach and her head felt as though it was swimming in the clouds. Her mother appeared at her shoulder. "Kinsee has invited us to eat."

"I am not hungry," Lozen answered, her eyes affixed to where she'd last seen Gray Wolf.

Crooking her arm through her daughter's elbow, Besh-a-taye began to walk. "You are, just not in the way you think."

Outside Kinsee's tipi, the smell of cedar smoke, corn and meat stew greeted them. They ducked through the flap, entered and gathered around the fire. Lozen could contain herself no longer. "Have you ever seen an Indian like Gray Wolf? There is no other who rides so proud!"

"Not even Cochise, eh?" teased Besh-a-taye.

"He is a great chief, but old."

"Kayate is not old. He does not hide his feelings for you," answered Kinsee, as her little one sucked on her stew-flavored finger.

Lozen took a piece of corn from the ashes, nibbled at it. "Kayate is but a boy."

"How will you capture the Seneca then?"

Lozen's voice danced. "I will sing to the sun and he will stretch a spider's net to catch him."

"Your love power may not work, daughter. Gray Wolf's beliefs and customs are not ours."

"I will pray so he will take on the nature of the butterfly. He will think of nothing else and fly to my nectar." The women laughed.

Walking back to their tipi, Besh-a-taye spoke softly to her daughter. "I have lived many harvests, Lozen, seen many things. My only wish is that you be safe and happy in your life. Know this, and do with it what you want. A lone wolf will not stay in a strange den long. The Seneca will return to his people."

Lozen touched her mother's cheek with her lips. "*This* wolf will be mine."

That night she slept little, tossing and turning as frequently as her thoughts changed. Did Gray Wolf already have a wife? Did his tribe accept outsiders? Could she leave her own people?

She got up and went outside. Excesses of stars glittered around a beacon moon. "They are as many as my thoughts," she muttered. She walked past Taka's tipi. Gray Wolf's horse was tied outside and she wondered what it would be like to share his blanket, feel the strength and warmth of him next to her. She stared at the heavens, hoping the answers would fall from the sky.

Dawn came and she took a basket and went into the hills. She picked chokeberries, ripe raspberries, crimson strawberries and wild grapes. After setting her brimming basket in front of her brother's tipi, she gathered firewood, started a cooking fire for her mother, then fed and watered Victorio's horse. She had never forgotten what her grandmother told her. "Just because you are a warrior does not give you the right to place yourself above others, or forget your womanly duties."

The sun draped its warm mantle across the back of the Sangre de Cristo Mountains, and Lozen headed for the Smoky Water. It had been a long time since she'd relaxed in the spiritual waters, and she was hopeful they would clear her mind.

The morning was cool and the temperate mists rose like vaporous curtains, blocking a clear view of the springs. Lozen walked through the veils of gray and found a spot to her liking. Eyes closed, arms reaching for the sky and face uplifted, she prayed to the sun for spider strands and the love power of the butterfly. She then sat in a lotus position, palms up and arms resting on thighs.

Breathing deeply she prayed again for the power of *Usen* to guide her.

The mists curled around her like tentacles of twirling ghosts. Streaming white clouds flowed across her mind, car-

rying her upon them as they billowed to the heavens. An eagle passed below and she dropped onto its back as it soared closer to the sun. She was one with the universe, her spirit touching the ebb and flow of all things.

Suddenly, the clouds turned overcast gray. The sun dimmed and the eagle began plummeting.

She tried to focus harder. The sky turned black; the connection was broken. With a deep sigh, she opened her eyes. Warming air had turned the clouded vapors into transparent veils, and she could see a broad, muscular back. The figure turned ever so slightly, revealing a hawk-like profile. Her eyebrows shot up and her eyes went wide. Gray Wolf!

Surprised and disarmed, she was unable to check the words that blurted from her lips. "You there! Your presence here has, has . . . disturbed my prayers. Have you no respect for anyone but yourself?"

Without turning, Gray Wolf answered. "The steam rises from your voice as it does the water. If your ties to the Great Spirit are as thin as leaves, more prayer would be useful."

"Who are you to tell me how much I should pray and what I should do? I am a warrior and make my own decisions!"

"Decide to pray elsewhere then. You chatter like a pack of hungry geese."

Lozen's face pinched and she sprang to her feet. The pleasant tingles she had felt just a short time ago had turned into a bed of hot coals. She tried to sift out her clouded thoughts and speak, but her tongue caught in her throat. Fist clenched, she walked stiffly away.

Hoping the Mountain Spirits would provide an answer to her dilemma, she headed straight for the sanctity of Salinas Peak. The light lifting over the mountain was a sign that life was soon to begin its daily chores. In an oval clearing surrounded by fir and aspen, she came to her prayer site. On a rock nearby, an orange-gray lizard did pushups, its legs pumping up and down in staccato rhythm. As it warmed, the creature's leathery skin became brighter, the colors melding into a waving blend.

Not the least bit hungry, Lozen wondered why her stomach was growling and if the loud gurgling would frighten the lizard away. Sitting cross-legged, she tried to gather her thoughts. Her head a cocoon of conflicting emotions, she shouted in exasperation. "If this is what feelings of the heart are like, I was right not to want a man!"

"There is no pleasure that comes without some pain," a voice answered back, as Besh-a-taye emerged from behind a massive tree trunk. She had been fasting and praying, and was on her way to gather berries before returning to the village. "I have seen your manner many times, from many women. You are like a woodpecker without a beak, tapping at the tree until your head hurts. It is always the same, always about love." She sat next to Lozen. "Tell me what happened."

Lozen explained the morning's occurrences, then: "I did not understand your meaning about Gray Wolf. I've had no pleasure with him."

"Did your eyes not feed you a feast when you first saw him? Even though you are angry, does his spirit still not touch yours?"

"There is a buzzing in my ears and I can't think of anything else."

"It is as it should be."

Lozen touched her fingers to her eyebrows. "Since he has been here he looked my way two times, yet has taken no notice of me."

"There is good reason. He cannot see you are a woman.

See the lizard, there. It disguises itself to blend in with his surroundings, to hide from the eagle and hawk."

"My clothes!" Lozen shrieked, her face looking as though the sun had risen inside of it. She pulled at her shirt, at her loincloth. "He sees only a warrior!"

"Clothes are easy to mend, daughter. But you must change your ways as well, or you will always face his back. No man wants to be with an angry she-bear."

Grabbing Besh-a-taye's hands, Lozen jumped to her feet, pulling her mother up with her. "Teach me womanly ways!"

"Hah! I am not sure I will live that long."

Inside Victorio's tipi, another discussion was taking place. Victorio lit a clay pipe, took a long puff, then handed it to his guest. "This pipe is for all with red skins that come in peace. It is filled with dried leaves of white and red flowers, mixed with sage and sumac. We do not use tobacco from the whites or Mexicans, for we would breathe in war."

Gray Wolf inhaled the mixture. "My people are one with the five Nations of the League of the Iroquois, the most powerful of all Indian nations in our land. The eight Seneca tribes are Wolf, Deer, Bear, Snipe, Beaver, Heron, Turtle and Hawk. We are known as *Ho-man-ne-ho'-out*, keepers-of-the-door. We were the first guardians against enemies to the land, the *Nun-da' wa-o-no ga*. Our brothers are the Cayuga, Mohawks, Oneidas and Onondagas. Together we stood strong when the whites came. But they are as many as grains of sand and their soldiers are well armed. Many of our people have been slaughtered."

Victorio reached for the extended pipe. He took a long puff and exhaled. "Our big trouble comes from the Mexicans, the *Nakaiyé*. We have not had as many problems with White Eyes, the *Indaa*, but know of their treachery."

Loathing spread across Gray Wolf's face. "They are like poisonous plants that cause itching everywhere."

"I have many brave warriors. If the pale ones come, Apache tribes from our nation will join us in the fight."

Gray Wolf reached for a chokeberry. "I met one of your warriors today in the place where the wet clouds lay on the ground. He said I had broken his prayer and should not be there. I do not wish to dishonor you or your people, Victorio. If the waters are for Apache only, I will find a new place to speak to the Great Spirit."

"The springs that smoke are for everyone to share, Apaches and Seneca alike. What did this brave look like?"

Gray Wolf shook his head and held out his palms. "I faced the rising sun and my back was turned so I did not see. The voice was young and he yelped like a wolf cub."

"Humph. You have met my sister then."

"Your sister is a warrior?"

"Do not be fooled, Gray Wolf. Lozen has many skills and great courage. She can run faster and farther than any man, is deadly with the bow and other weapons. There is none among us that can match her on horseback."

Gray Wolf shook his head. "I respect your ways, but . . ."

"Challenge her to any of the things I told you, decide for yourself."

"How will I know her?"

Victorio waved the pipe and wisps rose from the bowl. "Like this pipe here, look for the one with smoke rising from her head."

CHAPTER NINE

MOON IN THE WATER

The sun dipped like a golden shield behind swirls of clouds, casting hues of ochre and pink across a streaked horizon. In the pastel light, a figure flowed through the village on winged feet. The red headband was gone, and the dull hair, having been washed in yucca suds and mint leaves, now gleamed like a black waterfall. Parted and drawn at the back, it was knotted at the nape in an hourglass. Two necklaces, one of turquoise and the other of laurel seeds, looped over a bright yellow blouse. A new pair of plum-beaded moccasins offset a buckskin skirt.

Reaching the edge of the village, Lozen headed for her secret, hidden pool. As a young girl, she had discovered it nestled among the cottonwood and fir on the far side of the stream. Water from melting mountain snows and warm summer rains had carved out a rugged oval in the rocks, and sheets of somersaulting drops cascaded through the wide mouth.

Farther down, other watery basins provided private places for men and women to bathe separately. Laughing and splashing, the merry sounds of mothers and maidens mingled with the hearty cries of men and boys nearby. When everyone was gone and the night lay still, Lozen would perch on the small sandy shore by the pond.

The moon, sitting upon the upside-down reflections of the trees, was a blue pearl at her feet.

When a breeze would dust the water's surface, the moon shimmered. When the breeze stopped, it was as though the Great Spirit held it in his hands. Moving left or right, Lozen could position the reflection in the notch of a tree, or place it between the branches like a beaming headdress. She often imagined herself to be a great warrior and medicine woman, that great chiefs would come from far to seek her advice. Now, different sensations stirred within her.

Hot and cold all at the same time, her skin changed from goose bumps to sweat and back again with every step. She had prayed for butterfly power, but not the ones flitting around in her stomach! At one point on her way to the pool, she heard the thumping of distant drums, then realized it was her heart pounding in her ears.

It had been that way since she left her mother's tipi, and saw Gray Wolf standing with Tezye. In spite of her nervousness, she managed to keep a calm exterior, even remaining somewhat aloof. Aware of the Seneca's stare, she had followed her mother's advice, given to her that morning.

"The doe does little to attract the buck, is never the aggressor. To capture a mate, it must only give off the right scent."

As Lozen walked to the pool, she let sweet-smelling pieces of mint leaves fall from her hand. She didn't need to see if Gray Wolf followed. She could feel him. Settling by the waterfall, she removed her moccasins, curling her toes into the sand. Moonlight edged from her toes to her nose. She heard Gray Wolf approach from the opposite side of the basin, and when he appeared, greeted him with a smile and a pleasant tone. "This place is for all Indians to share."

"You are the insulting woman my back met at the Smoky Water, eh?" he answered.

Coals ignited between Lozen's eyes, and it seemed as though bullets would fire from them at any second. Then she remembered what her mother had told her about the angry she-bear. "You surprised me there," she said, trying to sound convincing. When Gray Wolf didn't respond, she continued, "My brother says you are a big chief and have taken many coup."

"I have been fortunate in battle."

"What of your village, your family?"

Gray Wolf sighed. "We are called *onotowa-ka*, 'the-people-of-the-big-hill.' My village was known as *Cha-da-queh, T,* the Place Where One Was Lost. It is no more, but once lay where the lakes spread like open fingers, settled among the wooded forests and green hills. All of us were as one family, as much brothers and sisters as if our children came from the same womb. Many families lived together in the long houses."

"You live there no longer?"

Gray Wolf shook his head. Silver light lit his features and stern jaw. "The White Eyes came as fast as the river flows after a storm. *Ga-oh*, The Spirit of the Strong Wind, is said to be a messenger of the Indian God alone, *Ha-wen-ne'-yu*." He picked up a cluster of maple and gold leaves and cast them into the air. "Yet he blew them across our land like so many leaves."

"Victorio told me of the place you did not want to be, the reservations."

"For a long time we fought fiercely. One day a Bluecoat scout came with a message saying they wanted to sit in council. We went to their fort, met under a sign of truce." Gray Wolf fingered a silver-etched amulet hanging around his neck. "I wore this charm with two clasped hands signifying peace. My grandmother gave it to me when I became chief."

Lozen stood and moved to the edge of the pool. "The fort, what happened there?"

"The chief of the soldiers had a paper from the Great White Father in Washington, the leader of their nation. He said if we stopped killing the white settlers and fur traders, they would send no more soldiers and we could stay in our homes and villages. I returned as the-one-who-speaks-for-the-others. It was winter and we needed food and clothing, to be in a warm place. The council agreed to their terms. On the day we made our pledge, the gray garment of death disappeared from the sky and brightness shone upon my people. We lived under the Great Law of Peace and turned away from war."

For a long time he remained silent. Across the few feet that separated them, Lozen could feel his pain. Finally he spoke.

"Because of the paper, my people felt safe. The warriors went on a big hunt. While we were gone, soldiers attacked our village."

Lozen shivered as his next words wrapped around them like a circle of fire.

"All male children and half the women were shot as they ran from their burning lodges. A few girls and old ones escaped and hid in the woods." He touched his forefinger to his cheek. "Many were sick with the white man's illness that makes tracks in the skin, and died in the cold. My mother, sister and her infant were among them."

"Your voice is angry, but your heart is filled with grief and pain."

"There is more to tell. When we returned from the hunt, we were captured and taken to the reservation. They said we had stolen mules and spoils, broken the treaty. Later we learned that they knew it was untrue. Whites do not weep for others; their cries are only for themselves, for our land."

"Their promises are like tracks lost in the rain."

"I escaped the reservation. The Creator sent me to find a place where my people can live in freedom and the children can grow old. He does not wish us to live under the dark shadow of fear and death."

"Have you found that place?" she asked, hoping this was his last journey.

"I have traveled far and crossed the land of the Sioux. I met Tantanka Yotanka, the great chief known as Sitting Bull. I have been to the land of the Pawnee and stayed in their houses of dried mud. I have shared fires with Cheyenne, Crow, Blackfeet and now the Apache. In the four seasons I have been gone, I have seen no place where Indians do not have trouble with whites." He shook his head. "Soon the Seneca will be no more."

The heart tug Lozen felt swept over her like a warm bath. She hiked up her buckskin skirt and entered the knee-deep water. Coming to the edge of the basin, she slipped on a polished stone, and was falling when Gray Wolf caught her, lifting her as if she were a feather. He pulled her close. Clinging, she looked up. His dark wren's eyes beckoned.

"I am sorry for your troubles," she whispered.

"Do not wear a long face for me, Lozen. My people will survive." He stroked her cheek, then kissed her as light as a snowflake.

Lozen had never felt a man's lips before, and suddenly her

body rhythm changed from an easy ride to an eager gallop. They kissed passionately and a strange tingling shot through her like the twang from a bow. Her fingers dug into Gray Wolf's back and she could feel his hands searching underneath her skirt, his member pressing hard against her thigh. Heat rose from her loins and, stepping back, she dropped her skirt, then curled up her blouse and lifted it over her head.

Gray Wolf's loincloth fell from his waist, and he gently lowered her trembling body to the sand. Beneath him, she quivered with ecstasy as his lips covered her flushed skin. Then he was in her, thrusting, penetrating, pulsing. Her cries of rapture filled the air, her moans mingling with the sweet smell of honeysuckle. They made love many times during the night, the moon bathing them in a blessing glow of balmy silver.

Lozen awoke with her bosom against Gray Wolf's naked back. It was chilly and she hugged him close, kissing his bronze skin, inhaling the scent of her man. Passions fired again, she tried to wake him, nibbling on his ear. "The day waits for us," she whispered. He merely twitched and snored louder.

Easing away, she slipped into the water. She sang a morning song.

> *Lover, awaken*
> *Wash the night from your body*
> *Make your blood run fast*
> *Mine too!*

Emerging from the pool, Lozen dried herself with her blouse, hung it on a branch, then donned her buckskin skirt. Spying her moccasins on the other side of the water, she noticed something glinting in the early morning sun. At first she thought it was the beads, but the glitter was thin and moved with the breeze. Curious, she walked to the edge of the basin for a closer look. Her eyes blinked softly and a feathered smile touched her lips. The silver net of a spider's web stretched between the moccasins, and flitting on yellow wings, a butterfly hovered above.

In the days that followed, the couple spent every possible moment together. Lozen moved her belongings out of Besh-a-taye's tipi, and made Gray Wolf's her own. The camp teemed with womanly gossip and good-natured joking.

"Her head and feet are in the clouds, and she floats as if she had a dreamcatcher full of good omens, full of deer," Kinsee told a stump of a woman as they nursed their babies. "There is no time that she speaks when Gray Wolf is not stuck on her tongue like honey."

The woman chuckled. "The hive must be full, then."

The next morning Lozen and Gray Wolf left camp. They wanted to be alone, to discover one another, to find where their hearts and spirits lay. Lozen was anxious to show him the land of the Apache, and share new adventures.

Fall graced the land with dripping bouquets of yellow, cranberry and gold. Rains turned forests and rolling hills into glistening greens, and dancing fields of wildflowers unfurled in bursts of newborn splendor. For Lozen, the sky had never been as blue, the sun as bright, the vistas so exhilarating.

She rode the horse Victorio had given her upon completion of her warrior training. Emblazoned with a white star, the black stallion's head nodded up and down regally, and it high-stepped on prancing hooves marked by matching white socks.

Journeying south and west, Lozen and Gray Wolf took a wide berth around Fort Bayard, and the nearby white settlement of Silver City. Passing Pinos Altos, they climbed north to the upper slopes of thick spruce and fir. They had no interest in anyone or anything but their own world, and even Indian villages Lozen knew to be friendly were shunned.

In the fertile Mimbres Valley, they came upon a large herd of antelope grazing in an open field. The pronghorns were as fast as a fierce wind. To down them, the hunters would have to get close. Staying upwind and using dense trees as cover, they got within forty feet before they broke out of the bosques, and charged. The antelopes bolted.

Lozen raced alongside the fleeing tan and white mass, then pulled away and yanked her pony up short. Hundreds of bounding animals flew by in waves. As one began its flying arc, Lozen's bow sang. The arrow caught the soaring animal just behind its front leg, piercing its heart.

Lozen looked back to where Gray Wolf was standing by his kill. Skinning knife in hand, he was staring in her direction. She trotted her horse over to him.

"I have been on many hunts with many hunters," he said, a look of admiration and wonder crossing his face. "Yet none has ever made a kill in such a skillful way!"

"Yours was dead before mine," she complimented.

After cutting up the meat and wrapping it in the hides, they found a small creek with a pond. Broken branches and leaves had dammed the rocks and swirls of algae created patterns of lime green marble in the standing water. They built a fire pit and roasted the meat. Lozen's smile was constant, her mood light.

"I love this land. I love the mountains and valleys, rivers and streams, canyons and forests, the deserts and cactus. I love everything we can see and things we cannot. I love them as I do my family, for they are mother and father to me." She knelt in front of Gray Wolf and looked up into his eyes. "As I love you."

He kissed her and cradled her head against his chest. "You are the blood that runs in the rivers of my heart, Lozen."

"May the water flow forever then."

Morning found Lozen applying a thick paste to the horses' hooves. "Our ponies will need protection from the rocky ground and hot sand where we will next travel," she told Gray Wolf. "I have mixed the antelope's liver with ashes, and will apply it several more times. It will harden like the white man's horseshoes."

A week later, they were in high rim country, at the canyon-of-no-beginning-and-no-end. Condors with red beaks and ten-foot wingspans glided through the monumental abyss, their shadows swimming across walls of massive granite that jutted into the sky. Seamless layers of pinks, purples and reddish-browns stretched in rock rainbows to the cavernous gorges and valley floors. They followed the river that cut through the chasms like an indigo snake, and bathed under waterfalls that fed dazzling pools. Riding side-by-side, they headed out again, their only objective to wring as much pleasure out of life as possible.

"I am curious to know how you came to be chief," Lozen said.

"One of my ancestors was the grandmother of our great father, Hiawatha. She chose him to be chief, and I came to leadership in the same way. It is how all our chiefs are chosen."

A spark of mischief lit Lozen's eyes. "It is only right that women pick the leaders. It is because we are stronger, wiser and know best!" She punched her pony with her knees and it leapt forward, breaking into a sprint. She had only gone a hundred paces when something whizzed by her ear, thudding into a tree and splitting the bark. Her mount came to a quick stop, its front feet sliding and haunches buckling as she yanked back on the reins. Without a word, Gray Wolf trotted past her and wrenched free the tomahawk buried deep in the trunk.

"That is how you became the head of your nation, by throwing weapons at your women?"

Tomahawk in hand, he flapped his arms. "When a woman's tongue flies like a scared bird, it becomes necessary to quiet her."

"It's not the bird that's afraid, but the one who seeks to still the truth." She turned the butt of her horse towards him and trotted away. He caught up with her, then rode ahead.

Staring at his proud figure, she thought of the many things that endeared him to her. He was not only a brave warrior who fought for his people, but a man of truth, his pride muted by true humility. It was a striking change from the boastful warriors, who reminded her of a prairie chicken—puffing up its feathers and neck, fanning its tail feathers and strutting a dance, then booming a call—all to impress a female.

They left the northern roof of Arizona and cut back through the midsection of New Mexico. After passing the Rio Bravo River and Tropic of Cancer, they came to the Gulf of México. They galloped along a serpentine shoreline, their horses' hooves kicking up salty spray. The wind caught Lozen's hair, whisking it into spiraling furies that lashed her face and neck. Later that day, their bodies scooped out twisting shallows of sand—their passions rising and falling to the sounds of lapping waves and squawking seagulls.

"Our father watches over us even as he goes to sleep," Lozen purred, as a yellow-orange orb drifted beyond the wavering horizon. She told Gray Wolf of how White Painted Woman and Father Sun became as one, and the story of their children, Killer Of Enemies and Child Of The Water, who created Apache life.

"Our Great Father, the God *He'-no,* came from a place of the same nature. He lived in a cave at the mouth of Cayuga Creek under the great falls called Niagara." Gray Wolf spread-eagled his arms, playfully bumping Lozen's nose. "The water drops there as if the sea turned sideways and rained from the sky."

Lozen nipped his copper skin, kissed his arm. "You miss your land, your people."

In silence, they gazed at silhouettes of pelicans and gulls swooping to the sea, only to rise with flopping catches. Gray Wolf was the first to speak. "Let us remember the seasons. Without end, they return as often as they disappear."

Lozen rested her head on his shoulder and curled into him. Awash in a balmy breeze, they looked at each other with eyes that wished for eternal togetherness, but knew the inevitable truth.

With no specific direction in mind, they traveled north out of México, crossed the Pecos River and strayed east into the vast, wind-swept plains of Texas. The songs of horned larks filled the air, and chirping prairie dogs popped in and out of burrows. From a ridge, Lozen and Gray Wolf watched a sea of brown humps that rolled out before them. "I have enjoyed buffalo meat over a Sioux fire," he said.

"In the time of Little Eagles, a herd wandered into our homeland. That is when I learned to hunt them. We are now in the place of the Comanche and Wichita."

"Friends, or enemies?"

Lozen's eyes narrowed and she panned the green expanse for signs of prowling war parties. "Once, we were as one and banded together to fight the whites. But the Comanche are untrustworthy, and have signed a treaty paper with the pale ones."

Gray Wolf's voice was hollow. "The White Eyes have a

weapon worse than poisoned arrows, more terrible than bullets or the big-mouthed guns that spread death in a wide circle. First it was the Spaniards, then the English. Now the ones who call themselves Americans bring this cursed killer."

"Is it a weapon from the gods?"

Gray Wolf shook his head. "It is a sickness from places deep in the earth where the dark spirits dwell. If I could find this thing, I would kill it. But it hides inside the body where I cannot see. Our people have no defense, and die like flowers in the cold. Our medicine men have no answer." He gestured at the herd. "It is time to hunt buffalo. We can cut one out with our ponies, run it down and shoot it."

"You know many things, but killing the *Bo'LGi'Pt* is not one of them. They have lungs the size of boulders, and can run as far as the eagle flies. No horse can stay with them. We must get close." She lifted her arm, patted her ribcage. "Aim for the hollow beneath the shoulder where the heart lies."

From an awl attached to her quiver, Lozen pulled out two pieces of sinew, then handed him a length. "We will tie these around our horses' muzzles. It will quiet any sounds that may alert the herd."

They found a long drainage and followed it, using the deep sides as cover. A brisk breeze soughed up, and every so often Lozen would stop and pinch a finger of dirt into the air, testing it to make sure they were downwind, that their scent would not reach the buffalo. They came to the end of the gully—the herd was in striking distance. They could hear cows lowing, calves bawling. Untying the sinew from their horses' muzzles, they rode quickly from cover. In rippling waves the buffalo bolted, the prairie shaking under the hoofed earthquake.

By using his knees to guide his horse, Gray Wolf's hands were free to handle his bow. He gained upon a thundering

114

male, but got too close. As if doing a pirouette, the massive bull whirled and charged. Too late, Gray Wolf quartered to his left. The horse cried out as a short horn swept by, cutting a red furrow in its chest. Eyes wide with fright, nostrils flaring, the animal reared hard to the left. Off-balance and twisting sideways, Gray Wolf was thrown to the ground. Scrambling to his knees, his arms braced in front of him, he remained motionless as rapids of shaggy death surged around him. Cloven hooves churned up the prairie, pelting and showering him with grit and ground.

Lozen had picked her target and was riding full pelt, when a horse's shriek caused her to relent. What she saw next sent snakes crawling up her backbone. Running in the midst of the stampede, was Gray Wolf's pony! Reversing her track, she whipped back along the fringes of the herd, scanning for a sign that would tell her where he'd fallen. Desperate eyes met with undulating chaos; the only thing she could see were hills of thatched humps racing by. She gathered her knees under her, and then stood on the back of her galloping horse. She spotted a gap near the herd's center, and dropped like a cannon ball onto her pony. Cutting through an opening in the thundering flank, she headed diagonally towards where she'd seen the break. Suddenly it was directly ahead, the buffalo like muddy water opening and closing around a sandbar. She pulled back on her bowstring, the feathers of the three-foot arrow touching her ear.

In front of a kneeling Gray Wolf, a cow thudded to the ground. Blood gushed from its nostrils and mouth, staining the black beard and earth, oozing between his planted fingers. He stared at an arrow buried to its feathers between the short ribs of the carcass. As the last of the herd parted and passed, he could see the four white socks of Lozen's stallion walking towards him.

"You have done a brave thing," he said, standing, wiping the muck from him. "Your horse could have stepped in a prairie dog hole and you would have been thrown and trampled, yet you risked your life for mine. I will not forget."

Lozen dismounted and patted the neck of her slathered horse. The drenched animal looked like it had been plunged into the foamy suds of the yucca, and moisture spewed from its nostrils in flaring heaves. She and Gray Wolf crossed the short space between them, and in the brightness of the noon sun, hugged one another tightly.

"My pony?" he asked. They turned, saw the horse standing near a cedar, the red scar clearly visible against its mustard chest. "We must tend to the wound quickly, or it will fill with evil and he will die."

As they approached, the animal raised its neck. Eyes wildly rolling, it stamped and snorted. They sat on their haunches in front of the trembling creature. "The cut is long, not deep," Lozen ascertained. "I will take leaves from the tree here, grind them with stones." She gestured at the creek that ran through the blue gama and buffalo grass. "Bring water. I will mix the powder and lay it on the wound to heal."

Chanting softly, Lozen edged towards the wounded horse. The stallion threw its head back and stamped again. Still singing, she moved forward. The pony calmed and put a wet nose into her extended palm. Stroking its muzzle, she tied the reins to a branch.

Gray Wolf returned with the water. While Lozen readied and applied the poultice, he skinned the buffalo. He cut out the huge liver and they ate it raw, savoring the tender taste.

"One day a Sioux brave and his wife entered our camp," Lozen said, her lips dripping red. "They told us the whites were slaughtering the great herds as fast as the blinding snow that buries the earth."

"They shame the buffalo's spirit, take only what they can sell, leave the rest to rot. When I was with the Sioux, their chief Yellow Wolf said whites do the killing on purpose. In that way, Indian nations will not be able to feed or clothe themselves, and will dry up and blow away like feathers in the wind."

Lozen gnashed her teeth. "It is easier than hunting Indians down, for we are better skilled in fighting. The White Eyes are thieves, murderers, and cowards! *Shi—zooleh—na—ee—sheesh!*"

"I do not know those words."

"It means, 'the blood goes to my throat from anger!' "

Gray Wolf's words grated against one another. "The light-skinned ones think they are superior and smarter than those whose covering is darker. They believe we possess little in the way of intelligence, the ways of the wise. Yet it was the red-skinned Wampanoags that taught them how to survive when they first came here. The whites have no gratitude, only greed."

Lozen shivered in the wind. "Already the chill comes like angry water, and soon darkness will be upon us. I will scrape the hide. We will need it to keep warm."

The pickings on the wind-blasted plain were sparse, but by the time the sun's ruddy glow dimmed to dusk, Gray Wolf had gathered enough wood for a fire. Using dry buffalo dung to catch a spark from the flint and powder he carried, he started a fire in the drainage, then returned to help Lozen. Wrapping several heart ribs and tongue in the thick-haired hide, they returned with their prize and began to cook.

"It is said the Comanche are cunning thieves, and can steal a man's horse from under him," Gray Wolf said.

Lozen sneered. "One night I crept into their camp. Around each man's wrist was a lariat leading to his horse. I cut them, took the horses while they slept." She bit into a piece of meat. "They were left with empty hands."

The wind picked up and changed direction. Where the dirt walls had served as cover and protection, they now turned the ravine into a howling funnel of bone-wracking cold. The fire was snuffed out as if The Creator had dropped an empty hill over it, and they finished their meal under the heavy robe. With Gray Wolf next to her, Lozen fell asleep, praising *Usen* for the gift of life.

She awoke shortly after the first glimmer of dawn, and felt under the dense cover for Gray Wolf. Not finding him there, she glanced down the gully where they had left their horses tied to a cedar. Her stallion was still there. His was gone! Threads of fear rapidly unspooled in her brain. Had he left to return to his people? The faint sound of moccasins on stones caused her to turn with anticipation.

Like winter spruces stripped clean, the expressionless faces of four Comanche stared back at her. Three had long braided hair, twisted into buns at the top. Their leader wore a chief's bonnet, thick with trailing feathers. Armed with lances, knives, war clubs and bows, their wickedness hovered.

Lozen reached for the knife at her side, but before she could grab it, the tip of a spear was at her throat. Lips stretched taut, the leader smirked. "The Apache dogs are becoming weaker. They send women into enemy land, the land of the *ne-me-ne*, to do their hunting."

Lozen had learned Comanche from her grandfather, and her tongue unleashed a scathing challenge. "Which one of you is brave enough to fight *this* woman!"

"They not only send squaws to hunt, but to fight for them," the chief mocked. His scarred face looked like it had been dragged through agaves, and when he spoke, needles of scorn flew from his eyes. "Apaches do not belong here! But we will show you the place of a squaw, a woman's place!"

Two warriors quickly moved behind Lozen, and powerful hands wrenched her backwards, pinning her to the ground. The lance moved from her throat to her crotch, slicing the cloth between her legs. The leader dropped his pants. Her body twisting and bucking, Lozen tried to break free. "*Ahagahe!* I will kick out your heart!"

"We will do with you as we wish!" the bare-butted warrior rasped. "Stop struggling, or my blade will end your woman-hood!"

Just as he began to lower himself, a whistling sound sliced through the air. Rooted in place, he stopped in a quarter bend. His mouth dropped open, and blood spurted from under his headdress and down his forehead, streaming into his eyes and yawning, paralyzed mouth. He pitched forward at Lozen's feet, a hatchet blade embedded in the back of his skull.

An arrow hissed, and the Comanche on her right slumped over. Her arm free, Lozen pulled her knife, jamming it into the other warrior's abdomen. He clutched at his spilling in-testines, then fell over, the gurgling sound of death coming from his lips. Lozen's eye caught a war club raining down, and just before it was about to crush her skull, grabbed the wielder's wrist. Kicking up and out, she caught her assailant flush in his chest. He fell backwards and she was upon him, slicing his jugular in a sweeping stroke. Catlike, she was on her feet, a snarling puma ready for the next attack. None came, for the only warrior left standing was Gray Wolf, his bow resting in his hand. They stripped the bodies of their weapons.

Lozen walked to the bloody-bonneted Indian, pulled off the pants wrapped around his ankles, and replaced her ripped ones. She did not like the feel of the Comanche on her skin, but it was better than the piercing cold.

"On my return from prayer, I saw their horses on the other side of the arroyo," said Gray Wolf. "They crept up on you from there."

"They wanted to steal my body. Now, they will creep no more," Lozen sneered.

Gray Wolf laid his hand on her shoulder. She calmed to his touch and drew close to him. He raised his eyes to the lingering wingspans tilting overhead. "Others may be close. Buzzard will guide them here."

"I will get the robe and my pony, then we will grab up their horses and leave this place."

In stark contrast to the howling night before, the air hung as still and lifeless as veinless leaves on a dying tree. The sun split arrays of shifting clouds, the sky swapping shades of bright light with gray shadows that dropped over their six-horse caravan. They passed the buffalo's remains, the blue-black ravens that cawed and squabbled over its eyeballs.

They rode warily, constantly searching for approaching signs of danger—animals or birds rushed from cover, or a dust spume triggered by many hooves. Once they saw a storm of spiraling powder, but it was only a herd of antelope on the move.

No words were spoken as they traveled towards the safety of Apache territory and Ojo Caliente. Deep inside, Lozen knew it was their last journey together. Over the past few moons she had sensed a certain tension in Gray Wolf, like some great, unseen force was pulling him from her. Her eyes searched his, trying to probe the inestimable, or prolong the inevitable.

After two days of steady travel they left enemy land, and found a place to camp by a reed-filled pond. Between the surrounding bushes, Lozen strung an ankle-high chain. Made from small bones taken from the buffalo, the skeletal alarm would give warning if intruders tried to sneak close.

Exhausted, she and Gray Wolf crept under the buffalo robe. Had they been as one, they could not have slept closer. Lozen wanted to inhale him, draw his spirit into hers. She tried to discard the pain invading her heart, bring her warrior mentality of toughness to bear. Each time she attempted to stifle her feelings, they grew stronger. She heard him arise before dawn, felt his gentle brief touch on her cheek. She couldn't bear to see him go and, pretending sleep, bid her love a silent farewell.

For a long time after the hoofbeats faded, she stayed still. Finally, she rolled up onto her knees. Underneath one of them was something smooth and cool. Picking up his amulet, she stared at the two clasped hands of peace. Tears misting her eyes she held it skyward, praying to *Usen* for Gray Wolf's safe return home.

CHAPTER TEN

DECEIT

Leading the Comanche ponies, Lozen tried to concentrate on her own homeland, how happy she would be to see family and friends. It was impossible, the eye of her mind focusing on images of her love. She could see his proud bearing, the commanding way he sat on a horse, his beckoning eyes and muscular body. His face appeared in a gentle swirl of blue-green algae, and his whispers tore at her. "You are the blood that runs in the rivers of my heart."

Like a cactus wren with a broken wing, Lozen's thoughts floundered. *I should have run after him, called his name! Would he have returned to my side? Should I have gone with him?* Tumbling leaves of doubt whisked through her mind and she shifted on her pony endlessly, as if a burr underneath was exacting mindless vengeance. She stopped at a drying tree, its roots exposed and ready to topple. *Like me,* she thought. She had never felt so alone, so abandoned. The sun on her face did not warm her, and that night when it rained, Lozen felt as though the sky was weeping. The place of joy she once knew was now a cactus bed full of stinging thorns. She refused to bed down without her love, and for three days stayed on her mount. Depleted, hugging her horse's neck, she slipped and fell off. Curled up under the reins, she slept in the dirt.

She awoke to a parched throat, and realized she hadn't stopped to drink since she'd left Gray Wolf. Rainwater glinting from a rock basin beckoned, and she crawled to it, quenching her thirst. Suddenly, she was struck by the reflection staring back at her. Eyes dull, the face withdrawn and sunken, it was someone she did not recognize. *Who am I? What has happened to me?* Alone with her thoughts, she took a strip of buffalo meat from a pouch at her side and began nibbling. It wasn't much, but combined with the water, the food helped to refresh her. She watered the horses, remounted and headed for Ojo Caliente.

Two more days and she came to the outskirts. She was familiar with the places where the rocks crept together, obscure, yet strategic vantage points from which Apache sentinels kept watch like cached ghosts. There were no warriors among the sentries she spotted on her way, only young boys and novices. She nodded to those who raised their weapons in welcome. They were positioned farther out than usual from the village, and there were more of them than needed for a normal watch. *Something was wrong!*

Approaching camp, the familiar smells and sounds penetrated her senses, yet the underlying rumble of male voices was absent, the throbbing pulse of the vibrant village stilled. She passed the tipi she and Gray Wolf had shared. She would live there now, alone with her memories.

Kinsee saw her first, and with toddler in tow, waved and ran to greet her friend. "It is Lozen!"

At the shout, Shonta turned from brushing his horse. Recognizing the distinct markings of the Comanche horses, he muttered approvingly. "She returns and brings *nohwik' edandiihi* ponies with her."

By the time Lozen reached the center of the village, a crowd had gathered. Den-me almost hugged the life out of her. "I did not lead you in your feast to see you run off and marry a Seneca from another land. Here, the wind knows your name."

"Victorio? Where is my brother?" Lozen asked, her head swiveling. "Where is Tezye, the other warriors?" Silence fell over the crowd like the padded footfalls of a puma.

Besh-a-taye eyed her daughter's thin frame, the dust-covered hair that hung like a tattered black bag over her shoulders. "I will tell you as you eat, for it appears you have lived only on the recollections of love for many moons." Lozen followed her inside the tipi. Her mother ladled hot acorn stew into a bowl. Lozen ignored the food. "What has happened?"

Besh-a-taye folded her arms across her chest. "You do not eat, I do not talk." Lozen had seen that manner many times before, and knew arguing would be like trying to roll a dead cow uphill. Suddenly she was ravenous, and ate as though she had never tasted food. "In the two seasons you have been gone, daughter, much bad medicine has happened. Again Apaches trusted Mexicans. Again we were deceived."

Lozen stopped eating, her taste for food suddenly gone. "Who died?"

"Soon after you left here, a message came. Geronimo and his family went with others to trade at Casas Grandes. It was to be a friendly trip, as promised by the *Nakaiyé*. On the way, they camped outside Janos, and the warriors went to the village. When they came back, crying and bleeding women and children ran to meet them. Drunken Mexican troops had swarmed down from the hills, hacked and stabbed them with swords and bayonets. Geronimo found his wife Alope and their three children scalped, bathed in a lake of their own blood."

Lozen's face was as bitter as poisoned water. "Mexicans are always drunk on greed, on hate."

"There is more bad, *izee'hi*."

Lozen stiffened. "What more news can be so terrible?"

"Two moons past, the same hands murdered more than forty of Mangas' people, including two of his wives. Victorio and our warriors have joined him to hunt down their slayers. White Eyes did the killing as well."

"Gray Wolf, he said they were everywhere," Lozen growled, her blood rising.

"What has happened to the one who carries your heart?"

Lozen waited a long time before she answered. Her blood cooled, warming to another passion. She related past events, hoarding private details for her own bed of cherished memories. Yet the pain was still raw, and her words were like cries of lost wolf cubs. Besh-a-taye laid her palm against her daughter's cheek. "The wind, the sky, the mountains change for no one. You cannot fight them any more than you can the wounds inside you. Every storm ends. You must ride with it, not let it ride you."

Lozen stared blankly across the tipi. "It is not the way I thought it would be."

"Things happen as they must. There is no shield against destiny."

"I will catch up to Victorio, help hunt down the enemy."

"You are like the desert without rain, daughter-of-mine. Rest, then go. The *nohwik'edandiihi* will always be there." Sagging over on her side, Lozen felt like a spent arrow at the end of flight. In the warmth and comfort of her mother's home, she finally fell into a fitful sleep.

That night she visited her hidden pool. Clouds had turned the surface of the pool to liquid ink, and there was no reflection of the moon. Lozen inhaled deeply, trying to gift herself the sweet smell of honeysuckle, to bring back the wonder one last time. The bloom was gone, the fragrance long faded. A breeze sighed through the pines, a song of sadness playing in her heart. Saddled by the tempest in her soul, she slept by the pool, curled up on the sandy beach.

On the second dawn after her return, the sun lit the crescents of granite clouds that clung to the peaks, while Mother Earth's hands pulled them lazily across the mountains. Ready for war, a single white band of paint swept across Lozen's cheeks, down her nose, and below her raven eyes. Her bow and a quiver of thirty poisoned arrows were slung over her shoulders. She had bathed the tips with the spoiled blood of a coyote, mixed with crushed spines from a prickly pear. On her way out of camp, she stopped at the Smoky Water. Among the rising mists, she prayed.

> *Great Spirit, creator of all that lives*
> *Whose voice I hear in the wind*
> *Whose breath gives life to the earth*
> *The path to freedom and peace is dark*
> *Show me the way, so I may help my people*

She opened her eyes, blinked, then blinked again. Sitting tall and proud on his horse, Gray Wolf smiled at her. As she ran to him with outstretched arms, a hard wind sprang up, dissolving the mist of her love and carrying him away.

The Thunder People grumbled over the mountains, and the air became heavy with the smell of rain. Digging her heels into her stallion's sides, Lozen bent into the whistling current and blowing dust. The storm had come abruptly, a sign of more bad news, of death. Galloping towards the billowing clouds that dropped over the peaks in a hood of swirling darkness, she shook Gray Wolf from her mind.

Two days later, nature provided an early-morning respite. From behind clusters of yellow-flowered brittlebush, Lozen watched a gray wolf lead her cub to a stream. The mother drank, then eased herself down onto a patch of sand. The cub plunked down next to the water. Lolling on its back, forepaws curled above a stark white stomach, the tip of its tail drooped into the freezing brook. Lozen laughed as it bounced to its feet and whipped around, trying to bite the creature that nipped at its tail with stinging cold.

Lozen gazed at the she-wolf, into the wren-brown eyes that reminded her of her man. *I see him everywhere, yet he is nowhere,* she thought. She drank from her calfskin pouch. The water, sweetened with flour ground from dry mesquite pods, had always been pleasing. Now, it had no more taste than air.

Later that day, a single column of smoke rising from a cliff caught Lozen's attention. The Apache call for identification would have to be answered rapidly, or she could be mistaken for an enemy. Gathering dry sotol wood and dewed grass, she made a smoke-filled fire. She was careful to build it to her right, indicating that she was a friend. After scattering the smoldering remains, she hid behind a mesquite and fitted an arrow to her bow. Enemies that wanted to trick her could also send smoke signals.

As Lozen waited, a bluish-gray Sonoran whip snake dropped down from one of the tree's branches and slithered away. Noiseless as the reptile, two warriors appeared from a wash, stopping in front of the ashes. Their faces were streaked with deer blood, arms and chests with mescal juice. Both were armed with a bow, two full quivers of arrows, lances and war clubs.

Recognizing Kayate, Lozen rode from cover. He flashed a surprised, meager smile. "You have been gone as long as the sand stretches in the desert, Lozen."

"It is good to see you, friend."

He nodded at the other warrior, a Coppermine Apache. "This here is Blue Raven." Lozen thought the man looked like a tree stump with arms and legs. "Do you know of Mangas, of Chihuahua?" the man asked.

"Only that two of Red Sleeves' wives are no more. They died, along with many of your people, at the hands of the *Nakaiyé*."

Blue Raven spat. "We have been looking for those Mexicans, and for the White Eyes. They share the same mask of treachery. I was there; I saw what they did."

Kayate broke in. "Victorio is with Red Sleeves at his stronghold. They await our scouting report. We must go." The trio wheeled south towards the mountains of *Tres Hermanas*.

After a half-day's ride, they stopped to water their horses. Lozen shared her dried pemmican. She had made the long-lasting staple from pounding the buffalo meat, then mixing it with boiled juniper berries. "Say what you know," she said to Blue Raven.

He nipped off a piece of hard, chewy meat. "The Mexicans were mining copper, taking the ore to Durango to sell. They built a large ranch with a fort, corrals and houses for workers and their families. A message was sent from a colonel named Espinoza, the one in charge. He invited us all to a great feast. It was to celebrate, to thank Apaches for letting them work in peace."

"Mangas trusted them?"

Blue Raven shrugged. "There had been no trouble between us, so Red Sleeves accepted. When we arrived, we were greeted by sounds of music. People were dancing and the smell of roasting calf filled the air. Tables in the square were piled with fresh fruit, corn and bread. New rifles leaned against the tables, bands of ammunition next to them. There were blankets, bracelets and necklaces, even toys for the children. The women rushed forward. Most of the warriors were untrusting and stayed back."

He waved his hands. "The *Nakaiyé* had filled jugs with mescal and sotol juice, mixed in the white man's alcohol. It was much stronger than our gray water, our *tiswin*. The day was hot. Soon many were drunk. No one saw that the Mexicans drank little, or that they slowly left the square. There was a great explosion. Hot pieces of sharp metal rained, cutting our people down. Wood from the heavy tables turned to straw, water jugs to dust."

Fear swept over Lozen like wildfire on a parched plain. "The women, the children?"

"Those who were not killed lay on the ground, bleeding from their wounds. We could see a gun barrel big as a log hidden behind some trees. Whites rushed out from there. They finished off the dying with revolvers, beat in their heads with clubs. Everyone was scalped, even the infants. Their screams stilled the blood in my heart!" He raised his knife, jammed it to the hilt in the dirt.

"People were running, falling. A boy stood at the edge of the square, bleeding from a gash in his forehead." Mimicking a gun, Blue Raven put his finger to his temple. "A white man ran up to shoot him. Before he could pull the trigger, Mangas threw his knife. It caught the White Eye in the throat. Mangas snatched up the boy and led us to safety."

Lozen frowned. "You did not fight back?"

"We were few against many." Blue Raven spit into a swarm of ants that were crippling a grasshopper. "That is what we will do when we find those who slaughtered our people! We will break their legs, eat them alive!"

The warriors remounted. The sun sank in the late day haze, trading places with the star-that-sits-in-front-of-the-others, lending the moon a warm glow. Nearing the fringes of the encampment, the threesome was immediately shadowed by several braves. As they began their climb into the mountains, silhouetted sentries raised spears against a low-lying yellow moon, granting passage.

Once inside the stronghold, Lozen and Kayate rode among clusters of dark figures, searching for their clan. Bonfires lit braves applying war paint and readying horses, weapons and food. Shields were stacked in tipi fashion, lances leaning against them, the blades thrusting into the night sky. Suddenly, Victorio's voice burst from a pocket of men. "Little Sister? Do my eyes deceive me?"

Lozen swung down from her stallion. Another, older man limped forward with his cane. It was her uncle, Nana. "You have come just in time to fight the enemy. *Enju!*"

"Where is the Seneca?" Victorio asked.

"Gray Wolf has returned to his people."

"As you have returned to yours."

A mountain rose from another circle of men. At sixty, Mangas Coloradas was still a daunting figure. Tall as an oak and wide as a thunderhead, he roared with fury. Even at the far edges of the battle-ready multitude, he could be heard clearly. His voice was so powerful Lozen thought she saw the moon tremble.

"In the dawn we will take revenge for the killing of our people. From this day, no one is to be spared. No mule trains or wagons will cross this land. No one will be allowed to settle as far as our horses can ride!" He nodded towards the chiefs. "When dawn comes, Victorio and Loco's bands will ride with me. Juh is here from his Blue Mountain stronghold in the Sierra Madres, and will lead his *Nednhi* warriors. The rest will follow Nana. My son-in-law, Cochise, watches from his stronghold in the west." Making a circle with his arms, he gripped his forearms, squeezing them to his chest. "We will close in on the enemy, draw the noose of death like the rabbit that strangles from the hanging snare!"

Approving cries of "Yee, yee, yee!" shot through the ranks. Her adrenaline coursing like a river of hot lava, Lozen became as one with the multitude that began to circle the bonfires. She stepped, twisted and chanted to the drums that beat the *?katsita?*, the dance of death.

"Think of fierceness, fighting, killing those who stand against us!" Kayate shouted.

"A man is worth nothing, if he is not willing to die for something!" yelled Victorio.

Juh strode into the dancing circle next to Lozen. He was a virile man, tall and thickly built, with braided hair that hung to his knees. "The past and the dead speak through us. We will take revenge on our enemies!"

Shaking a rattling gourd in each hand, a medicine man foot-stepped forward. "I see the *Nakaiyé* and *Indaa* falling from our arrows. They flee in front of our horses, scream for mercy under our knives. Their dead are already crawling to the underworld!"

It took until half the night was gone, before tempers and fires cooled. Walking through the camp, Lozen spied Victorio sitting atop a rock formation. Together, they watched the shards of brilliant light that splintered the darkness in the distance. "The gods light the sky. It is a sign for us to punish the enemy," he said.

"Why did they attack Mangas? He was peaceful; there was no trouble."

131

Victorio's voice filled with contempt. "The governor of Chihuahua placed a large bounty on Apache scalps. He also commands the ground from which they take the copper, so the miners had to do what he said. The White Eyes had the long gun. A blood pact was made. The Mexicans lured our people to the *rancheria;* the whites killed them and got the bounty. That is the way it happened."

For a long time, neither of them spoke. Lozen thought back to the story Nana had told her, the Legend of the Black Path. "There is none that can stand before the onslaught of Apache warriors with one direction. Happy songs of birds turn to shrieks of death. Skies turn yellow with sickness. Hills tremble. Trees bend in fear. Even the Spaniards who conquered the Mexicans could not stand before us, and fled."

Lozen touched her brother's arm. "The *nohwik'edandiihi* have chosen the Black Path."

"We will strike the enemy as fast as the speckled nighthawk, bring death like the burning arrows that shoot from the sky," came the lethal reply.

Dawn, the next morning, and Blue Raven rode into camp. He had found the Mexican troops camped in the center of a wide hollow surrounded by steep cliffs, and counted them to be two hundred. They were Colonel Espinoza's Militia of the Fourth Guard, the same that had been at Chihuahua. "Leave none alive!" ordered Mangas. "Not even the dogs!"

As if they were one, the Apaches mounted for the warpath. The attack force rode hard, scaring black-tailed jackrabbits from their hiding places behind tarbrush and whitethorn bushes. A falcon soared on dark wings, looking down on the heavily-armed men. They crossed the dry, scrub plain of the Chihuahuan desert, forded the Rio Grande and passed by the shifting dunes of Ciudad Juarez. Two nights later, three hundred warriors had positioned themselves among the murky hills overlooking the soldiers' encampment.

Surrounding the enemy in a three-quarter circle of assault, the warriors took cover behind the curled leaves of ten-foot agaves, or secreted themselves between boulders, and the tall pitahaya cactus that looked like saguaro. On the side where the gap was left open, another hundred waited on horseback with Nana. Once the enemy began to retreat, they would be driven into the hole and his men would charge, closing the jaws of death.

Dawn broke, and the revenge-seekers waited until the blinding sun was at their backs, then began their descent. The leading groups crept to within a hundred paces of the bivouacked tents. The half-dozen sentries had fallen asleep, their backs leaning against rocks and tree trunks, rifles nestled in their arms. Their *compañeros* snored in their tents. Even the mourning doves had stilled their woeful cries.

"They will soon be as dead as their campfires," Kayate whispered to Lozen. *It is too quiet,* she thought.

The semicircle closed like a bull's horns, the flanks of the formation curling into tips of sneaking death. Juh and Loco led two sides of the assault, Victorio and Mangas the other. Creeping behind them, Lozen's fingers began to tingle. She directed her face towards the heavens, mouthed a prayer.

> *Creator, I search for the enemy*
> *Grant me the power to hold the eagle in my hands*
> *To see what it sees*

A pang of uneasiness struck her stomach and surged upwards, her heart began pounding in her throat. She cast a stone in front of the chiefs and, as they turned, held up a pair of blue hands. "It is a trap," she whispered. "Many more

Nakaiyé come on horseback. They bring the *Indaa,* their long gun!"

Victorio's eyes blazed. "The guards play the sleeping fox to trick us. We must warn our men!"

Lozen snatched an arrow from his quiver, bent and ripped out a fistful of bunched grass. Binding it around the shaft, she thrust it at her brother. "Make a fire arrow, shoot it to the other side. Our warriors will see it, know something is wrong. Hurry, the long gun draws near."

Mangas nodded to the west. "After, gather our forces, meet in Guadalupe Canyon."

Fishing two flints from a pouch, Victorio struck a spark. The grass lit and he nocked the arrow, aiming at the heavens. The fire arrow soared into the sky.

By the time the arcing flame reached its zenith, Lozen was halfway across the compound, heading for the Mexicans' horses. One of the sentries jumped to his feet, and dropped just as quickly as the butt of her lance hammered him between his eyes. Simultaneously, the streaking arrow plunged into a dry creosote. The bush burst into flame; the camp became alive. Shouted orders catapulted armed troopers from the tents. Sleeping decoys rose and bodies of men wheeled and kneeled in different directions, shouldering long-barreled muskets and firing into the hillsides. Hundreds of rounds peppered the hills, the half-inch lead balls ricocheting and whining off stone crags, shaving splinters of granite that caught unsuspecting flesh.

Acrid smoke from the .50-caliber weapons was dense as fog. Using it as cover, Lozen reached the remuda without being spotted. Tearing free the reins holding a roan, she jumped onto its back and sped along the tether line, slicing through rawhide and ropes. With a shrilling cry, she stampeded the horses into the soldiers. Off guard, they broke and scattered. A dozen went down under trampling hooves.

Lozen speared a musket-loading trooper through his heart, shot another in the temple with her pistol. A trooper fronted the roan and grabbed its halter, trying to yank her down. The horse reared with flailing hooves, kicked him dead. A running figure broke from the pall of smoke. Lozen aimed and pulled the trigger. Misfire. Pulling her war club from her belt, she whirled the stone-headed weapon. Galloping alongside the fleeing soldier, she brought it down in a crushing loop. Colonel Espinoza's skull split open like a ripe melon. Before the body had crumpled to the ground, she was whirling in the opposite direction, ready to do more battle. There was no need. Her plan and diversion had allowed most of the braves to escape, leaving the soldiers to take pot shots at the last of the fleeing band.

Still using the smoke, she galloped from the camp and rode to a ridge. There, she watched and waited. Below, troopers rounded up the scattered horses, while others sifted through the wreckage of ripped tents. A doctor tended wounds. The dead officer and four soldiers were slung over pack mules and tied down.

On a mesa parallel with Lozen's view, a wagon came into view. In the bed was the long gun. Behind it, dust clouds stirred by a thousand infantry and cavalry mixed with the trailing musket smoke, turning the sky from bright blue into a haze of brownish-gray. At first, Lozen thought the smoke was playing tricks with her eyes. She squinted, peered harder. Her head snapped up. Near the long gun, an Indian with stump-like limbs gestured at a Mexican officer and white man. The officer gave Blue Raven two rifles, and a soldier brought up a loaded pack mule, handing him the reins. The betrayal was clear—Blue Raven had sold his people to the enemy! As he began to ride away, the white man shot him in the back. The wagon circled, heading back in the direction from which it had come.

Lozen made for Guadalupe Canyon. In the past, she and others had used it as a hideaway for raided livestock. Now the deep ravines would provide a sanctuary for the war party. She reached it at dusk, and entering its mouth, was met by Tezye. "Your brother has been wounded."

"Take me to him."

Victorio lay under a rock shelf, twisting from side to side and mumbling incoherently. When Shinash-a-too saw Lozen, the medicine man stopped chanting over the body. He motioned to her with a smoldering sage stick. "Your brother has fever talk, speaks of things that have no meaning."

Kneeling, Lozen carefully removed an oozing red cloth that was wrapped around Victorio's shoulder. The wound from the miné-ball was vicious, the wad of lead leaving a charred hole the size of a man's thumb. She rolled him on his side; spoke to Tezye. "He is lucky; the bullet passed through. Bring *nopal*. Chop off the thorns."

When Tezye returned, a small fire was going. Using two long sticks as tongs, Lozen held the prickly pad over the flame to burn off the remaining spines. The cactus cooled and she sliced it. With Tezye propping up her brother, she sandwiched Victorio's wound between the fleshy sides of the pads, and bound his shoulder with strips torn from her loincloth.

"Our chief will live, aya?"

Lozen tied off the dressing. "I saw our *shimaa* do this to a pony that was shot in the flank. The next day, it limped like Nana. The following moon, it was running."

"When Victorio heals, we can ride him, then," Tezye said dryly.

Darkness bled the canyon of light. With sentries posted at

both ends and along the ridges, leaders and warriors held council. Fire shadows jumped along the cliff walls, creating warped images of the men. Lozen had told Tezye about Blue Raven. While she tended her brother, he related what she witnessed.

Mangas' eyes went wide as an owl's, then turned to slits. "It was Blue Raven that convinced us to attend the feast at Chihuahua. He is also the one who brought news of the Mexican troops and said it would be an easy ambush, that we outnumbered them."

"Umph," grunted Loco. "He tricked Kayate into thinking he was searching for the *nohwik'edandiihi,* yet knew where they were all along. He turned his back on his people for a few horses and weapons."

Nana thumped the ground with his cane. "Blue Raven's treacherous ways did him no good; he is no more." He pushed up the tip of his white, short-brimmed hat. "Without my niece, we would all have shared his fate."

"Lozen's hands told us of the enemy; her bravery saved our lives," Mangas rumbled.

"Mexicans are everywhere; more whites come every day. With Lozen, we will have no fear of a surprise attack. We need her more than ever. She deserves to sit in council." Nana finished by sweeping his hand before him. "We must vote."

In the morning, with her brother asleep at her side, Lozen awoke to the great leaders standing before her. Juh's stone chest thrust out from the blanket wrapped around his shoulders. Mangas wore his crimson, long-sleeved shirt. Nana leaned on his cane. "Until now, your mother has been the only woman allowed to join the Circle of Influence," he said.

Mangas stepped forward. "At twenty-five harvests, you are the youngest to ever become a member of a war council.

No other has achieved such an honor."

Humbled by their decision, Lozen bowed her head. When she raised her eyes, she had another reason to be grateful. Victorio was sitting upright, drinking from a water pouch.

Later in the day, standing atop a boulder that overlooked the various bands, Mangas issued a final decree. "Wherever Mexicans and whites go, we will find them, scalp them with fire and take revenge for Chihuahua. Fear will live in their hearts and they will not dare enter the land of the Apache. There is no path they can travel, no lair they can hide in to escape!"

CHAPTER ELEVEN

THE FORETELLING

To replenish their strength and gather supplies, the clans returned to their homes. Soon, war parties were scattering across the land. Like an army of foraging ants, they moved in roving tentacles of death, obliterating those that stood in their path. Across the territory, blistered bodies hung upside-down from tree limbs or were spread-eagled on wagon wheels, the charred skulls roasted from burning coals. Screams of the dying pierced the air.

A year passed, and Mangas issued a new order that the vengeance killings be stopped. He then made peace with the Blue Coats—a bond that was both surprising and disturbing to the Apaches. At Ojo Caliente, a council was called.

In the Circle of Influence, Lozen took her place of honor. She sat cross-legged, accepting the pipe passed by her mother. Like Besh-a-taye, she wore a squaw dress and calico blouse.

Victorio was the first to speak. "Red Sleeves has made

friends with the Blue Coat chiefs, puts his mark on their treaty paper."

"That old fool," Nana snarled. "When Mangas went to Pinos Altos, he told the miners he came in peace, that if they stayed away from his people and caused no more trouble, he would lead them to the yellow metal. They didn't believe him, beat him with ox goads until his skin was cut into pieces of red meat. The soldiers were supposed to protect him and did nothing. Now, he trusts whites again."

A fly landed on Lozen's arm and she grabbed it, then cast it away. "There is no humility worse than the whip. Later Mangas found those miners. They are no more."

Loco swept his hand before him. "Not all Blue Coats speak with a twisted tongue."

Nana threw him a burning look. "When you killed that bear with your knife, I thought you were brave—" he turned to one side and, showing his butt, mimicked wiping it, "—now I think you sat in *Shosh*'s leavings and came under its evil influence."

The claw mark above Loco's cheekbone twitched and his good eye flashed dark with anger. Lozen was glad he was at the far end of the council, for he always smelled of dry urine and sour sweat.

Tezye touched his brows, gestured to the sky. "Loco, how many eyes does it take to see the moon?" He pulled on his lobes. "How many ears does it take to hear the elk? White Eyes' words are like rain running off a tipi."

Outside a devil wind eddied, and Lozen could see dust swirling above the smoke hole. She put her hand to her chest. "This heart is heavy. The whites stir up Mother Earth, cut out her heart. Their cattle and soldiers trample her flesh. They commit grave insults to our people and defile our hunting grounds."

"They do not come to Ojo Caliente. We have nothing to fear," Loco argued.

Shonta's face tightened into a hard cinch. "It is the time of the hunters. Cougars track deer. Coyotes steal rabbits. Snakes swallow lizards. Eagles feed on snakes. Apaches catch eagles. Whites come for Apaches."

A groan of agreement went up.

Nana rubbed his lame foot. "Cochise's people cut wood, trade it for goods at the stage place near the spring by Apache Pass. He lets White Eyes travel through his stronghold. It is only a matter of time before they come here."

Victorio lit his smoking pipe, blew out a puff. "Our brother Gray Wolf told how the Five Nations of the Iroquois were forced to surrender their land, that many other tribes would follow. The Sioux, Blackfeet, Utes, Shawnee, Cree, Ojibwa, Comanche and Kickapoo have all signed treaties. Lipan Apaches have done the same. Blue Coats tell them where to go, how they should live."

At the mention of Gray Wolf, Lozen sighed inwardly. It had been a long time since his name was spoken, and she had managed to still her longing for him. Hearing his name brought back indelible memories. Her mother caught her look, blinked an understanding, then spoke.

"The pale ones come like winter snow, stay like the long moons of summer. They take scalps, feed Indians whiskey, cheat our people, steal our women and children. Then they bring their soldiers to protect them—from us!"

Jaws clenched, murmurs of discontent turned into a volatile buzz.

"When they signed the treaty with the *Nakaiyé* at Guadalupe Hidalgo ending their big war, the Blue Coats told them Apaches would not raid in México," Victorio scoffed. "That promise was not theirs to give. We will do what we have always done, go where we have always gone." From a quiver behind him, he took an arrow. "If they leave us in peace, we will do the same, for we have many to protect and feed." He thrust the arrow into the ground. "But if they come to this place, we will take their hearts!"

Lozen's eyes glinted as if they were pieces of mica lit by the sun. Wrenching the arrow free, she stood, bringing the shaft down over her uplifted knee. It snapped with a resounding crack, and she held up the broken ends. "Red Sleeves and Cochise, their trust in the *Indaa* will be broken."

CHAPTER TWELVE

TIMES OF REFLECTION

From a high slope overlooking the village, Lozen looked out on the abundance provided by the Life Giver. Across stretches of dark, rich earth, a budding bonanza of gold, purple and red unfurled, the flowering multitude swerving across rolling contours. Tawny, rolling grasses were alive with edible seeds while stands of oak, pine, spruce and aspen grew in close-knit friendship. On an outcropping no bigger than a blanket, two bighorn lambs butted heads. Below, horses grazed in green fields, and colts kicked up their heels. Farther down near the timberline, a wolf regurgitated breakfast for her cubs. It was the time of the great hunter, He Brings Many Good Things With Him.

Lozen thanked Mother Earth. "You give birth to the cedars, pines, juniper and forests. You suckle the saplings until they grow into trees. You take the breeze from the Great Spirit, give breath to the flowers, direct the waters so the land will grow. From you, all creatures get what they need for life."

Walking back to the village, she was overcome with gratitude, and tears edged her eyes. For five years, there had been no war or killing, and her people were happy and safe. Lozen fingered Gray Wolf's amulet that hung around her neck. His spirit was there, laughing, whispering, and she could hear him in the leaves rustling around her.

She thought back to her recent trip with Kinsee and another woman. They had gone to México to harvest pitahaya. The sweet cactus fruit with its bright purple insides were one of Lozen's favorites, along with the red berries of the algerita.

"It is safer when you are here," said Kinsee, her horse winding through clumps of magenta hedgehog cactus. "We feel more secure with you at our side than when the men ride with us."

The other squaw flicked her wrist. "What do we need them for anyway? We do all the hard work, then after, when the day is done, they want to take us to their sleeping mats."

"*That* is what we need them for!" joked Kinsee.

Immersed in thought, Lozen rounded the edge of a tipi. There, sitting in a rocking chair, was her grandfather. A palomino shirt fell loosely to his waist, and around his neck was tied a black bandana, the ends slipped through a large turquoise ring. On his lap was a horsehide blanket striped with alternating strands of iris, blue and white. Taking a pull on his pipe, he held it between stained rawhide fingers, and motioned for Lozen to sit. He patted the arm of the chair. "Your last raid was good to me, granddaughter. It is you I have to thank for this seat with the bows on the bottom."

Placing her hands under the blanket, she massaged his brittle knees. He closed his eyes and a hum of appreciation passed his lips. "You have become a good healer, a good medicine woman. These days my bones ache and I shuffle more than I walk. Washing up at sweats no longer does me any good. Your fingers take some of the pain away."

Rubbing him, Lozen reflected on her days as a child, the privilege he had afforded her at the *tachih nada.*

Although she was not allowed to participate in the baths, he let her assist in building the low, dune-like sweat lodge with its oak frame and brush-and-pelt roof. Inside, near the entrance, she helped dig the pit in which hot stones would be placed. Water, to be cast on the stones for steam, was placed nearby. Outside the dome Lozen made a cedar fire, heated four large rocks, then carried them inside on a forked stick.

Carrying mesquite bean drinks, eight men wearing loincloths and sage headbands entered the lodge. Lozen listened to their chants and songs, and when they emerged at day's end, watched them race to the nearby stream, plunging their sweaty bodies into the refreshing water.

"We do this to cure ills, for cleansing and to keep fit, to make swift runners and give them stamina. You are already fleet as the wind, and have the lungs of a galloping horse," her grandfather had told her.

A creaking rocker interrupted her thoughts. "I have a favor to ask you, child."

Lozen looked up into a face chewed up by time. "If it is in my power, it is yours, *shichoo.*"

He fingered the kerchief. "Like others of my years, I wear this to fight ghost sickness. Yet I know soon I will go to the hereafter and wish to take this seat with me, so that I may rest like the easy branches swaying in the breeze."

"Your death will be hard for me. Your request is an easy thing to do."

His silver mane blowing in the breeze, he nodded towards the mountains. The sun cut a ragged hole in a charcoal sky, bathing them in a shaft of light. "I have lived many harvests, seen many things. While I am not strong as when I was a colt, my days are simple and full of joy." His voice crackled with mischief. "Each day is the same now. I rise with nothing to do, and when the day has split in two, I have already finished half my tasks."

Just then, Besh-a-taye walked by, curious as to what her father and daughter were cackling about like two chased chickens.

That afternoon, Lozen was called to the tipi of a bereaved woman, whose man had been ambushed by a Pima raiding party. "Aye-yaaa!" cried the widow, clutching her husband's medicine pipe and the fringed vest he'd left behind. Next to her, a small boy sat motionless. Lozen's voice was soft as tanned buckskin.

"Bury your husband's possessions, and never speak his name again. That way his ghost will not return to reclaim them, and bring sickness and death." She made a fire, immersing the tipi in smoke. As the ashes cooled, she scattered them around the boy. "This here is powerful medicine. The sage smoke will protect you and Round Son from harm, and the owls will not bother you at night, calling, 'That dead person is here again.' " The woman calmed, her cries turning to weeping.

Lozen picked up the boy. "Your eyes are rimmed red with sorrow, but your son's gleam with happy innocence. Focus on your child and the bad feelings will leave you. Know he gives us all more strength, more hope. Raise him well so the tribe may grow and prosper from his offspring. Have faith, *Usen* will watch over you, and the one who will soon be at your heel."

The woman managed a weak smile, and took her son from the medicine woman.

Exiting the tipi, Lozen cast back upon the first time she had seen death.

The elder's dying eyes were milky gray, his lips thin, skin wrinkled and pale. Clothes draped his wasted body like wet wash.

"What has happened to the old one, shimaa?*"*

"Daaztsaa," answered Besh-a-taye, explaining that his life had ended. She ran a finger down the lines on the back of her hand. "The blood has been washed from his veins; his heart no longer beats in the four directions like the drum. He is no more in this world."

"Where will he go?"

"He is being put away, under the rocks."

"How will he keep the dirt out of his eyes then?"

Besh-a-taye smiled and laid a palm upon her daughter's head. "He does not need to see; Usen *will guide him. He will dwell with his ancestors in a place with mountains, rivers and game. He will hunt, sing, eat and dance. Do the same things he did here."*

Lozen passed the spot where her grandfather had been sitting, the now-empty chair. *You too,* shichoo. *When your time comes, you will go to the Happy Place.*

The horse did not check the momentum of its charge, or change direction to swerve away from the naked baby crawling in its path. Unaware of the impending danger, Round Son picked up a shiny stone and plopped down with his newfound treasure. The pony bore straight on, pummeling hooves churning clumps of dirt that flew in the air.

At the sound of drumming hoofbeats, Lozen turned away from the badger pelt she was scraping. Her eyes swept past

147

the infant and, in the same instant, caught the horse. Air blew from its flaring nostrils, white foam whipped from the yellow hide. Legs gathering underneath, the horse was a stride away when Lozen dove for Round Son and scooped him up, spinning to a stop in the dirt. In the lingering dust, she examined the infant. Except for a ruddy bruise where his cheek touched the ground, he was otherwise unharmed. Lozen carried him to his mother, who was standing rigid by her tipi. Dazed eyes awoke, and spoke their gratitude.

Kayate had chased the horse down and was leading it back. Head down and hobbling, the stallion's haunches, flanks and legs were caked dark with blood. A rider with an arrow through him sagged over the withers. Kayate called to the gathering crowd. "This one here is a *Tchok-a-nen,* one of Cochise's people." The warrior slid sideways and Kayate caught him, lowering him to the ground.

Lozen assessed the wound. "He must be tended to quickly or he will not see tomorrow's moon." She fingered the feathers jutting out of his back. *"Yudaha."*

"Those Navajo take revenge for the *Tchok-a-nen* stealing their wool, burning their sheep corrals," said Tezye.

Following Lozen's instructions, two men carried the wounded warrior to her tipi, then left. With a honed, wedge-shaped rock, she sheared off the blood-encrusted arrowhead sticking through his chest. Moving around to his back, she gripped the feathered shaft. Using all her strength, she pulled it free. Holding it before her, Lozen studied the sodden arrow. It was smooth—the warrior would not die from splinters left inside.

From a basket, she took several stones of various sizes. Each was round at the top, tapering to a slim end that narrowed to a point. Between thumb and forefinger, she measured them next to the entry and exit wounds. Choosing two, she wrapped them in healing herbs, then inserted one into his abdomen, the other in his back. Just enough of the plugs protruded so she could remove them once he was healed.

"Will he live?" asked Victorio later that night.

Lozen shrugged. "My thoughts are divided. The arrow was buried under his ribs and missed those places that make the blood rush from the wound. It is not the color of death as when it goes to a killing place. Yet his fever is strong. Only the night will say if he lives."

Upon awakening, Lozen was surprised to find the warrior's red-stained mat empty. She walked outside. The brave was leaning against the tipi, staring at the rising sun. At the sound of her footsteps, he turned slightly. "I didn't think I would see another dawn. You have strong healing powers."

He started to walk, stumbled badly. Lozen caught him. "Your wounds were like dried mud; now they leak again."

"Much bad medicine has happened, I must speak to Victorio."

For the first time she noticed his features—a wide forehead, strong chin, arms knotted like bamboo. "Rest, or the fever will not leave you. I will gather my brother, bring him when you are well."

Leaning heavily on her shoulder, the warrior rasped, "You are his sister, Lozen. I have heard of your Power Of The Blue Hands. I am Chaco, same as the canyon."

She braced him, led him back inside. He drank from a water pouch, then held his forefinger over his eyebrow, making the sign for whites. "Cochise has been tricked by the Pony Soldiers. They killed his brother and two nephews."

Lozen shook her head. "My heart moves in me like black clouds." Behind her medicine drum was a clean mat of reeds and soft mustard grass, and she pulled it forth for Chaco. For two days, she bathed his feverish body with cool water, rubbing the pollen of life and renewal over him.

In a collective effort to help, people would come to chant and drum. "Pray so your good thoughts will please *Usen*," she told them. She smoked a ceremonial pipe, blew puffs to the four directions.

This man is wounded
I will tell you something now
Your power must go into him so he may live
If he stays in his fire, he will lose his way, and wander forever

On the third day, the fever broke; on the next, Chaco downed a meal of boiled potatoes and mesquite beans. That night, he was able to sit in council. Twenty attended. The chiefs, Victorio and Loco sat cross-legged around the center fire, along with Lozen, Besh-a-taye and several warriors. Others stood behind them, arms folded across chests or holding lances. Nana was absent, having left the previous night on a raiding party into México.

Chaco explained that on the way to carry Cochise's message, six Navajo ambushed him. His wounded horse was so frightened, it outran the enemy. He rode a long time before shadows dropped over his eyes and he fell into the hole of darkness.

Victorio nodded with his chin. "Speak of the *denchq'e*, the ugly news you carry about the White Eyes."

"A white chief from Fort Buchanan called Cochise to meet him in Apache Pass. There had been no quarreling with the Blue Coats; our chief saw no threat. He only took his brother, two nephews, a woman and child. They met in a big tent. Then the *nantan* Bascom accused Cochise of stealing a boy from a ranch. The White Eyes had much anger; they had searched for four years and could not find the man-child."

Tezye scratched his cheek. "They are like Bluff Over Belt, whose belly is so big he can't see his own penis."

Chaco continued. "Cochise told them we took no part in the stealing. The *nantan* would not listen. Soldiers surrounded the tent and stopped him and the others from leaving." He made a slicing motion with his hand, silently winced at his wound. "With his knife, Cochise slashed through the canvas and ran through the soldiers. Many shots were fired. He was wounded but escaped."

Shonta thrust his cane in the air. "The *Indaa*'s flag of truce is as full of holes as a blanket eaten through by insects!"

"We took captives from a wagon train to trade for our people. The white leader said we had the boy and would not agree."

Lozen picked up a hollow gourd, rapped it with her knuckles. "The pale ones have no brains in their skulls. Ignorance and arrogance live in that empty place."

Chaco turned his palms upwards. "More soldiers gathered in Apache Pass. Cochise feared that they came to kill all our people. As a warning, we killed three hostages, marked them with lances and left them to be found. To take revenge, Bascom hung Cochise's brother and nephews." Venom spilled from Chaco's eyes. He clenched his fists and pumped his arms back and forth, indicating war. "When I saw this, my heart beat hard and fast. Cochise's own heart burned and he yelled, 'I will splatter their brains for this!' Since that time, we have killed many whites. Now, more forts have been built, more soldiers come."

Looks of shock registered among the council and they went silent, their faces like stone. The only sound was an occasional whoosh from the fire, caused by downdrafts from the smoke hole. Lozen's insides knotted, and she could feel the fire of hate running through her. Finally, Victorio spoke.

"The winds of time carry the words Little Sister spoke many harvests ago. Cochise pays for his trust. What does he want from us, Chaco?"

"Cochise and Mangas plan an ambush in Apache Pass, ask that you join them."

Victorio swept his hand in front of him. "Tomorrow we will decide. This here council is over."

Lozen took her time walking back to her tipi. She gazed at the moon. Small and silver, it cast a ghostly glow. She passed by the home of Round Son and his mother. Would the boy live long enough to father another, or would the whites take his life?

The argument whether to join in the ambush at Apache Pass had been dragging on a half-day, and was no more resolved than when the war council started. Lozen's tone was stiff.

"Red Sleeves is past the time of seventy harvests. He no longer carries the skills and powers needed to win a big fight. We should turn down his request to join him. He and Cochise will be defeated by the Blue Coats."

"You have lived half the years of Mangas, tell chiefs what is to be and what is not?" Loco snarled. "You know more than Cochise now? The men here, we will decide!"

"The pass is narrow and there is no cover to hide," Tezye said with authority. "The enemy will be like ponies strung out on a rope line, and can be killed with bullets and arrows from above."

Loco gripped the handle of his knife. "They will die under our knives."

"We cannot win," Lozen insisted.

The scar under Loco's eye twitched, and his blade started

to come out of its sheath. "You walk on my words woman, I walk on you."

Besh-a-taye intervened, her voice calm as still water. "All the village talks of Lozen's courage, saving Round Son from the horse."

Voices hummed in approval.

Besh-a-taye scanned the warriors. "She has always known things others have not about the enemy, saved many Apaches at Chihuahua, fought fiercely and with cunning."

More approving voices, but not from Loco. "We are not concerned about what happened in the past. This here is a war council about what to do next!"

A steady gaze passed from Besh-a-taye to Lozen. She hoped the many lessons she'd taught her about how to negotiate with men had somehow gotten through her daughter's thick skull.

Lozen acknowledged Loco with a head nod. "Loco's words carry strong meaning. He is a fearless chief with many warring skills." She gestured to the council. "I have gratitude for the ways and teachings of the great Red Sleeves and Cochise, the lessons I have learned from them, from those here. Without you, I would not be in this place of honor."

In rapid succession, she touched her lips and eyebrows. "My words carry only the truth of what I saw. Seven moons past, I hunted in the Dragoons for lion. Many Blue Coats were coming up from the whites' village in Tucson. I got right on them, stayed hidden and watched. They traveled with those long guns of a fierce and powerful nature, headed for Apache Pass."

The image hit Victorio like a bullet. "Our fighters will be blasted from the rocks, forced into the open. The soldiers will be waiting to shoot us from below."

Besh-a-taye spoke. "It is for the *men* to decide then. Stay, or join forces with Mangas and Cochise."

The count was swift, only Loco dissented. Outside the tipi, away from the earshot of the warriors, Besh-a-taye spoke to Lozen. "Once you know a man's weakness you can use it, achieve the outcome you want."

"What weakness?"

"Pride. They like to think that they have the answers to everything."

Lozen's face lit up like a bright star. "They think it was their idea not to go and waste our warriors' lives!"

"Aya, daughter. And you. First your mouth was like mad water, then you became the voice of still breezes." She pulled on Lozen's sleeve. "You did well. Loco is a powerful man. To make an enemy of him would be unwise."

Lozen thanked her mother for her help, then went her own way. At her hidden pool, she sat on the sandy bank. The breeze touched her brow and the air rose on wings of butterflies. A bright green hummingbird hovered, then zipped away. With her bare toes she drew circles in the sand, and as she did so, her mind traced a memory of Gray Wolf. She sought to bring him into her consciousness, but a screech owl trilled and her reflections shifted to the recent hunt near Cochise's stronghold, the place where the Rocks Sleep Standing on Top of One Another.

Needing a hide for quivers, she had camped at Mountain Lion, known for its abundance of cougars. Searching for her prey in the early dawn, she climbed upon a high column of stacked boulders. Below, a family of quail scurried. No sooner were they out of sight, than a jackrabbit bounded from a clump of sagebrush. Had the cougar not moved from between the boulders, Lozen would have missed it, the tawny hide blending perfectly with the rocks. The big cat played a rousting game. It caught the rabbit, held it down with a padded paw, let it free and pounced upon the furry prey again. The action was repeated several times, and when the rabbit could no longer run, the cougar killed it.

Was it a sign, Lozen now wondered? Would the Apache people, the people of all Red Nations, be doomed to a similar fate at the hands of the whites? She flipped a stone into the pool, watching the circle of ripples until they disappeared.

Thirty moons went by, and a messenger came from Cochise's camp. The chiefs had been defeated at Apache Pass; Mangas wounded. Both escaped.

CHAPTER THIRTEEN

SKULLS

Six months passed and Victorio decided to visit Red Sleeves' camp, taking Lozen with him. They traveled north past Silver City, rode up piney mountains then down to the Mimbres River. The winter sun was so bright it hurt Lozen's eyes and, shading them with her palm, she leaned forward, peering through her stallion's twitching ears. A tree stretched gray and dead in the shallows, debris clinging to a high fork. Downstream, a white egret on stilt-like legs hunted for food, its long beak stabbing the water.

Lozen and Victorio crossed the river, climbed a bench and came to Mangas' camp. Wickiups stood between a breech of hills, the largest belonging to the reigning chief of the Apaches. Like the others, it was covered with hides, brush and branches. A wildcat pelt with the head still attached hung inside the doorway, and Mangas ducked out to greet them.

Healed from his battle wounds in Apache Pass, he wore a new black sombrero, multi-colored *serape* and red Chinese sandals the size of snowshoes. "Got all this in México, paid only one necklace," he boasted, grinning. After treating his guests to a rare meal of mountain goat meat, plus corn and tamales, he told them what he was about to do. "A message came from the whites. The Blue Coat Shirland wants to talk peace."

"Those treaty promisers believe Indians will cease to be as a people. They care nothing about us, our way of life," Victorio told him.

"Red Sleeves," Lozen said, touching his arm. "They are killing us because of the color of our skin. Yours has not changed."

The chief took off his new hat and donned his white, straight-rimmed sombrero with the small square crown. Lozen thought his head looked like a boulder with a pebble on top.

"I remember the treaty I signed in Santa Fe, eleven years ago. The whites agreed to friendship, and we saw that for a while. Before I leave for the world of the Great Spirit, I must try again. The Star Chief Carlton rounds up Mescaleros, holds them on a reservation in Bosque Redondo. Blue Coats seek Apaches like snakes hunt mice. I will not refuse to talk with them. It is for the good of all our people."

"Our prayers go with you then," she answered.

They spent the night, and in the morning, Lozen attended a sorrel that had gone blind. To restore its sight, she cut the veins leading down from its eyes. "Soon it will see again, kick up its heels like a colt," she told Mangas.

As brother and sister left camp, the day unfolded in a blue-gray. "I have something to tell you, brother. I did not tell you before, because I wasn't sure of the signs."

"And now?"

"Before we came here I spent four moons on Salinas Peak.

I fasted, prayed to the sun, moon, stars and Mountain Spirits for good omens. I saw only the blackness the whites bring with them."

"It is good you speak of this, Little Sister. Signs sent by the Great Spirit cannot be ignored." His hard eyes shifted to the timberline. "War is as close as the forests. We must be ready."

But they weren't ready for what came next. No one was.

Lozen was rubbing Shonta's rheumatic knee with a warm mixture of grease and red ocher, when a brave rode into the Warm Springs camp. Lozen immediately recognized him as Mangas' most trusted and respected warrior. Although just a shade taller than a horse's back, He Knows Many Things was a courageous fighter, and a clever one as well. A superb strategist, he had outwitted many an enemy, and saved his chief and band from disaster on more than one occasion.

But it wasn't a proud or confident man that dismounted. The head that had always been held high was bowed, the erect shoulders and thrust-out chest sunken as though sucked down by a whirlpool. He walked slowly, trancelike, and, following him, Lozen was drawn into an inexplicable sense of dread. As he wove through the pathways of the encampment, people were pulled from their work and tipis as though by some invisible thread. By the time he reached the center of the village, a great, yet hushed throng had gathered.

A boy brought He Knows Many Things a water pouch, a woman a basket of fruit. He paid them no attention, and with a glazed look in his eyes, began to speak. At first his voice was no more than the drone of an insect. But in a few moments it became a torrent of angry water, rushing out of his mouth, overwhelming his listeners with disbelief and horror.

He told his story how it happened, exacting in every detail.

He told it as though he hadn't really been there, as though someone else was willing him to tell the tale. But he had been there. The ragged hole through the center of his palm was irrefutable evidence of that.

Behind the cover of trees, ten warriors and their brightly clad chief sat on their horses, watching the Blue Coats' camp in the early twilight. With his spear, Mangas pointed at a white flag fluttering from the peak of a tent. "They show the cloth of friendship."

A warrior half the chief's size growled. "Did you forget what they did to our people, what they did to you? Do not go to the snake pit of the whites."

"I will be safe, He Knows Many Things. Stay here until I return." He urged his horse forward and, as he reached the encampment, a smiling officer appeared from one of the tents, his hand raised in friendship.

He Knows Many Things shook his head. "Our chief is drawn like the moth, fooled by the flame of death."

The words had barely left his lips when soldiers rushed out from the tents, forming a cordon of leveled rifles at the chief. The officer came forward and, with pistol in hand, motioned for him to dismount. At the same time, thirty more Pony Soldiers broke from a bosque on the opposite side, heading for the warriors. They wheeled, the troops chasing after them.

To lose the soldiers, the band split in half, each going in a different direction. Darkness dropped like a blanket, affording them an easy chance to escape. While the others rode for reinforcements, He Knows Many Things snuck back to the whites' camp. For two days, he tracked his captured chief, watching as he rode shackled in the bed of a wagon. When they came to the Blue Coats' fort, he hid himself be-

hind a thorny thicket, waiting and watching. A wagon might come, and he would be able to run and hide himself under the canvas, sneak inside the gates and free Mangas.

Suddenly, the gates swung open. In the dim light of a shrouded moon, the warrior recognized his chief's shadowy bulk. A dark mass, this one as big as the prisoner, followed. Three smaller soldiers emerged. They pushed and struck the chief, and one of them brought his gun butt down into his back. He fell to his knees and they prodded him, laughing as he struggled to his feet, pricking him in the buttocks with bayonets.

He Knows Many Things nocked an arrow and sighted down the shaft. His bow was at full arc, yet he stayed his fury, for the dark barrel of a pistol was pressed against Red Sleeves' skull. A guard staked his bare ankles to the ground with chains. The others spread out, gathered wood, piled it in a heap and started a fire. It gained momentum, lighting the blackness. He Knows Many Things winced. On his knees, legs hobbled, Red Sleeves' bloodied shirt hung like a tattered tent.

Hauling a water-filled kettle, two more soldiers came from the fort and placed it over the flames. One had a thin, snarling face, reminding the warrior of a cornered coyote. The other was younger, with long hair the color of straw. They thrust their bayonets into the coals and, when they began to glow, withdrew them. They pressed the scorching blades against Mangas' legs and bottoms of his feet.

There was nothing He Knows Many Things could do— the soldiers were too many. He could smell burning flesh and, screaming inside himself, gripped a branch with such might that a thorn ran through his hand. He wrenched it free, steeling himself to his chief's yelps of anger and pain.

"I am Mangas Coloradas of the Mimbres, leader of the

Apache Nations! You cannot treat me this way!"
The soldiers raised their rifles, fired into his chest. The
big white chief emptied his pistol into the slumped-over
body, which twitched until the last shot. He said something
to two of the soldiers, then returned with the rest back into
the fort. The straw-haired one drew a Bowie knife, sawed
off Mangas' head. He spiked the skull with the tip of the
knife, whooped, walked to the pot and dumped it into the
boiling water.

It was the longest and most agonizing story Lozen had
ever heard, or ever wanted to hear again. His death weighed
heavily on her heart; and in the corner of her mind, she could
see the sombrero on his head, the Chinese sandals he'd worn.
Her face wrapped in sadness and anger, she joined the other
women by the creek. For the rest of the day and into the
night, their sorrowful cries of "Aye-yaaa!" filled the air.

The night passed with warriors readying weapons and
horses. In the predawn chill of morning, twenty Apaches
sought the trail of revenge. They rode to the eastern corner of
the valley, went north over the shoulder of a hill, then traversed through a series of bluffs and flatlands towards the
Santa Fe Trail. Some wore vests over bare chests, others
long-sleeved shirts. Their war-painted faces were grim, set to
the task at hand. As they rode, ravens rose from the trees like
black ashes.

No one knew where He Knows Many Things was. He'd
disappeared as unexpectedly as he'd come.

Laughing and joking, the two soldiers paid little attention
to their surroundings, or the bird calls that came from above
the trail. Suddenly, two arrows slammed into their pack
mule's neck. The animal brayed, high and screeching. Before

it fell dead, the troopers were surrounded.

Kayate snatched their weapons, while Lozen ripped open a burlap sack with her knife. An immense, fleshless skull tumbled from a red and green serape. "These ones here," Lozen snarled, "they are Red Sleeves' killers!"

A circle of arrows and lances closed, pinning the soldiers tight. Nana slid his hand into a saddlebag and pulled out a square-rimmed sombrero and a pair of sandals. His cane whistled, and the soldier next to him screamed, clutching his broken collarbone. Tezye moved to finish him.

Victorio, his brow knitted fiercely, held up his hand. "They do not deserve to die quickly. Take them."

As the prisoners were led away, a gust of wind kicked up. It took the page of a newspaper tucked into the bottom of the torn burlap sack, swirled it in the air and jammed it onto the spike of a palo verde. The full-page ad in the *Santa Fe Gazette* flapped in the wind.

ANY CLEAN APACHE MAN'S SKULL—$200!
CASH ON DELIVERY!
A CHIEF'S HEAD GETS YOU AN ADDITIONAL $200!
WOMEN'S AND CHILDREN'S
WILL FETCH UP TO $100!
JOHN WHARTON, PHRENOLOGIST
Send to 2602 Ballantine Street. Washington, D.C.
Payment to be made when skull is identified as Apache
Send any corroborating information for authenticity

Their plan foiled, wrists bound tightly behind them, the soldiers squirmed in their saddles. War clubs hammered their rib cages and kidneys; spears jabbed into torsos, legs and arms. With Victorio leading, the horses slowed, then stopped. Ropes were thrown over the prisoners, and they were yanked from their saddles. Nearby, a raised circle of ground moved as if it were alive.

Lozen and Kayate grabbed the coyote-faced soldier, threw him belly down over the anthill, then bound his arms and legs to stakes. Facing him on the opposite side where he would have to watch, the other trooper was being hog-tied. His arms were pulled taut behind him, wrists bound to his ankles with a short strip of rope so that his shoulders and legs were off the ground, drawing his head and neck up into a tortuous, curving bow.

Silent, their eyes burning with hate, the Apaches squatted on their haunches.

The ants crawled up their victim's throat, across his stubby beard, onto his chin and lips. They crept up his nostrils and he futilely tried to blow them out with snort-like "phtts." They moved up his cheeks, crawled under and over his terror-stricken eyes, stinging his lids.

A quarter-inch demon entered his ear canal and tread upon the drum, biting him. The soldier screwed his head around with such ferocity he almost wrung his neck, and his piercing screeches frightened a cluster of nesting doves that took to wing from a nearby tree. As he screamed, ants swept into his mouth and down his throat. Gagging, he choked on his swollen tongue. Massed inside the heavy uniform, the ants stung with straight, needle-like spikes, thrusting until they ran out of venom.

"Let's turn him on his head so the ants can drop onto his testicles, sting him with bad influence there," Kayate mocked.

Tezye spoke of an old Apache belief. "He must have urinated on an anthill as a child, for now he has bad luck with them."

Victorio was in no mood for humor. "These here will take

no more Apache heads; they will die before their evil grows further."

"Red Sleeves cannot hear, taste or smell the spirit world, enjoy the hereafter," Lozen said bitterly. "Where the cool stream flows and the green trees stand in line, is closed to his eyes. The big sand hill blocks off his next life and he will journey in darkness, forever."

By dusk, the ant-ridden soldier ceased writhing. While Kayate and Lozen pulled him from the mound, two other warriors went for the straw-haired one.

CHAPTER FOURTEEN

WAY OF THE SPIDER

It was The Time of Little Battle and back at Ojo Caliente, Lozen's heart felt light. She wore a bright blue vest over a yellow and white calico shirt, pants with a breechcloth tucked in, and beaded moccasins. As she walked through the village, children skipped light-footed before her. She inhaled deeply, enjoying the smells from roasting meat, mescal and agave hearts. Her grandfather was in his rocking chair and she waved to him.

Away from the encampment she strode past the hill named Two Old Women Are Buried, and in a clearing surrounded by oak and alligator juniper, prayed.

> Usen, *we are thankful for this time of rest*
> *Show us the path of no anger*
>   *so we may happily dance the Sacred Dances*
> *Bless our people that they may live in peace;*
>   *be happy and prosperous*

For a while she remained in the quiet, savoring the fragrance of the woods, then took a looping trail back to the village. Suddenly, a twisted clump of grass flew into the air. A small arrow pierced its center and a shout rang out. Rounding some bushes, Lozen found the youthful marksman collecting his companions' missed arrows—his reward for a successful target hit.

"You will soon be ready for novice training, Little Tachita," she called.

The eight-year-old held his arrows above his head and his bare chest was thrust out with pride. His black eyes jumped. "My mother said she trained with you, but could not continue because I was in her belly. Do you think she carried a warrior?"

Facing Lozen, he backpedaled as she walked. She nodded past him. "If you break those spider sunbeams behind you, we will never know." Kinsee's son froze in his tracks.

"Do you know the strength of Spider?"

Little Tachita gulped. "It has great power to harm."

"Damage a spider web and Father Sun will weave strands inside your body and you'll die. Kill one and another will take its place, seek revenge. Walk to me now, away from the web." The boy came forward. "I am on my way to visit your mother. Go practice with your arrows."

By the time Lozen reached the village, an icy wind had sprung up. She was glad for the fire inside her friend's tipi. She sat cross-legged next to Kinsee's three-year-old daughter, Her Eyes Brown. The girl's dark eyes flashed with delight and she reached up and touched Lozen's cheek. A green bracelet of fern circled her wrist and pine needle earrings the size of small leaves hung from her ears. Lozen kissed the child's hand, tapped her nose.

Her Eyes Brown giggled, and focused again on her lesson.

Her mother was showing her how to make beads from wild-rose hips, round cherries and the scouring rush plant. When strung together, along with twists of panic grass, the beads would form a doll's figure.

Lozen glanced at a tipi made from plants, and the finger-sized dress next to it. "Your daughter learns the ways of a homemaker, aya?"

Kinsee stroked the girl's hair. "She grows like a fresh sapling. I remember that time when we rolled her on the ground in the four directions, so she would always know her place of birth."

The two friends smiled at each other. Born within a week of one another thirty-five harvests past, they could have easily been mistaken for sisters. Both wore waist-length hair stolen from a blue-black night. The slight difference in their features was that Lozen's nose was more tapered, her cheekbones higher. "Where is Kanda-zi?" she asked.

"My husband scouts with Kayate, searching for those whites that might come." She placed a hand on her daughter's head. "I am worried for my family. In the night, I sometimes wake, for my heart beats like the wings of a frightened bird."

Lozen handed a bead to her goddaughter. "Where the Blue Coats go is uncertain." Her eyes turned hard. "The Star Chief Carleton has stolen that place where the Mescalero Apaches once lived. He put them on worthless ground near the Pecos, at a reservation called Bosque Redondo, where there are no mountains. The White Eyes take all the land thick with game, water and trees, claim it as their own."

Kinsee formed a piece of round cloth for the doll's head, tied it and sewed animal fur to the top for hair. Smiling, she handed it to Her Eyes Brown, who dressed the toy in bits of blue and green cloth. "I think your *benagolnehe* looks like Lozen there."

The girl held the doll up next to her godmother. "Indian women wear dresses, not loincloths. My doll doesn't look like her." The women laughed.

Outside, the wind howled savagely. Kinsee cocked her head to one side. "The sun runs swifter in his moccasins, the days grow shorter."

Lozen cradled the girl-child against her chest. "I think maybe ours too."

CHAPTER FIFTEEN

WHERE IS THE VIRGIN MARY?

Up and about; women were lighting cooking fires, while small girls brought water from the stream, pouring it into pots. Maidens returned from bathing and combed one another's hair, the glistening black strands tinged purple by the rising sun. Wives brought weapons and medicine bags to their husbands; bleary-eyed elders poked their heads out of tipis. Two boys raided a drying rack, snatching several strips of deer meat before being driven away by the stick-wielding cook.

Walking with her brother by the creek, Lozen looked past the forests, beyond the reaches of alpine peaks cloaked in white. "The night brought us the lightness of female rain; the spring here grows out of the mountain's foot and the sky glows."

Insects flitted over an eddying pool, and Victorio gestured at them. "The *Indaa* are like the water skippers, come fast from every direction."

Lozen cupped a handful of water, swallowed and took another. "It has been three years since their Big War against one another in the East ended. Now they come here like unwelcome fingers of a bad flood, bring more soldiers, build more forts and cattle ranches to feed their people. The best land is where Indians live, and they take it for themselves."

Victorio spat. "I signed that treaty paper that came from the Big White Father in Washington, agreed not to make no trouble, lived my word. They promised us a thousand new blankets and food." He gestured at the sky, then spat. "Have you seen these things? Their words are like the clouds, thin and without substance. Now they say we must go to the Mexican pueblo of Canada Alamosa with a thousand other Apaches, live under their rule."

"Each time they come here to Ojo Caliente they bring more Blue Coats. The last *nantan* said they will force us if we resist."

Victorio picked up a stone and threw it into a bush splattered with birdsquit. "The council has agreed that we must go to save our people. I do not like it."

Lozen put her hand on her brother's shoulder, looked into his handsome face, his piercing black eyes. "I have a plan, brother-of-mine." As they sat on the mossy bank, Lozen explained what she wanted to do. "Take most of the braves and elders to the mountains. In that way, if the soldiers mount an ambush, you will have the warriors and wisdom needed to escape, to fight."

"Good," said Victorio. He wasn't smiling.

Leading her pony, Lozen walked through the encampment at Canada Alamosa. Smoke from hundreds of fires curled upwards into a pall that hung dark and wide. Stretching in every direction, wickiups and tipis were partially covered in brush and pelts, while Apaches in tattered clothing went hungry, trembling in the cold. Settlers and miners rode in and out of the camp, mingling with the soldiers that came from nearby Fort Craig. They smoked, gambled, fought over the prostitutes who frequented the camp. On crates and from the backs of wagons, Mexican whiskey sellers hawked their wares.

Propped against a wagon wheel, a warrior set his jug to one side. His wife walked by, accidentally knocking it over and spilling the remainder. He screamed, broke the jug on the wheel, then chased her with the ragged piece. Suddenly he stopped and collapsed in a drunken heap.

Nearby, a boy of six was pulling on a meatless bone, trying to snatch it from the jaws of a mongrel. Its paws digging into the ground, the dog backed up. With a great tug, it wrenched the bone free and ran away. Just then, a trapper passed with his son, who was chewing on a cooked chicken leg. The Apache child jumped up and tried to grab the chicken. The white boy, who was older and bigger, pushed him to the ground.

Her eyes surveying the misery, Lozen glanced at a baby desperately trying to feed on his mother's shrunken teat. Another bawling tot sat in his own leavings. Her stomach churned and, clenching her teeth, she was struck with a mixed tempest of sadness and hate. If whites suffered this way, they would not call it peace, or the broken pledges prosperity.

Near the camp's center, she found Kinsee and her children. Flesh poked through holes in their moccasins and filthy clothes. Lozen looked into the blank faces of Her Eyes Brown and Little Tachita. The brightness was gone out of their eyes, out of their small souls. She tried to sound cheerful. "In the morning I will hunt. You will have food, hides for new mocca-

171

sins to keep your feet warm and dry."

Kinsee nodded across the way to where Round Son slumped against his mother. "The Blue Coats give us only enough food for sparrows, and the belts of our children are cinched tight. I will pray for your success."

That night Lozen slept on the bare ground next to the family. At first light, she headed away towards the sullen high reaches. She climbed her horse to the mid-section of a mountain, found a sheltered spot among a stand of conifers and tied up her pony. From here, she would go on foot. Though her horse was unshod, the cold cocoon of silent winter woods would ring hollow with the sound of hooves, alerting wary prey. To match the color of her quarry and blend in with the surroundings, she had dressed in dull gray and white. Over her shoulder were a bow, and a quiver with twelve cane arrows. She glanced at the sky. Thwarted by a brooding blanket, the sun struggled to waken the land.

Lozen followed a brown furrow that crawled through the center of a snowy field. The deer trail led her into a copse of naked aspen, pale as a dead body. She trod noiselessly, searching between the trees for signs of prey. Squatting, she felt through a smattering of leaves until she found one that was dry and flexible. She folded it and, holding the leaf to her lips, blew, imitating the cry of a fawn. She waited and tried again, hoping the call would attract a doe.

When the trick didn't work, she moved on, the reed-like path edging along a creek, its banks pockmarked with patches of ice. By the lapping tongue of a small waterfall that dropped into a pool, steam rose from the frozen earth. Lozen nocked an arrow, moving past the fresh droppings and up to a clearing. Out of the corner of her eye, a slight movement. Gray as the sky, a doe sifted into view. Head up and ears twitching, its wide black nostrils flared to catch a scent.

Lozen stood still as the trees. The animal moved to the center of the clearing and began feeding on stubbles of exposed grass. Lozen raised her bow, aimed for the heart. Unexpectedly the deer turned, the flicking black tail facing its killer. The doe's head came up and it froze in the middle of a chew. "Come around so I can see the place of your heart," Lozen mouthed. As if in answer, her prey turned and resumed feeding. Lozen pulled back on the bowstring.

Like the crack of a gunshot in an empty canyon, the sound of a breaking snow-laden branch shattered the silence. At the same instant the doe sprang sideways, Lozen loosed her arrow. The obsidian head slanted into the flying deer and the animal's cry of pain and fright was almost human. In mindless panic it bolted, crashing through the dead underbrush. Lozen tracked the crimson splotches on white snow, the tips of bare bushes stained livid.

Reaching the fringe of a long meadow, she spied a black tail disappearing into a shelterbelt on the opposite side. If she moved quickly, she could slay the mortally wounded deer while it rested. Halfway across the pasture, a polar wind picked up. White cloaks fell and swirls of fleece eddied around her. Visibility was becoming dim. Even if she found the doe right away, she would still have to get her horse to carry the carcass. With the storm worsening, she would be caught without shelter or dry wood for a fire. Reluctantly, she began backtracking. The wind rifled through her clothes in a freezing blow, the cold scurrying under her skin. To keep warm, she ran. Her warrior mind worked unerringly, directing her over the rapidly-disappearing trail. When she spotted the black hide of her stallion through the white curtain, she let out a breath of relief.

A darkening sky told her it was far past midday. Victorio's camp in the San Mateo Mountains was closer than Canada

Alamosa, and she made for it. Wind-blown pellets of ice stung her face and she ached from the cold. Hunched over her horse's neck, she guided the animal as best she could through the sleet and snow. "You have been there before, Great One," she whispered. "Know the way better than me."

Just as light escaped the day, she entered the small camp. Sparsely cloaked tipis dotted a swath of ground between two hills. Above, three caves yawned like ice-ghosts, their mouths covered with frost. There was no smell of roasting meat or simmering acorn stew, no ash bread to be dug out of the coals. There was nothing but heated voices coming from a tipi. She dismounted, pulled back the blanket that served as a door and warmed by the fire. Solemn nods greeted her.

"The Blue Coats put too many of us at Canada Alamosa," said Victorio. "They tell us to exist on the rations their government supplies, yet our people must creep like the coyote at night and steal green corn from the fields of the Mexicans to survive."

Loco's argument leapt at the council. "The Indian agent Piper says more food will soon come. He also says if we agree to go to the Bosque Redondo Reservation and live with the Mescaleros, we will not go hungry again. I believe him."

The cords in Victorio's neck tightened with anger. "My friend Crook Nose lives there with his tribe among our enemy, the Navajo, who the whites also ordered to that place. They don't care that the Mescaleros are hundreds, that the Navajo outnumber them many times. They steal Apache horses, clothing and food. The soldiers give them the sickness that makes blisters and fever that burns like the sun. Then they throw the dead bodies into the water they drink." His eyes blazed. "This, then, is where we should go, Loco?"

The round-faced chief with one eye, shrugged. "You have a better plan, eh? Our people are dying a slow death."

174

"In The Moon of the Big Leaves I listened to your words; again during The Season of Large Fruit. I washed my mouth and hands with fresh water to show the whites my words were true, that we would do no harm. I promised we would wait for the words of the new White Father Grant, asked only for clothing, food and to stay at Ojo Caliente." He threw up his arms. "None of these things happened."

"Piper says we must return cattle and horses other Indians stole, or we will receive no more food," snapped Tezye. "They accuse us of things we didn't do. It gives their chiefs reason to plan against us."

"They think if we give back what we don't have, then we can eat what they don't give us," Lozen said.

An ally of Loco's, a stout warrior with a flat face, spoke. "Cochise has fought for many harvests. Now he can no longer feed his women and children, and seeks peace at Canada Alamosa."

"Peace?" Besh-a-taye hissed. "Cochise trusted them and they hung his brother. Red Sleeves trusted them and they cut off his head! We should believe what the Blue Coats tell us, go to another place where they will boil our skulls and those of our children in pots?"

A mutter of misgiving swept the tipi.

Nana pulled on his chin. "The White Eyes plan their next ambush behind their promises. Their lies hide behind the ugly fur on their faces." He leveled a gaze at Lozen. "Niece, what do your thoughts say?"

Lozen's eyes wicked from member to member. "Those Indian agents argue with soldiers and accuse them of stealing our supplies. We fight with the agents for food, while soldiers fight with traders over whiskey. Whiskey sellers do not let Apaches alone and cause families to fight. Soon we will be killing ourselves."

Shonta leaned forward, his weathered face like a cracked riverbed. He pinched his nose between thumb and forefinger, his voice twanging. "It is better to stay upwind of the whites' stinking promises."

Loco retaliated. "I will wait and keep the path with the White Eyes clear until they give us a place of our own to live."

"Eskiminzen, chief of the Aravaipas, thought in the same way," scoffed Victorio. He reiterated a story the council knew well, but was determined they never forget. He told of Lieutenant Whitman, the Blue Coat who had a good heart for Apaches, and promised Eskiminizen his people would be safe up the creek from Camp Grant near the San Pedro River. They grew crops, traded with the fort and caused no trouble, waiting for a decision about where they would go.

Besh-a-taye took up the story. "One day while the warriors hunted, angry and armed people from Tucson came and brought our enemies, the Papagos and Mexicans. The whites said the Aravaipas attacked the mission at San Xavier, stole horses and later killed four Americans."

"Once again they blamed those not there," cut in Tezye. "They attacked, forced themselves upon women, beat in their heads and those of the children. Wounded were shot, stripped naked and mutilated. One hundred forty Apaches died. The Papagos captured twenty-seven children, sold them into slavery in México." He glared at Loco. "*That* is what you wait for."

Lozen tented her fingers and put them to her chin. "The Papagos follow the way of the whites, do evil things, then ask forgiveness from their Christian God. My grandfather told me what Cochise once asked the general, Granger. 'Tell me, if your Virgin Mary walks all through this land in peace, why has she never entered the lodge of the Apache?' "

Victorio held up a closed fist, then opened his hand. "The

176

excuse for the raid on Eskiminizen was revenge, the reason greed. Whiskey sellers, gun traders and ranchers do not want to settle things, for it means fewer soldiers, fewer riches. The *Indaa* fill their pockets from the bodies of dead Apaches."

Loco remained steadfast. "Another Indian agent comes from Washington. He carries the power of the Great Father who is said to have decreed peace, and wants to protect us. In two moons, I will take this agent Colyer to Ojo Caliente. He will see the land is full of good things, that we should be allowed to stay there."

The council over, Besh-a-taye and Lozen walked outside. "*Usen* doesn't help us, *shimaa*. Things are getting worse."

Besh-a-taye pulled her blanket over her head. "He can't hear our prayers through those thick clouds, doesn't know we are running a footrace against a hard wind."

There was no more fire that night; all the wood was wet and there was little horse dung. To keep from freezing, Lozen made her pony lie down and slept close to him.

In the morning, she went to one of the caves. Inside, her grandparents hugged in a sheet of ice, frozen in one another's arms. She gently ran her fingers across their frail faces, and as she brushed back the white hair, tears iced against her cheeks. Sobbing, her breath blowing smoke, she fetched her mother. For a half-day they keened in high-pitched voices, their death chants filling the air. Later, with Victorio and Tezye helping, they buried the elders in a deep crevice, covering them with rocks.

In reverence, mother and daughter cropped their hair short. Facing one another, they held each other's elbows. Lozen's face was a mask of torment. "I killed them. It was at my suggestion that the elders come here."

White snowflakes covering her black hair, Besh-a-taye bowed her head. "It was better to die here, with their family.

We can honor them by remembering their teachings and words. They live in us as we walk their path in our hearts."

Lozen's heart felt like the tree falling not far from them, its trunk splitting in great creaks.

A week passed, and an angry and disillusioned Loco returned from his meeting with the Indian agent, Colyer. "Their government has ordered all tribes to Fort Tularosa, high in the mountains to the west. We must go down the mountain, gather our people right up and leave."

The band broke camp. As they headed to Canada Alamosa, Loco waved his hand. "The whites take us from here, put us there, move us wherever they want. We no longer have any say in our own lives. We should kill them!"

Nana's voice was filled with contempt. "You are like a drunk who can't decide what to sing. One day you say, 'Trust them.' The next, 'Kill them'."

Riding behind them, Shonta had another sense of it. "I too want to fight the whites and stay in our homeland." He tapped his thigh. "But my legs can no longer climb steep hills or run away from the enemy, and my arms are not strong enough to scale mountains. Many of us suffer in this way. Our tribe grows weaker."

An image burned deep in Victorio's memory. "I have been to Tularosa. The ground is hard and the sun flees the days before its time. Only thick-coated elk go there in winter. In summer, flies feast on horses' eyes."

He reined in, motioning for Lozen to follow. When the last man in line was out of earshot, he confided, "Hunger claws at our bellies and nips at our heels more fiercely than the soldiers. Our shoes are rags and we dress badly. I do not trust whites, yet only their path appears." He gestured at a lizard that moved in a series of jerking starts and stops. "My thoughts about what to do are like that whiptail there."

"Brother, the eagle cannot fly with the wings of the sparrow. To survive, we must come by a way other than resistance, go where the Blue Coats say for now. You are Chief of the Red Paint People, the *Tchi-hénè*. They will do as you say."

That afternoon, under a slate-gray sky, they rode into Canada Alamosa. Lozen found Kinsee and the children. She dismounted, then helped them onto her horse. Victorio gave his to Round Son's mother. Bit by bit, they made their way through the encampment, gathering their tribe.

The clan stretched in a tired yet disciplined formation, warriors at the front and rear, everyone else in-between. Most traveled on foot, having traded or sold their horses for liquor, or killed them for food. The ponies that were left went to the elders, ill and pregnant, and to small children who rode three to four on a horse, hugging as if they were one. Other than babies in cradleboards, there was little else to carry.

To ward off the cold, people clothed themselves in makeshift outfits. One squaw was shrouded in canvas stolen from a trader's tent. Another wore a long beaver coat with more holes than fur. Beside her, a man with a raccoon cap trudged along, his legs wrapped in pieces of tied army blankets. The clan needed rest, but with a buffeting gale and no wood or shelter, they had to keep moving. The well-fed, warmly-clothed United States Cavalry that herded them, kept their distance.

By noon of the third day, they had completed the last of a tortuous climb. The caravan of three hundred slogged into the narrow valley of the Tularosa River, seventy miles from where they'd started. Snowbound mountains stared at them with bleak faces, sloping downwards in scowls. Apache spirits sunk to the ground.

Her clothes hanging loosely on her gaunt frame, Lozen

stood by the river that ran with the color of shadows. She grabbed a handful of withered vegetation, rubbed it between her palms. "These leaves hold no more strength than that Big Peace Order signed by the White Father," she growled. Her eyes shifted across the river, where a bear fed on a dead horse that it had dragged down from a snowfield. She stared at the sky. In black spirals, misfortune hovered on the wings of red-necked buzzards. She felt a tug on her shirtsleeve.

"My mother says we are all made the same inside," said Her Eyes Brown. "Why then does the color of our skin call us enemy to the whites? Are there no *Indaa* with good hearts?"

Lozen knelt next to the young girl. "We are not the same. Apache babies are born in dry grass; whites in soft beds. They take what they want, when they want it. Ones with good hearts for Apaches have little power. They are like owls in the night; we don't see them much."

Her goddaughter pulled a small wooden knife, brandished it in the air and yelled, "The enemy won't grab me up, or my brother. I will cut out their hearts first!" She slipped her knife back in her belt, then held Lozen's hands. "My father Kandazi says you have the Power Of The Blue Hands; you know when the enemy comes." Her eyes burning with hard questions, she cocked her head towards a white mare on its front knees, its ribs protruding through a thin veil of hide. "If you have the power to know when enemy comes, why can't you make them die like that pony?"

"Waah." The emotion of sadness escaped Lozen's lips. Each day the children grew more afraid and angry. Her hands closed around the small fingers. "I don't know that ceremony. The medicine men say if you use a power not yours, you might go crazy, leap into fire, stab yourself or jump off a cliff."

Like we will all do if we stay here for long, she thought.

The pony swayed and toppled over. Lozen drew her skinning knife. Tough meat was better than none.

The band traveled onwards, reaching the grounds below Fort Tularosa. In a low, mud-caked depression where the hills would buffer the wind, they made camp. At the north end of the plain, a lone mountain with a gnawed peak hovered, its middle striped by a cloud of gray. At its base, the bottom slopes curled inward like dead pincers.

Using blankets and hides supplied by the army post, and branches from naked trees and bushes, they made crude shelters. There were no rations, and that night they had only bits of fruit and grain that they had saved in pouches.

Wild animals were hungry too, and when campfires burned, the ember-like eyes of prowling wolves could be seen in the darkness. A horse strayed too far, and soon after, the snarls of a feeding pack broke the icy stillness.

For the next few months, the clan hunted in knee-high snow. They existed on rabbits, fox and occasionally an elk. Dogs fought over food scraps, and if they weren't quick, were soon bones themselves. When the harsh winter finally ended, fifty *Tchi-héné* had been buried in the mountains—too late for the promised rations of dried meat, corn and flour that finally came from the Blue Coats.

On a morning when deer pawed through melting snow for new shoots, Victorio sent a boy to gather the warriors. Downtrodden, their moods like black ice, two hundred men formed a thick circle around their leader. Standing atop a boulder, Victorio raised a hand to the sky. "Hear me! Loco and I have given our word not to raid against the whites. We have kept that peace." His voice grew stronger. "Nothing was said about south of the border!"

Lozen climbed up beside him. "We live with the call of the wild in our blood. To turn away from that voice is to ride a fast-setting sun in the dead time of winter, never to return. México waits!" The men whooped and yowled. Kayate and Kanda-zi danced in place.

A quick council was called. Tezye noted that because of the harsh winter, only twenty horses were strong enough to make the long journey. Victorio quickly chose his raiders. Loco would stay behind with the remaining braves to provide a defense should white intruders mount a surprise attack.

To send the band on their way, Three Holds Sticks made a ceremony, and with other drummers beat on calfskin hides until their arms ached. Singing and high-stepping, Lozen joined the men around the bonfire. Encircling them, the clan chanted, clapped and yelled. Weapons and horses were readied.

Their spirits freed from the high mountain prison, the raiders rode a fast wind. After crossing the Rio Grande into México, the gods sent them a gift.

High on a bluff, the warriors surveyed a caravan of three wagons. From a leather case tied to his horse's mane, Victorio pulled out a Long Glass, a present from a slain Mexican officer. Extending the telescopic sight, he put it to his eye, then spoke to Lozen. She slid off her horse, and with nine others, ran in the direction of the train. A while later, Victorio followed.

In the lead wagon, the driver, a burly white man with a drooping black mustache, was talking animatedly. He chucked the wagon reins, flashed a broad smile that revealed a gold tooth and patted the thigh of the Mexican woman next to him. She returned the smile, then adjusted the infant in her arms so that it could better suckle on her teat in the jouncing wagon. The trader rubbed his fingers together as though he was counting money. The woman laughed and as she did so, he reached back, pulled forth a new rifle from under a tarp and thrust it into the air.

It was still there when Lozen's lance rammed him through the center of his chest. The blade pinned his torso to the back of the wooden seat and he hung there, impaled next to his family. Blood drenched his shirt and a trickle oozed from one corner of his mouth.

Covered in clay and wearing bear grass on their heads, Lozen and the warriors rose from the dirt not ten feet on each side of the three wagons. At the sight of the armed braves, the other drivers threw up their hands. From a nearby arroyo, Victorio rode forth with the rest of the raiders.

Holding her infant, the woman in the lead wagon jumped down and ran. An arrow thunked between her shoulder blades and she fell, the baby rolling out of his blanket. It lay naked, crying in the long footprint of a four-toed jackrabbit.

With her pistol, Lozen motioned the captives off the wagon seats. Two braves took their guns and forced them to their knees. A second woman cradled her newborn to her chest. A brave plucked at her blouse and she shirked away, holding the child even tighter. The raiders clambered over the tarp-covered goods, slicing through the ropes. They tore through packages and boxes, whooping and hollering as they held up new blankets, knives and guns. There were four sixteen-shot Henry rifles, plus several lever-action 1866 Winchesters with all-brass frames. Another crate held Colts.

Kayate picked up a heavy box and threw it down. The wood broke, revealing necklaces, jewelry, blouses and clothes. Lozen pulled out a buckskin dress, fringes hanging from the wide sleeves. The dancing colors spoke to her, its symbols expressing a woman's respect for nature and life. At the top of the dress, two gold-beaded crosses represented the morning star, while underneath a wide swath of indigo designated a lake. The design of a white turtle was inlaid on top. She fingered a hole where a bullet had gone through, just over the heart.

Another shattered box gave up small pairs of moccasins, brightly beaded in purple, gold and blue. "The dead feet of Apache children offer little resistance to stealers-of-toes," Lozen mumbled.

Kanda-zi reached into a carton packed tight with straw. He shouted with glee and pulled out a bottle of tequila. Dancing atop one of the boxes, he held his prize aloft. Victorio shot it through the neck with an arrow. The stunned warrior stood there with the stub, a dark stain running down his arm.

"Leave the whiskey," snarled Victorio. "We do not need it to put us to sleep so our enemies can kill us in the dark." His steely eyes caught the two remaining traders and their wives, the mother still clutching her baby. "Kill them."

Kayate jumped down from the wagon and ripped the baby from its screaming mother's arms. The kneeling men stood to protest. Tezye shot one through the heart, the other in the head. Kayate held the infant by its heels and swung it sideways. The baby's skull barely made a sound as bones and brains splattered against the wagon wheel. The mother, and the infant wailing in the dirt, were lanced to death.

Standing to one side, Lozen's heart felt like it had been ripped open by cactus. She knew that to leave the mothers alive as witnesses was unwise, that the babies weren't old enough to do slave-work, and would eat food meant for Apaches. Yet pity, sadness and humiliation enveloped her and she felt like a snake cut in half, each side writhing desperately to find the other and become whole again.

"Cut the horses free," ordered her brother. "We will use them as pack mules. Take all the weapons, blankets, food that you find." He chambered several rounds into a Winchester, cocked the lever and, shouldering the weapon, shot at nothing in particular. He patted the stock. "Good gun."

Jabbering with excitement, the men followed his instructions. They gathered up the rifles and ammunition first, slung ammunition belts over their shoulders, strapped gunbelts to their waists. Kayate rifled through a box of knives, testing each blade on his finger for sharpness. Others stripped the dead bodies of clothing and boots. Lozen's focus was on other things. She stuffed a burlap sack with small beaded moccasins, then took the squaw dress with the dancing colors. They would make welcome gifts for Her Eyes Brown and the other barefooted children. Kinsee would have no trouble mending the hole in her new dress.

With their spoils in tow, the raiders made for the border. Moonlight bathed the silvery sand as they forded their way back across the Rio Grande and headed to Tularosa.

CHAPTER SIXTEEN

WOOD THAT SINGS

A season was born. A season died. When and *if* food and supplies came, they were always late. A half-dozen white chiefs and agents had come and gone—their promises the same as their lies.

On one side of the council fire, Nana thumped his cane in the dirt. "The *Indaa*'s words scatter like partridges when they see the hawk."

"They accuse us of raiding in places we haven't gone," sneered Victorio, "and know nothing of the places we steal from."

Not intending to be funny, Tezye slapped his knee and said, "Whites do not know from where the smell of their own shit comes."

His remark took the members by surprise. Victorio almost swallowed his smoking pipe. About to gulp down a mouthful of water, Lozen spit it out, spraying her brother. Besh-a-taye drew her own blood with a spiny sewing needle stuck through a lion hide.

The council roared. Each voice caught the others and sent them back to their shaking owners, capturing them in loops of laughter. It had been a long time since they had anything to be joyful about, and they laughed until their sides, stomachs and throats ached. Once again, their emotions gave way to more serious tones.

"The new Indian agent Dudley wants us to go to Fort Stanton on the Bosque Redondo Reservation, live with the Mescaleros," croaked Loco. "It is no better than here."

Lozen stood and putting one foot atop the other, moved forward a few clumsy and tilting paces. "They do not know life moves in circles, step on their own feet and forever walk a crooked line."

Nana responded with a snort. "Whites like to tell others what to do. Their talk is not the Long Talk of the council, where we decide things for the good of our people."

"*Hou,*" echoed the members in agreement.

Later that day, when shadows dropped over Apache shoulders, a Chiricahua runner came. A lean warrior with a face burnished by wind and sun, he carried devastating news. "Our great chief Cochise was sick for a very long time. The pains in his stomach chewed at him like wolves tearing at live meat. He knew he was dying and said he wanted to ride one last time. We helped him to his horse. He was in a terrible way and we rode close to keep him from falling. At the top of a high butte, where he could see the Chiricahuas to the east and Dragoons to the west, he lay down and died during the night. The next morning we hid his body in a canyon. No one will ever find it there."

In the gathered throng, heads bowed, and women's tears drizzled down somber faces. The men stood impassively, blinking in disbelief. They stood there for a long time, then slowly and silently, shuffled away. Standing in a tight knot with Lozen and Besh-a-taye, Victorio shook his head. "Cochise was a good friend, a leader to all Apaches. We will never speak his name again, for it would only bring sorrow, make people feel bad."

"I remember the first time I saw him, when he came to my *dai-a-dai*. My eyes will keep him as he looked then—proud, fierce and strong, with eyes that spoke wisdom," said Lozen.

Eyes wet, Besh-a-taye looked at her children. "I knew him for forty years, and the hurt circles my heart. I will miss him." She wiped her nose with the back of her hand. "Though he's inexperienced, it falls to his son Tahza to lead."

"Geronimo is brave and fierce, has proven himself as a warrior and medicine man," answered Victorio. "It would be better if he were to head the Chiricahua."

Besh-a-taye raised one eyebrow. "That one, Goyolka, drinks too much, does crazy things. He is no chief. Cochise's people will look to you, my son."

To her surprise, Victorio did something Lozen had never seen before. He hugged his mother tenderly, holding her close. "I will offer them my leadership, with Little Sister as my right arm."

Two weeks fled, and on a sunlit morning when water gushed down the slopes from melting snow, a Blue Coat scout entered camp. A Tonto Apache, he wore a red headband, an army coat buttoned to the neck, dark trousers and high-topped moccasins. In a voice filled with gravel, he gave the white chief's message—the band had three days to ready themselves for their return to Ojo Caliente. To keep angry settlers and miners from attacking the tribe, Pony Soldiers would shadow their return. It was all for the good of the *Tchi-héné*, the clan.

The unexpected good tidings turned the camp into a

bustle of renewed energy. Chattering women began to pack up food and possessions. Braves collected their spoils and weapons, young boys ran to gather and feed the horses. Lozen's heart was light as a moth's, and her spirit chirped like the gap-toothed marmots that stood in their hillside villages.

Victorio knew better, knew that the smile on the thin lips of the messenger hid the *Indaa*'s real reason. With Lozen at his side, he walked to where a trickle of water meandered between new blades of grass. "It is not because the whites' hearts are one with ours that we are being allowed to return. It is because it costs their government too much to bring rations and supplies here. Our homeland is closer, cheaper for them."

He thrust his chin in the direction of the Apache scout, who had unbuttoned his coat and was leaning against a rock. "The army may be planning an ambush. Those brainless Tontos do not care; they will do anything for a handful of bullets."

"I will see that we are prepared, brother." She left him as hurriedly as she had spoken. Each warrior was cautioned to be weapon-ready. Knives were given to mothers, children and elders, who hid them under their clothes and blankets.

On the day of departure, Lozen rode up and down the fringes of the strung-out column, her voice high in spirit and hope. "Soon you will be on the ground where you were born and held in the four directions. You will be able to kick off your moccasins and wiggle your toes in the sacred water." She began to sing.

Honor the sacred
Honor the Sun our Father, the Earth our Mother
Honor the water from which we came to be
Honor the elders

Honor four-leggeds, two-leggeds, winged ones
Walk in balance with water skippers, swimmers, crawlers
Walk in harmony with plants, rocks, mountains
Dance the Dance of Life

The clan took up the song, repeating each line after it was said. Parents held small children close to them and bounced them to the chant. Old ones picked up their tired heads. Three Holds Sticks brought out a drum. Those on foot tramped to the beat. Others clapped and swayed to the music.

An elder took out a fiddle he had made from the wide stalk of a dead century plant. His rickety arms were thin as the sumac bow that followed, his veins taut as the horsetail-hair string. He ran the bow across the sinew tied over the hollow of the fiddle, cocked his head to one side and began to play. "Follow the wood that sings!" he yelled.

Several girls danced and twirled in no particular fashion. A warrior grabbed his bow, put the string in his mouth and began to tap it with an arrow. Another did the same. To Lozen, it sounded like Apaches singing.

Songbirds picked up the gaiety and, on sweet voices and flitting wings, carried it back and forth. At the sound of the cheerful chorus, a herd of pronghorn antelope feeding in a belt of gold and green raised their heads. Floating on its back in a pond, an otter paused, then continued to munch with whiskered contentment on a fish held between webbed paws.

As Lozen rode alongside the procession, Her Eyes Brown came running from the other direction. She reached down, swept the girl up and rode to the crest of a nearby butte. Below, a herd of wild ponies galloped under the arc of a rainbow that held two mountain peaks together. There was a dun with a spotted red clay rump, a brown-and-white splotched paint, two ponies of snow and several mustangs. Flying manes and tails streamed as they chased a swath of rain that fled the tableland.

"Where is the rain going?" asked the girl.

"It lives on the other side of the doorway of many colors."

"I will dream about deer, summer, everything green, fruit and pollens. I will dream about all the colors. Someday I will go there and bring them back, so our lives will always be bright," said Her Eyes Brown. Lozen embraced her. It was a good dream.

Four moons passed, and just after dark, the band reached Ojo Caliente. Lozen wanted time alone, to think and pray. She immediately sought out her secluded pool. Memories of Gray Wolf floated in the calm of a reflected moon. *Da go Te,* it called to her in a welcoming greeting. As she sat cross-legged, a blustery wind blew out of nowhere, lashing the water's surface.

Moon and memories broke up in tiny pieces.

CHAPTER SEVENTEEN

BLACK BLOOD

An early-morning breeze tickled Lozen's toes, and she opened her eyes to a brisk blue sky. The bright canary face of a tall sunflower stared down at her, its yellow pistils tipped in purple. Thousands of male cicadas buzzed on every side. The short-horned grasshoppers had emerged from their underground incubators to lure females.

She stretched, long and lazy, with arms and legs off the ground, fingers and feet extended. The breeze spiraled around her and she reveled in the coolness, knowing the day would soon turn hot and muggy. A few feet away, a muddy pond reflected saplings that waved from the surface.

Lozen pulled on her moccasins. From a bush, she picked a handful of dark red squawberries. She popped a few currants in her mouth, savoring the sweet taste. Voices filtering through the bushes drew her to where Kinsee and five other women were harvesting the spear-flowered stalks of agaves.

On the ground was a three-foot stick with a flattened end.

Lozen picked up the crude shovel and pointed at a plant devoid of buds and petals. "Better not to harvest those man plants that do not bloom," she explained to the two girls who were helping.

"They are like men that behave badly and leave us with a bitter taste," complained a laboring woman, sweat dripping from her brow. "It is better to dig up these blossoming women plants here that give us sweet syrup and juice."

"Mmnh," chimed in a stout woman with twinkling eyes. "It is more proof that women have a better disposition than men."

"It is good to get away from them and their boastful talk," said Kinsee. She pulled down on a sword-like leaf and showed it to the girls. "Be careful. One small bite of this will put a big fire in your mouth."

A dawn of understanding came alive in her daughter's eyes. "We should have a big feast then, invite the White Eyes. We can dry these mescal tops, roll them into round shapes. We will tell the whites it is candy, feed it to them until they burn away."

Eyebrows went up and Lozen patted her on the head. "She is practicing to be a strong medicine woman and will soon turn enemies into cattle."

Kinsee hacked off flowers from a fallen plant. "One time my aunt roasted mescal, but they did not cook well. My aunt said that I was not following our set ways and traditions, and had sex with my husband during baking time."

Lozen nudged Her Eyes Brown in the ribs. Her voice crinkled with humor. "*That* is how you came into this world, from the tops of undercooked agaves."

The girl looked to her mother. "Does that mean when plants are badly cooked, Apache babies begin in their mothers' stomachs?"

Lozen leaned on her shovel with such force that it snapped. She fell to the ground, folding in half with laughter. The others held their sides, or onto one another. Tears of mirth mingled with the sweat on their cheeks and liquid dripped from their noses.

Not sure what all the merriment was about, the girls looked at each other with curious smiles and puzzled eyes.

Near day's end, the harvesters began their return to the encampment. Caught between a flat horizon and low bank of clouds, the sun blazed in a spiral cross of pointed light, painting the sandstone cliffs in a rosy flush. As they approached the village, Lozen could see Victorio's rapidly-moving figure silhouetted against the horizon. She gripped her bundle and ran after him. "It has been a day of plenty," she called. "We have gathered lots of mescal, berries and potatoes."

"Bah! It is a day like all the others, full of people who do not belong here. We are fenced in by the *Indaa*'s presence. Soldiers and forts surround us. Each season there are fewer warriors. It is more difficult for wives to bring up their children in the right way." His stride kept pace with his frustration, and Lozen hurried to keep up.

"Agents with two tongues steal our rations so they can sell them for a profit. The worst are whiskey sellers who come like those insects with stinging beaks after a rain." He stopped and kicked over a decayed log. Black bugs, termites and wood beetles scurried.

"Our homeland has become an open wound full of rotting things, brother."

Victorio scratched his chin. "The whites' big council that sits in Washington says there will no longer be treaties between Indian nations and the United States."

A butterfly with turquoise wings edged in green flitted in

194

front of them. Lozen imitated its flight with her fingers. "They have stolen our sacred grounds and have no need to make peace with Apaches."

"Our friend, the White Eye Jeffords who Cochise trusted, says they live by their 'Constitution paper.' It promises what Americans' rights are, and is kept in the big house where the Great White Father lives. We must not be Americans then, for that dwelling has no door for Indians."

Lozen held out her arms, palms up. "Before they came, we lived by the *begodih,* the means of *Usen*'s power. We held our destiny in the hollows of our hands." She spread her fingers wide. "Now freedom escapes like water through a cracked gourd."

They went their separate ways then, and Lozen sat by a boulder that was blanketed with red and black ladybugs. Watching them, her mind chewed on her clan's predicament, the fate of her people, her own embittered emotions. Her thoughts were abruptly interrupted when Kayate galloped by. A few moments later, he caught up to Victorio. Lozen ran to hear what he was telling her brother.

"The soldiers with curly hair come from Santa Fe, travel with a white chief and *Yudaha* scout."

"Give weapons to all those old enough to carry them. Our enemy will hear my words and see their meaning."

On a dog-day afternoon filled with creeping clouds, the troops arrived. Led by a white lieutenant; twenty black cavalrymen of the Ninth Regiment rode straight and tall. Their bedrolls were tied neatly behind their saddles, and sheathed knives clung to their sides. Dressed in caps bearing a crossed rifle emblem, each wore a yellow neck bandana and a dark blue shirt. Lighter colored pants were wedged into over-the-knee boots. A young private carried the U.S. Coat of Arms, the silk standard of an eagle under thirteen stars fluttering in the breeze. Inscribed in yellow, on a red scroll held in its beak, were the words, *E Pluribus Unum.* An olive branch and bunched arrows were clutched in the talons.

The women, children and many of the men had never seen a Buffalo Soldier before, and they gaped at the troopers. Lozen thought of Gray Wolf's description when they had hunted buffalo on the plains.

Victorio met the cavalrymen in front of his tipi. Like spider's legs about its victim, the weapon-bristling warriors curled around the small force. Neither the Navajo scout, nor the army officer dismounted. It was a sign of disrespect, but Victorio had things that were more pressing on his mind. He glared at the scout, who cradled a Spencer carbine in his arms.

"Not long ago *Yudaha* warriors raided here and killed a squaw, stole horses. If it were not for the Blue Coats, we would have tracked your people down, cut their throats."

Eyes the color of peach pits flicked and narrowed. "You Apaches have warred against us since the beginning of the ancients. Revenge walks two paths."

"And a blade cuts two ways," Lozen hissed.

Victorio shifted his gaze to the officer. As he spoke, the Navajo translated.

"Our women harvest and our men hunt, yet still there is not enough food, for your people cover our land. We have received no rations for more than a season." He reached behind him and, bringing a young boy forward, placed his hands on the small shoulders. "I have no power over my warriors when our children cry from empty stomachs. If food does not come in the next seven moons, we will make war again. You may someday kill us all, but you will bury five of your own for every Apache."

The officer cleared his throat. He was a thin man with eyes of emptiness and a strained face that looked constipated. Finger by finger he pulled off his yellow gloves. When he finished, he hooked them in his belt. With his forefinger, he pushed a pair of spectacles high up onto the bridge of his nose, and managed a counterfeit smile.

"The United States Government does not seek hostilities with your people, Victorio. This time you can rest assured you will receive your supplies because they will come from the army, not the agents." He adjusted his hat, resting his hand on the hilt of his saber. "*That* is what I have come to tell you."

Kayate whispered in Lozen's ear. "His words ride a pale pony that disappears in the clouds. We should kill them now, take their horses and weapons."

"We cannot get out of a hole by digging a deeper one. Many times their number will come."

Victorio looked at a stocky, powerfully-built soldier. His eyes were as hard as the muscles that bulged the sergeant's shirt and stretched the yellow stripes across his arm. Keeping his gaze fixed on the trooper, he spoke to the scout. "Tell the one big as a mountain to get down."

The words were interpreted, the lieutenant nodded at the trooper and Sergeant Henry Coombs swung from his horse. The full-chested Apache chief moved close. "I was told the one who gave you freedom said in a big talk that all men are created the same. Did he not count those with red skins?"

Coombs waited for the translation, then said, "Tell him I believe he did." Lozen thought his voice came from the Thunder Gods stamping on top of the world.

Victorio rubbed two fingers across the soldier's forehead. The sergeant's eyes flared, but he remained still. Victorio grabbed his wrist and put the tortilla-sized hand on his own face. "My color does not wipe away any more easily than yours." He waited a drumbeat, then pulled his knife from its sheath. The sergeant stiffened and his free hand dropped towards his pistol. Troopers' hands went for their holstered Colts. The warriors, their weapons raised, moved in tighter. Sharp clicks of hammers coincided with the Navajo's abrupt warning. "Do nothing, or we will not leave this place alive."

Victorio pulled the man's hand away from his face, sliced into the rough-hewn palm, then cut his own. Neither of them flinched. "Look at our blood, the color is the same." He jerked his head in the direction of the officer. "Whites seek to skin us from our ways, our religion, the land we love. Your people suffered in the same way, yet you take their side against those with darker skin." He released his grip and slipped the knife back under his belt.

Coombs shook the blood from his hand, shook his head. "We're soldiers now, finally got free from two hundred fifty years of slavery. We fightin' for the rights of all people in these here United States. The army pays us thirteen dollars a month, gives us food, allotments and clothing. We done got back our manhood, our families. A few of us even owns land now and aims to keep it." He turned to the scout. "Tell him."

Victorio's mood turned inky as the soldier's hide. "Yet you would keep us from ours. Whites still own your people." He waved his hand. "Go. Never return here."

With the scout and officer leading, the soldiers turned away. At the outskirts of the village, Coombs lit up a corncob pipe. He took a long draw, glanced at his blood-encrusted palm. "Shit."

"Coombs!" The sergeant rode forward and pulled abreast of his superior, who was rubbing his nose between thumb and forefinger. "Make sure those rations get here in seven days. I don't want or need any hassles from the Apaches, or crap from the captain."

"They'll be here, sir. I'll see to it personally."

His lieutenant coughed, then took a swig of canteen water. The senatorial-type speech he was about to give needed to be loud and clear. "Indian Commissioner Smith's report to Congress aptly states the problem. We have in the midst of the Southwest thousands of Indians. They are the least intelligent of our population, not subject to any laws except their own. We spend millions trying to civilize them, to no avail. Therefore, Indians should be subject to the laws of this nation only. No ancient beliefs or customs should shield them from those laws."

He shifted in his saddle. "It has been decided the best way to do that is to concentrate all Apaches from all tribes in one place, at the San Carlos Reservation in Arizona. They can be confined there and kept under control."

His tone turned disapproving. "The Indian-lover agent there, John Clum, convinced the military to withdraw troops and replaced them with Apache police. They even have their own damn court system. Won't last though. Indians aren't smart enough to be anything but savages."

Riding closely behind them, the Navajo thought, *Trying to keep Apaches in one place is like trying to tie sap to a tree. They will never stop costing you money, costing you lives. Maybe you're the ones who are not so smart.*

CHAPTER EIGHTEEN

MOCCASINS, MONSTERS

Taking a walk far from the village, Lozen felt the thunder beneath her feet. Her heart took a hard thump. Could it be a surprise attack by Blue Coats, *Yudaha* or both? She looked at her hands; they weren't tingling, hadn't turned blue. Preceded by an oncoming dust cloud, the rumbling became louder. A warrior emerged from the brown haze, and Lozen recognized the familiar, log-like body of Geronimo. He raised a rope in greeting. More warriors appeared, and Lozen counted at least eighty horses. Like a gusting tumbleweed across an open plain, she raced alongside a gray pony. Grabbing a handful of mane, she swung onto its back.

"You have had good luck, Goyolka," she said, riding up next to Geronimo. Wide-nosed and full-cheekboned, a headband encircled his short-cropped hair.

"My Power tells me to raid and fight."

"It must be a good Power then, for in all this time you have never been wounded."

He smiled, thumped his chest. "I am blessed with strong war medicine and sleep soundly after defeating my enemies." Like a dog pawing at a flea, he scratched his head. "I remember after your lion hunt in the Dragoons, when we rode with Cochise. It was a good time; we collected many spoils from those lying naked in the dust."

"Aya. I remember you were drunk and killed a man for no reason."

Geronimo kneed his horse, urging it ahead. "He wanted to steal my liquor." Lozen could smell it on him, the same as when they'd raided.

They drove the herd on. A sentry on a high outcropping waved his rifle in greeting. As they rode into the encampment, dogs scampered and created a racket, while parents ran to grab wandering children. Tipi flaps flipped open and people hurried outside to see about the commotion. Women scrubbing clothes laid their work on sunlit rocks and hastened towards the noise; warriors put aside their shield painting.

While three warriors rode out to take charge of the herd, the riders dismounted. Flanked by the council, Victorio greeted them. "You have captured many fine ponies, Goyolka."

Geronimo thrust out his chest. "There were lots more. I sold them to the whites, along with cattle and guns that we stole from the Mexicans."

"You sell our enemies weapons to be used against Apaches?"

"If they come, we will kill them, steal the guns and horses back, sell them again."

Lozen could see Victorio's jaw muscles clench and knew he was like a dog with raised hackles, ready to bite. She moved next to him, her voice low. "Do not argue; we have

201

much to learn from him about the whites."

Victorio grunted. His tone changed slightly. "You and your men must eat. When you finish, we will smoke, make the Big Talk."

"My men will eat. I will drink, and talk." He pulled a bottle from a saddlebag, pulled the cork and took a swallow.

Inside Victorio's tipi, a woman brought a basket filled with tobacco and paper. Shonta expertly rolled a cigarette and lit it with a burning stick from the fire. Shadows flickered and danced across weathered faces. Victorio took a pull on the smoking pipe and handed it to Geronimo. "Speak of what you have seen of the White Eye, the one called Crook."

Geronimo blew out a puff of smoke. "That general is stubborn as the mule he rides, clever as a fox. His soldiers no longer travel with heavy wagons, now carry supplies on pack mules to move faster. They do not ride in straight lines as before—are not as easy to ambush."

"He takes lessons from Apaches," boasted Nana.

Geronimo flicked a thumb against his nose. "He hunted Delshay and his Tontos for two seasons. When he could not find that tribe, he hired other Apaches to track them down. They brought the heads to the fort at San Carlos. Crook stuck them on tall poles with the heads of other Indians for all to see." Holding the pipe, he made a wide circle in the air. "That one rounds up White Mountain Apaches, Tontos, Coyoteros, Chiricahuas, Pimas, Pinals, Aravaipas, puts them all on the reservation there. Lizards hide from the sun in that place."

Loco scratched under his bad eye. "We have heard the Indian agent, John Clum, has honor, a good heart for Apaches, pays them for the work they do."

Geronimo moved his head back and forth in a bobbing motion. "That gobbler puffs himself up and squawks about many things. He also forbids weapons and *tiswin,* and no one can drink that beer. He makes money telling Apaches what to do and how to live. He is no more honorable than Apaches who become reservation police for a handful of ammunition."

Tezye, who now had the pipe, pointed the stem at Geronimo. "You ride with the Chiricahuas. Why are you not at San Carlos like them?"

Reaching into his jacket pocket, Geronimo withdrew several oblong tags and threw them into the center of the council. "Those metal pieces there carry names of dead Indians who tried to escape the reservation. They were made to wear them like the marks white men burn into cattle, so they can tell where they belong. I did want not live like a cow and escaped to México."

Leaning forward, Lozen picked up a tag, fingered it and flipped it into the fire. "Our ancestors would die many times again over these things you tell us."

Victorio looked squarely at Geronimo; the red and black paint that streaked his forehead and ran under his eyes and down his cheeks. "We have nothing to do with Tontos, Coyoteros or the others. We try to live here in peace. You are like a bear that stirs up the bees' nest, raiding along the border killing Mexicans and whites."

He gestured at Geronimo's blue soldier's jacket. "You are not a chief but play like one, wear the clothes of those you've killed. Young warriors think you are brave, follow you, die for your glory. We are grateful for the horses you bring, not the whiskey and bad medicine."

"I take what I need, look to no White Eye!"

"They look for you," shot back Victorio, "and where they find you, they have a reason to come for us. Big trouble follows wherever you go."

Bristling, Geronimo stood. "The *Indaa* harvest Indians the way Zunis gather corn. I do not bring them; they come for all Apaches." He strode out of the tipi, collected his small band and rode away.

Lozen and Victorio walked to the pasture. It was the Moon of Fat Horses, and ponies grazed on blue-green grasses that bent in the wind. Under puffs of cottontail clouds, an eagle turned a slow circle, wings spread against the brilliance of a sapphire sky.

"Goyolka walks only in his own moccasins," Lozen said.

"He left us twenty horses, and does not speak with a split tongue. We will wait, and watch."

The scout that dog-trotted into camp a week later was a sturdy, mean-looking man with scars on both sides of his face. Although the camp had not yet stirred, there was no hesitation when he entered Victorio's tipi. A few moments passed and he exited, Victorio at his heels. The warrior took off at a flying pace, stopping briefly at several tipis.

Still in the early throes of slumber, Lozen sensed something afoot. Pangs of anxiety ran through her and she rolled from her blanket. Pulling back the tipi flap, she came face-to-face with her brother. Silver streaked his ebony hair, and his face was marked by a silent strength. "Goyolka and his braves have been captured by Clum at the Ojo Caliente agency. Loco and I must go there, talk to that agent, see if our people are in danger."

Lozen put her hand on his arm. "I am afraid for you; do not go."

"If I do not, Crook will send soldiers. Our people will lose their heads."

"I'll go with you."

Just then, the scar-faced warrior, who was accompanied

by Loco, Nana, Tezye and five braves, rode up. Three were armed with six-repeater Winchester .73's, the others with carbines. Bare-legged and breech-clothed, the tails of their long shirts flapped from underneath ammunition belts. Victorio took the reins of his horse from Loco and slid onto its back. "Stay here, Little Sister. If we have not returned by the time the sun begins sleep, lead our people to the mountains."

Before the hoofbeats had faded, Lozen was calling for added sentries. Enlisting the help of Little Tachita and other novices, she prepared the band for a fast escape. Warriors stacked lances tipi-fashion, shields resting against them. Bowstrings were tested for tautness, arrow quivers replenished, ammunition checked. Women filled food pouches, children water bags. Horses were brought up from the pasture and tethered close. By midday, all was in readiness.

As Lozen walked through the village for a last inspection, uneasiness sifted through her. Had Geronimo's capture been a trick to lure the leaders away so the whites could kill them? She shuddered at the thought that they might already be hanging from long nooses, their feet jerking in the last throes of death. Suddenly, she was struck with the fact that she might be the only one left to guide her people. She had led small pods of warriors before, in skirmishes and raiding parties. But to lead hundreds in an escape! Would she be able to keep them out of harm's way? How would the women, children and elders eat, the clan keep warm and survive?

Coming to the village outskirts, she climbed a short bluff and surveyed the camp. Convinced all was ready, and that trouble, if it did come, was a day away, she ran down the slope to her hidden pool. A short time later, under a leafy canopy of oak and aspen, she dropped out of her clothes. The sun filtered through an opening in the trees, caressing her in soft light. Surrounded by cattails that bent in the breeze, she slipped into the pool. Ripples nudged her breasts, and she took handful after handful of water, letting it fall through her fingers and over her head. She needed this—the quiet, the contentment, the refreshing of her spirit. She ducked her head under, brought it up and stroked back her hair. Finally, she waded to the bank and sat on the grass. After the wind had dried her, she dressed and walked upstream into the sun's bright light. A shadow moving speedily over the ground caused her to dodge away—had she been caught in the vulture's shadow, bad luck and misfortune would follow.

Giggling came from around a bend in the brook, and as she rounded it, spied several pubescent girls splashing each other in ankle-deep water. Hair fell to their shoulders and bangs shadowed their eyebrows. Bare-chested, their plum-like breasts were just beginning to ripen. Each wore a long muslin skirt tucked at the waist.

"Lozen, tell us a story," Her Eyes Brown shouted, spotting her godmother.

"Tell us about how the days and nights were created," piped up another maiden, scooping a handful of water at her playmates.

"Come out of there, and I will tell you."

Their skirts drenched, the girls sloshed to the bank. Curious as prairie dogs, they perched on their knees. Lozen began. "In the beginning, before White Painted Woman and Child Of The Water, there were only monsters, birds, four-leggeds and snakes. A contest took place, monsters on one side, the other creatures against them." Her eyes swept the maidens. "Who knows by what name it was called?"

"The Moccasin Game. I have heard my grandmother speak of it," said a girl with a smile as ample as her girth.

With a stick, Lozen drew a round shape in the ground. "Each player took one of their own moccasins and threw it in the middle of a big circle. There were lots of players; the pile grew high."

The girl jumped up and stretched her hand over her head. "Taller than me, I bet."

Lozen's voice filled with mirth. "Aya. In one way you're lucky, in another not so fortunate." She raised her eyebrows three times. "Short people get rained on last, drown first."

The girls laughed.

"Grab up your shoes, toss them in the circle," Lozen instructed.

Playfully jostling each other, six maidens ran for their moccasins. Lozen made a winding design in the sand, and slid the stick under the pile that was being dropped. "A snake with a bone in its mouth slithered through the moccasins and hid it there, where no one could see. Each side got one chance to guess which moccasin held the bone. If the monsters guessed, they would win and the world would be forever in darkness. If the others chose right, there would always be sunshine."

"But we have both," said a questioning Her Eyes Brown.

Like a stalking cat, Lozen crawled around the drawn circle, her head poking in and out. "A monster and bird went round and round the pile, trying to see the bone." She then fell sideways, into the heavy girl's lap. "They became dizzy and tired, and had to lean against each other. Both looked into the middle, spying the bone at the same time."

Her Eyes Brown's face lit up. "Each side won; today we have light and darkness!"

As Lozen righted herself, she was caught under a fleeting shadow. The vulture banked and headed for the village.

CHAPTER NINETEEN

NO COVER

Later that day, the envoy returned. Except for knives, all were naked of weapons and ammunition. Shoulders sagging and ponies plodding, they made their way to the village center. Victorio dismounted as though the weight of his mount was upon him. Above, cranes in formation flew across a peach-clouded sky, feet extended behind them like toed twigs.

From the far reaches of the village, people began to drizzle in. Dogs went silent; children were hushed. The only sound was the drone of an occasional bee. When the clan had gathered, Victorio related the white man's orders—the band had seven moons to pack up and go to the agency at Ojo Caliente. As he spoke, heads bowed, shaking in disbelief and anger.

"Clum says we must then go to San Carlos in Arizona, that his government has ordered all Apaches to that reservation. He says soldiers and settlers will not bother us; we will be able to hunt and there will be plenty of rations, clear water to drink."

Shonta went livid and, stiff-jointed as he was, whirled his cane in the air. "I trust nothing the whites say. We must take our people and escape to Juh in the Sierra Madres, where they will never find us!"

"In two moons as many soldiers will be here as there are hairs on a rabbit. We do not have enough weapons or warriors to fight them. Goyolka is held prisoner in a corral with others. I saw them."

"Penned like the cow he did not want to be," Lozen brooded.

"I told Clum we would make no trouble, that we want to remain here, close to Ojo Caliente. I said, 'Look here, white man,' " Victorio spread his arms, " 'this is where we want to live. It is the homeland of our ancestors. We are connected to it as a parent to a child, a husband to a wife, a relative to a relative. We do not want to go to San Carlos, for we know nothing of that place or those people.' " He put his hands to his head. "His ears were closed."

"Bah!" Besh-a-taye exclaimed. "Getting the *Indaa* to hear Apaches is like prying open a dead man's eyes, thinking he will see."

"We will hide our weapons in the mountains," Lozen said, "bring in only enough to satisfy the whites. Someday we will return to fight again."

"Strike the village," Victorio instructed. "All must be at the agency office in seven moons to be counted."

At his order, the scar-faced warrior, followed by six braves, mounted their horses and galloped away. Lozen watched them go, then muttered, "They are angry and will become renegades like Goyolka, be hunted the rest of their lives."

In a pall of despair, the clan began to ready for the journey. Possessions were collected and packed, tipis stripped of hides. For the sick and those too old to walk, crude drags were made by stretching skins across downed lodge poles, then lashing them to a horse's sides. On the day of reckoning, four hundred fifty Warm Springs Apaches began the trek to the agency.

Shonta had adopted a black derby, the arrowhead tear in the center clearly visible. Tezye wore a white man's red vest, Kayate a single-breasted cavalry coat with the brass buttons opened down the front. From beneath empty gunbelts surrounding the warriors' waists, tails of cowboys' flannel shirts whipped in the wind. Victorio draped a gray wool blanket over his shoulder, the stamped indigo letters *U.S.* clearly visible. "The Blue Coats will see that our surrender does not come without a price."

Riding at the head of the column with him, Lozen looked down at her frayed calico blouse, the worn cotton duck trousers. "They will know the cost has been their own kind lying naked in the dust." She glanced back at the plodding, human river. "We are caught between the white man's world and our own, brother."

Three miles farther on, they came to an expanse of flat ground banked between low, rolling hills. From the porch of the agency office, a man rose from a wooden barracks chair and headed out to greet them. Victorio nodded at him in greeting. "It is the *Nantan* Clum."

Lozen was surprised at the man's youthful appearance. Unlike the older Blue Coats and stiff-mannered agents previously encountered, he wore a small mustache instead of a bushy beard, and dressed simply in a high-peaked sombrero, range pants, gray shirt and pebble-grained leather boots. He was armed with a hunting knife, Colt .45 and cartridge belt. She was even more surprised when he greeted them in fluent Apache. He then passed among the clan, welcoming women

210

and dour-faced braves alike.

Off to one side, Lozen could see a hundred Indian police. In white pants, dark shirts and a variety of hats, they stood in a disciplined show of force, .45-caliber Springfield rifles over their shoulders, pistols at their hips. Nana came up behind her. "That Clum is smart. He chooses White Mountain, Coyotero and Tonto Apaches, Indians that have no ties to our tribe. They would not hesitate to follow his orders, shoot us if necessary."

Lozen glanced at the corral nearby. Sitting on the ground, their legs in iron ankle traps, were Geronimo and eight of his followers. In an open field beyond, hundreds of ten-foot-high, conical-walled tents stood neatly arranged in rows—houses for the Pony Soldiers. She walked over to a line of wagons and peered inside. Some carried stores and provisions, another cots and blankets. Her head tilted with the off-balance thought that Clum was a white man that might be trusted. On the opposite side of the wagons, pack mules were being loaded. A soldier, his foot braced against an animal's ribs for balance, hauled down hard on a diamond cinch strap, securing the load.

Shortly after dawn, the four hundred-mile pilgrimage began. Heading out of the valley, Lozen glanced back wistfully at her homeland. No more would young women be sprinkled with pollen and run around the Sacred Basket during *dai-a-dai*, the Feast of Maidens. The Crown Dancers' chants, and happy squeals of children diving for sweets, would be stilled, as would the blessings, holiness and healing powers given by *Ish Son Mah glash eh*—White Painted Woman. No more would she sit by the Smoky Water, or bathe at the hidden pond where images of her love floated in the water. With a heavy sigh, she turned away.

Led by Clum, the mile long caravan headed east, a dozen of his police filtering among the clan. Bringing up the rear were wagons on creaking wheels, plus a rear guard of twenty soldiers. Walking next to Lozen and his mother, Little Tachita spoke fiercely. "The police and whites are few; they would be easy to overpower and kill."

Kinsee's scowl could have turned an oak to firewood. "It is one thing to be a novice, to learn to ride and shoot. It is another to know how to behave as a man." She cuffed the side of his head. "The white *nantan* honors his word, brings only a small force. Your chief has given his word that we will keep the peace. You are insolent to think he would backtrack on his promise."

She nodded ahead to where Her Eyes Brown struggled under a pack. "Go help your sister there, great warrior." As her son skulked away, she tugged at the back of his loincloth, "And do not lose the cover of your manhood on the way."

"Your sharp tongue pierced his pride," said Lozen, as they watched Little Tachita take the pack.

"Youth is an excuse for ignorance, not stupidity, for that is what kills Apaches. I do not want my son to die."

"You are a good mother, a wise teacher." An orange-bellied oriole flew by, white wing patches flapping like small moons.

The caravan twisted and turned around bends, through forests and streams. They climbed up and down rolling hills and steep inclines. Parents carried small children on their shoulders, holding them by their ankles for balance. Dogs chased rabbits and squirrels, boys, lizards. Twilight fell, and as the clan passed under the moon shade of oak, spruce and elm, pale light dappled them in spots of silvery-blue. Against a yellow moon, women carrying cradleboards looked like calves walking on two feet.

In a meadow with a stream meandering through the center, the Apaches and their enemies made camp in an unusual alliance. Horses were watered and let out to graze. Girls and soldiers replenished water pouches and canteens, women struck fires. The police distributed rations of beans and hard-tack. Drawn to the aroma of food, a bear wandered on the fringes of the treeline.

After Lozen and her mother finished their meal, Besh-a-taye eased down on her back, gazing at the sky. "The moon ate the stars tonight. It lights our way with a full belly."

"I see nothing but darkness, *shimaa*." Lozen curled on her side, and in three blinks, began to dream.

A river of blood snaked from her neck, and her stomach was caved in by a thousand blue uniforms that marched without bodies. A naked woman held her dead baby high— a massive raven perched on the small head. Trees had clawed limbs, and as she tried to run, they clutched at her, ripping her skin.

Twitching with each vision, Lozen awoke in a cold sweat. Besh-a-taye's head rested comfortably against her stomach, while Her Eyes Brown slept at her feet.

Within the next several days, Apaches began falling sick. Shinash-a-too danced around a feverish girl on a litter, the eagle feather in his hair dipping up and down. He took a pinch of pollen from a vest pocket, herbs from another, and sprinkled them over the girl. Waving smoke from a smoldering stick, he chanted.

This maiden is in a bad way
She is searching for good health
Your Power, the one you promised me can keep her from harm
I will tell you something
Put it in her right now,
*   so she will be well and live a long and fruitful life*

213

Helpless and hopeless, Lozen stared at the shivering girl. Only a few days before she had been playing in the stream, listening to the moccasin story, holding the storyteller in her lap. "The sickness makes bad skin with spots, Shinash-a-too."

"The evil strikes with heat, with ice, and repeats itself. Many scratch their hides away until it bleeds. I have made the pollen cross on her chest, fed her agave juice and put it on the sores that burn her skin." He waved the stick towards the rear of the column. "Clum sends the fallen to that wagon with the red mark. Soldiers do not let me go there to put up a dance, sing a song, heal the dying. The same Indian scout always takes away the dead to bury them. No one is allowed near."

The weeks dragged on. Youngsters, who had started out with jumping beans in their shoes, slogged along as though they were caught in deep mud. More litters were put together for the elders, for the pregnant who could no longer walk. The stricken girl had recovered, but a half-dozen others had died. To the west of Santa Fe, on a high path between Horse Springs and Stein's Peak, the caravan came upon the burial scout.

Lozen was near the head of the column and the victim was close. She gasped, threw her hands to her mouth, then squinched her eyes shut, trying to blot out what she'd already seen. Distorted limbs jutted in anguish from the gas-bloated form, and hard sacs of pus covered the body from head to foot. The skin was the color of charred wood, peeling off in layers. Encrusted, blackened blood funneled from the mouth, nostrils and ears.

"Make a wide berth!" yelled a policeman, waving his arms at the column. Lozen was already beating a hasty retreat when she suddenly fell to her knees, and wretched. The Tonto Apache came up behind her. "It is called smallpox.

You do not have to touch it like hides of evil animals—the bear, coyote or snake—to get it. It is not like when you are afraid, so the entrance of evil influence finds an easy path into your body. This here sickness attacks on the wind."

Lozen wiped the back of her mouth with her sleeve. Standing, she fingered a fringed buckskin amulet filled with creosote leaves that hung around her neck—a childhood gift from her grandmother to guard against sickness. "There is no cure?"

The man, who was thin and had the face of a weasel, shrugged. He nodded back past the halted column. "The White Eyes put the sick in that wagon there, so their breath does not spread the illness. It does no good." Lozen remembered the groaning she'd heard from the first day. Her blood boiled and her eyes went wide. The Apache policeman walked away. In his place, was Victorio.

Lozen's words ripped the air. "Clum walks among us, speaks our language, tells us we are going to a good place. But he pats no children's heads, offers no hand to touch in friendship, for he is afraid of catching the sickness. He said no harm would come to us, yet he put death on our trail from the start." She gestured into the distance, her voice a vacuum. "Our keening fills the canyons of the Burro Mountains, Apache tears run with swift streams."

That night, someone set fire to the ambulance wagon.

The dirt-caked procession trudged west. The air began to turn hot, and soon they were among clusters of prickly pear and staghorn cholla. From the desert floor to the high rocks, towering saguaros took footholds. Ocotillos with blood-reckoning thorns riddled the landscape; dust devils careened in grained corkscrews. A bony arm pushed up from a sandy grave, white skeletal fingers reaching for the blue sky.

Few took notice of a yellowed newspaper tacked to the side of a lone fence post, the photograph of two grinning ranchers. One of the men held up a burlap sack, the word *Poison* stenciled across it. The other stood in a similar fashion with a bag marked *Sugar,* his foot resting on the chest of what looked like a dead Apache. The headline in the June 16, 1877 edition of the *Arizona Citizen* rose like a mountainous gravestone over the picture. Underneath, bold-faced print and a one-paragraph explanation slammed home the deadly message.

YOU DON'T HAVE TO SHOOT AN APACHE TO KILL ONE!
Strychnine + Sugar = Scalps
Tucsonans and Arizonans!
Here's the surest way to get rid of an Apache and profit at the same time! Carry some quarter pound cakes of strychnine mixed with sugar. Wrap it up with a roll of crackers. When being chased by the Indians, just cut it loose and throw behind your horse. Return when it's safe, shoot the heathen if he's still twisting and get your hank of hair.

Inside the border of the margin, words were scrawled in heavy black ink.

Git the Apach out of Areezoner, or Buryem underneath it.

Where the San Pedro and Gila joined in a river of sand, the migration of misery finally ended. Scrawny shrouds of depressed cottonwoods hung over alkaline banks, and a yellowish-brown butterfly flitted among leaves of the same color. A molar of a mountain, its top chiseled out like an irregular tooth, welcomed them from a distance.

Slowly, the grim-faced clan filtered along the banks, into the riverbed. As if some force had paralyzed them all at once, they stared in dismay at the desolation around them. The baked bottomland was a torched tortilla, the edges burnt into a forest of black scrub. Rocks were coals to the touch, the floor a dirt furnace. Victorio bent down, picked up a handful of dead soil. He let the wind scoop it out of his fingers, then stood, looking after the dust. "This place will break our people's hearts."

Tezye, his wiry frame drooping, voiced his lament; "The whites have sentenced us to death."

"We are not the prisoners here." Lozen said. "It is the *Indaa* who are afraid of us. Our deaths free our spirits because our words are spoken truths. Whites' spirits are held captive by lies and choked by fear."

Nana's voice was gnarled as the surrounding trees, his words spiked in poison. "Better we should strangle them, end their suffering."

As they looked on, Clum, the police and the soldiers headed out. The Apaches had no choice but to follow. It wasn't long when they reached the agency office. On a dead piece of ground, two adobe buildings in the shape of an "L" butted corners. Hugging one wall was a long line of Apaches. Barefoot children in tattered clothing squeezed between the crowded legs of adults; mangy dogs sniffed for food scraps. In front of them, hundreds more sat in the dirt. Men hiked shirttails over their heads for protection against the yellowish-white ball overhead; mothers picked at fleas infesting small scalps. Under wagons and low-bellied horses, Apaches sought relief in the shade.

Curious as to what was going on, Lozen got at the end of the line. Next to her, a woman cradled a thin, sallow-looking baby. Lozen took out a lump of mesquite sap from a rawhide pouch and touched it to the child's lips. She smiled at the boy who struggled to suck the sweet candy. "By what name is he called?"

"He Knows Hardship, same as others born here," the mother snapped.

"Why do you stand here?"

"Today is ration day, the only time you can get food. The whites give us enough for seven moons, sometimes less." She hefted her baby in her arms. "Every week on the same day we come to be counted. Miss, and you do not eat."

Lozen's eyes swept over the landscape, over the people. "How did this place come to be?"

"The Creator had lots of flowers, fruit, trees, rivers, game and green places. He dropped them over the earth, then ran out. This is what's left."

From the building to the east, Lozen could hear loud voices. Suddenly Clum appeared in the doorway. He shook his fist at someone inside, then with angry strides, motioned for Victorio and Loco to follow him. At the edge of the compound, they huddled. All three seemed to shake their heads at once. After a short while, Clum threw up his hands and walked away.

Victorio and Loco acted as if they were planted in the ground. As Lozen approached, her brother placed a hand on her shoulder. "Clum said he argued with the Blue Coat *nantan*, told him we should be treated better, that he'd given his word. He wanted more than a week's rations and water for us." Victorio spat. "He didn't win."

Loco closed his one good eye, then opened it. "We are the last tribe of five thousand to come here. No good land remains and there is little water." He squeezed the bear claw around his neck. "We are being sent to a place fifteen miles away."

As though she hadn't heard right, Lozen cocked her head. "Fifteen miles? We have few horses; many of us are tired and weak. Are we to run here on ration day?"

Neither of the chiefs said a word. There was nothing left to say.

CHAPTER TWENTY

FOUR TO ONE

Lozen smiled in her sleep. She was flying above eagles, nestled in a bed of floating white feathers. A blue ribbon water-danced in the sky and speckled fawns mixed with spotted mountain lion cubs beside a stream. Apache, Mexican and white children scampered along green banks, their parents sharing meals and laughing over cooking fires. Suddenly, a dark shadow blotted out the peaceful glow, and wind from the beating of heavy wings blew Lozen's bed apart. Hurtling downwards, she grabbed desperately at the twirling feathers, the fear in her heart rising as rapidly as the cactus moving up to meet her.

Lozen woke with a start. Looming in front of her eyes, was an upright curved tail with a black needle tip.

She blinked, and the scorpion's segmented body and bowed legs moved closer. She thought about rolling away, but any sudden movement might bring stinging pain to her eye. Afraid to move, she stayed on her stomach. The sun wore on, baking her body into the ground. As if out of nowhere, the toe of a tattered moccasin kicked the scorpion away. A voice croaked down to her.

"Your wickiup you started there. When you finish, catch a quail and keep it inside. It will keep the scorpions, tarantulas and centipedes away. If you do not want them to fall on you in the night, pack mud in the open spaces above you."

Lozen sat up, spit out a thumbful of grit, then called to the squaw who was shuffling away.

"How do you make mud with no water?"

A pair of wrinkled hands waved at the sky. "Wait 'til it rains."

Lozen grunted. Each night she had prayed, hoping the Creator would tip the slice of moon so water could fall over the edge. Several feet away, an empty, broken cradleboard hung lopsided from the branch of a Palo Verde. Pieces of cholla wood and sage jutted from a torn pouch hanging from the frame. Lozen stared at the grim reminder—even the strongest of medicines could not protect a baby from starvation and the white man's sickness. Above the cradleboard, three cleaners-of-death sat hunched in shrouded cloaks of black feathers. She moved in the direction of the vultures and they grudgingly lifted off, huge wings flapping. Lozen recognized the sound as the one that had broken her dream. It had been a vivid vision and she knew the meaning carried danger—of something yet unseen.

She reached back and stroked her hair. It felt like the tumbleweeds around her. She touched her cracked lips, ran her fingers over the dirt on her face. She looked to the west, to the cool Pinal peaks; then to the north, where the lakes and sweet-smelling pines of the White Mountain Apaches lay. Her eyes roved again. Dozens of half-finished wickiups stood in disarray, their dome tops covered in meager brush. A few were draped in army blankets. Hardly any of the clan could be seen. As she stood there, Besh-a-taye came up beside her. "It is time for a council. Come, they wait."

They found them not far away, crouched under the shade of a mesquite. Victorio was given first voice. "The *Indaa* want us to become peaceful farmers, yet give us soil where only cactus lives. Cattle have little to feed on, and the meat is tough as the hide. We live in brush huts where insects, spiders and snakes crawl over us and devour our children. Before the palefaces came, we had little sickness and lived long lives."

"Pimas, Mohaves and Yumas attack us," growled Nana. "Cha-Thle-Pah sends his Tontos against us." He thumped his chest. "I had sharp metal waiting and killed three."

Tezye spoke. "Clum is wise and fair in his decisions and has made Victorio a judge. Apaches govern themselves, which is good for our people. But outlaw whites and Indian renegades come and go as they please on this reservation and pay no attention to any laws. Drunken soldiers from Fort Apache and Fort Goodwin chase them here. When they can't find them, they accuse us of things they've done."

"The Indian agent is honest, does not cheat us," said Loco. "He stands against soldiers on the side of Apaches."

"What you say is true," Victorio answered, "yet Clum has never learned to think like one of us, and cannot understand our fight to resist his ways. He caused us to move from our reservation at Ojo Caliente, same as he did others from theirs. His words were sweet, but his belly was filled with arrogant wind and his thoughts were ugly. I know this, for one of the police told me he gets more pay if we remain peaceful."

Lozen's voice was a mixture of exasperation and contempt. "Whites cannot shoot, cannot ride and smell bad. We have few horses, and without weapons and water, we will soon become like them. They kill the sense of who we are, and already we are becoming useless as old gums on a bone." She tapped her hand to her chest and swept it away. "Clum has quit this place and gone away. We should do the same."

Victorio stood. "Geronimo and his men still stay shackled in the agency guardhouse. One hundred fifty of us have been lost to starvation, disease and killings. Little Sister speaks wisely. It is time to leave."

"*Yoshte,*" the council chorused, voicing their readiness.

By sundown of the following day, three hundred Apaches had gathered in the shallow dustbowl designated as a meeting place. They carried paltry bits of grain, scant water pouches and a meager assortment of weapons. Yet hearts surged with gladness, for like the deep taproots of surrounding mesquites, their spirits were connected to the wellspring of their homeland, and hopes of freedom ran high. As they tramped away in a haze of their own making, a scathing wind blew grained heat in shifts, bidding them a stinging good-bye.

Fields of bear grass and poisonous crows' feet plants with balls of stinging nettles marked their southeast path. Passing the Holy Grounds at Ash Creek, the band longed to stop and pray, but kept moving to take advantage of the oncoming darkness. Farther on, near a dwindling waterhole, thirty horses were rounded up.

It took a full day and most of the next for the band to reach the slopes of the Nantanes Mountains—forty miles from where they'd started. A pale moon lifted into a long Arizona sunset, and peach clouds backlit buttes, filling in rugged swells. On a high ledge, two bighorn sheep banged heads with majestic, curved horns.

Besh-a-taye gestured towards several wide swaths in the hillside. "Those green places there, caves with water hide beneath. We can fill our pouches."

Like foraging ants, women and children spread along the base of the slope, disappearing into the underbrush. A young boy emerged and ran forward, handing a dripping bag to Victorio. He drank and passed it to Lozen. She took a gulp, then quickly took it away from her lips. "My hands tingle and turn blue. We are being chased!"

Victorio whipped his head around. "Blue Coats?"

Lozen closed her eyes, raised her arms to the sky. A breeze came out of nowhere, blowing her hair and brushing her face. "Not soldiers, Apache police and White Eyes . . ." A bullet whistled under her nose, slamming her words into the side of the cliff. A volley of shots followed. The band scattered for trees and boulders. Braves surrounded Victorio, and with Lozen leading, ran to take cover behind a hedge of rocks.

"We will fight to the death," said Kayate, his eyes splinters of steel.

Victorio looked at the hardened faces, brandished knives and single bow. "We cannot fight guns with knives and a few arrows. We must find another way."

Scanning the cliff wall, Lozen spied a wide crack. "I will see where the opening leads." She sprinted for the crevice, bullets nipping at her heels. She dove behind a boulder. Besh-a-taye was lying there like a curled leaf, blood streaming from her neck.

"No!" The word came out in a whimper—as a prayer, and Lozen fell to her knees, trying desperately to plug the bullet hole with her finger. In her mother's dying eyes, she saw her own fear and pain reflected.

"Raise me up so that I may see you clearly one more time." It was only a whisper.

Lozen helped Besh-a-taye sit against the boulder, brushing back the white, blood-matted hair.

"Listen to my words and remember them, Lozen. I will always be with you. You will never cease to be my daughter, as your brother will always be my son. If you need me, call on me, and the wind will carry my love to you. When you want to find me, look in your heart. I am there, forever."

A bullet pinged off the boulder. Besh-a-taye rasped, coughing and spitting blood. "Two deaths serve no purpose. Escape so you can help those not yet born."

Lozen rejected the thought. "I'm not leaving you."

Besh-a-taye reached out a weak hand. "Run, daughter," she urged, and then went limp. Lozen's heart went with her. She hurt all over, and her veins seemed to be running with tears. Eyes streaming, she drew Besh-a-taye to her bosom. "*Shimaa,* speak to me," she pleaded. No answer came.

In the midst of her sorrow, Lozen heard stealthy footfalls and clopping hooves. Two men were hunting her on foot, two more on horseback. She could feel the heat of lightning run through her body, and instead of fleeing, bent on one knee in her mother's blood and waited.

Pistol in hand, the first man passed the boulder. The sun glinted off the posse badge on his blue shirt, and his sweat-stained hat was edged up over his forehead. His eyes went wide as a knife-wielding demon sprang forward and, with blinding speed, cut him into ribbons. For a brief moment, he looked down at his dangling vest of shredded flesh, then crumpled.

An arm's length away was a fallen lance and Lozen grabbed it, hurling it at an oncoming horse. The point speared the animal in the eye. It screamed, reared in terror, threw off the rider. Veering away, it swerved headlong into a tree, the trunk driving the spear into its head and killing it instantly. Lozen grabbed the revolver from the dead man at her feet. With feral swiftness she was upon the toppled cowboy and shot him between the eyes. In her madness, she fired again. The gun clicked empty and she threw it away.

The other horseman and the one still on foot attacked simultaneously. An unearthly shriek burst from Lozen's lungs. Ripping a war club from her waist, she charged the man running towards her. She could hear pounding hooves, a lever cocking behind her—she glanced back and hurled the war club over her shoulder. The rock-weighted end caught the rider full in the mouth, mashing lips and gums into shattered teeth. His body did a half-somersault and his neck broke as he hit the ground.

Only twenty paces separated Lozen from the oncoming fighter. Big as a bull, his oak-like chest was bare; his thick waist stacked into a pair of cavalry pants. A flattened, crooked nose gave evidence a rifle butt had smashed it. In his right hand was a Bowie with a seven-inch blade.

In a killing rush, the two fighters went for each other. Lozen reached for the knife in her belt. It was gone, lost in battle! She ducked under his sweeping blade, hit the ground, rolled and came up on her feet. In her hand was the shaft of a broken arrow. As she turned, he was upon her. She sidestepped a swiping cut but the tip caught flesh, opening a long gash across her midsection. A flicker slower and she would have been cut in half.

The man hovered like a mountain over his one-hundred-twenty-pound opponent. He sneered, shifted from a half-crouch to a brazen upright stance, and flipped the knife to his other hand. In that blink of time, Lozen rammed the arrowhead through his wrist. He yelled and jerked back, dropping the Bowie. Before it hit the ground, she had hold of the bone handle.

With the ferocity of a wildcat protecting its young, she jumped at his chest, curling her legs around his back. She meant to stab the knife down into his skull, but misjudged his quickness. He wrapped his arms around hers, pinning them to her sides. With fingers locked and hands clenched, he began a crushing squeeze. Lozen could smell the stench of him, feel his sweat through her shirt. The jagged end of the arrow's shaft pressed into her spine and she thought her back was going to split open.

Her lips curled back and she lunged, clamping her teeth down over his ear. His eyes went hard and he bellowed, tightening his grip. Bedding her teeth to the bone, Lozen twisted savagely, ripping the flesh from his skull.

His scream ricocheted off the cliff wall and he dropped her. Easily dancing away from a swiping paw, she spit the ear into his face, and at the same time, thrust the Bowie into his stomach. Arms outstretched, he came on. Twisting and turning the blade, she drove it deeper; thick fingers wrapped around her throat, pressing into her jugular. Black clouds rolling over her eyes, she fell to her knees and lost consciousness.

She awoke to a loud, sucking sound, and realized she was gasping for air. Ignoring the fire in her throat, she rolled up on her knees and shook her head clear. A few feet away, her enemy was on his back. His fingers were closed around the knife handle, and his legs twitched like a sleeping dog bitten by fleas. He was still alive.

Lozen rose and walked unsteadily to the body. She kicked his hands loose and dropped to her knees. Two hands gripping the knife, she pulled the embedded blade free. "This is for my *shimaa,*" she hissed. She stabbed the blade just below the left nipple, slashing and rotating between the ribs, carving the wound wider. She reached into the cavity, seized his heart and tore it free. It glistened and pumped purple-red in her hand and she slammed it down, grinding it into the dirt with her heel.

"Aye-yaaa!" Her scream filled the caves and crevices, curled up the cliff, burst through the top of the butte. She raised bloodied fists to the sky, then clutched at her stomach. In the struggle, she had forgotten her own wound. The slice was wide, but not deep. She ripped off a torn shirtsleeve and wrapped it around her middle. Stained in crimson, she walked back through the carnage.

Lured by death, vultures were already circling overhead. Dense flies droned over the horse, and a coyote was tearing at one of the haunches. Ants and beetles picked their way along rivers of thickening blood, between mangled flesh. Next to Besh-a-taye, a raven hesitated, then lifted off as Lozen approached. The beat of its wings sounded like the beat of her heart, heavy and despairing.

Anger turned to sadness, and she felt as though there was a hole inside of her that could never be filled. She kissed her mother lightly on the forehead, rubbed her nose against a cold cheek. Weeping, she gathered large stones and placed them gently over the body. In the customary mourning way, she cropped her hair with the Bowie. Feeling ragged as the stripped ends, she whispered a last prayer and headed up the crevice.

CHAPTER TWENTY-ONE

"BAD THOUGHTS ARE LIKE WETTING YOURSELF"

Shonta had gone missing, and on an afternoon when the heavens were speckled with white like a new fawn, Lozen and Tezye went searching. They found him on a slope blanketed with pines, his body as gnarled and rigid as his cane. His pony stood over him, the reins still wrapped around his wrist.

"He must have fallen, couldn't get up," Lozen said tearfully. She brushed the cluster of pine needles from his face.

As Tezye untied the reins, a single tear slid down his cheek. "I told him not to ride anymore, that it was dangerous. He died out here with no one to hear his cries for help, to comfort him." He reached up onto the pony's back. "This was his favorite horsehide blanket." He bent down and picked up the cane. "This his best friend. We'll bury them with him."

The body was old and thin, and they had little trouble lifting it onto the pony. They took him to a deep cranny high in the rocks, and lowered him there, along with his possessions. Tezye placed rocks over the opening. "He is no longer old or feeble, and is a proud man of wartime, standing erect and strong. He was my good friend and I pray our paths cross many times, that we run, ride, and hunt together again."

Lozen wedged in a large stone. "He taught me many lessons of stealth. 'Creep and lie still, creep and lie still,' he would always say. Now he runs down prey on swift legs, leads the Great Spirit on trails he knows, follows on those never before seen."

When they finished, they brushed themselves from head to toe with sprigs of gray sage. "His ghost won't come back now," Tezye said.

"Aya. If we hold our sorrow too long, it might pity us, then return and try to lure us to its evil realm."

With Tezye leading the pony, they walked back down the mountain. He kicked a pinecone, and it rolled down the slope in front of them. "We have killed lots of whites, stolen many horses. The white man's posses and soldiers haven't been able to find us, yet each day it seems we lose another."

Lozen sighed. "We've been here in the Black Range for two years, ever since San Carlos. We have surrendered six times—to the fort at Wingate, the one in Silver City near here, to four others—just so our people could eat and keep warm. Then, when we cannot stand the whites' ways, we escape again. It is no good to live in this way. Sixty of our people have perished. There are no longer enough babies to replace them."

They reached the foot of the mountain. Tezye handed the reins to Lozen. "I am going to put up a sweat lodge, pray to the Great Spirit for my friend, for our people."

Lozen tapped the pony's neck. "Even in his death Shonta leaves us a gift. This one here will be the last of the horses to be eaten." As Tezye peeled off in the opposite direction, Lozen slowly walked back to camp. A mother quail and five chicks scurried across her path, and as a speckled shell with feet brought up the rear, Lozen chuckled. *Those quick-footed birds, they are like feathered mice,* she thought.

In a clearing, a raven pulled on the tail feathers of a bald eagle, which was feeding on a small carcass. Each time the predator turned to fend off its tormentor, the black bird would easily skip out of the way, then run in and tug at a wing. Soon the eagle was turning from one side to the other, confused about which side to protect first. Finally, it became distracted long enough for the raven to duck in, steal some food and fly off. Its jubilant caw sounded from a nearby oak.

The wily antics reminded Lozen of how she had played with Kayate when he came to her, asking for her help in courting Her Eyes Brown. The maiden had passed her flow, celebrated her puberty rite and was ready for marriage. As custom dictated, the suitor could not speak directly to the bride's parents.

"She is a fine lovely maiden, very industrious," Lozen told him, as she pulled fibers from agave leaves, twisting them into a rope. "What would she want then with the likes of you?"

Kayate pulled himself up to another two fingers in height. "I am a respected warrior and have proven my bravery many times in battle."

"Hmmph. You intend to fight with your wife, show her your strength then," she teased. "Like the time we wrestled and you tried to force me to fool around, like you did with those loose Comanche women."

"I was young and foolish."

Lozen braided two strands together. "And now you are smart?"

231

"Smart enough to own horses and blankets."

Still holding the braid, Lozen tapped his iron chest. "You have lived forty-five harvests, are as old and bark-hard as me. She is a young, flowering bud."

"Our hearts are soft for each other and we want to go around forever, have many fine Apache children. You are the godmother of Her Eyes Brown. Will you talk to Kinsee and Kanda-zi for me, or not?"

Lozen already knew the parents approved of the union, for their daughter had shared her feelings of love for Kayate. Yet she was having fun and, like the rope she was weaving, wanted to string him out some more.

"My thoughts are divided. Do you not keep a captured Mexican woman as a bedmate?"

Kayate blustered, and waved his hands towards the tipis. "As do many of the men here. I treat her well; she is accepted as one of us."

Lozen stared at the warrior, one eyebrow raised in question. "Her Eyes Brown does not object?"

"She does not argue, says the woman will be a help with the chores, when the babies come."

Lozen shook her head. "It will be difficult, but I will try to convince her family that you are worthy enough to be their son-in-law, and a husband to their daughter."

"I will turn out two of my horses in the pasture with theirs, to show my intent is honorable," Kayate answered proudly.

"It is good to bring them the burden gift." She paused, setting the hook. "Three ponies with saddles would make my words stronger."

"Three? With saddles?"

Lozen shrugged, and pretended to ignore his surprise. He stroked his chin, began walking away. "Three ponies with saddles," he muttered, "that is too many. I must give this proper thought."

A smirk crossed Lozen's face. "Your decision is wise. I will tell the maiden's parents that Kayate, the man who wants to go around with their daughter forever, the husband-that-someday-may-come-to-be, is considering her worth."

Kayate stopped in his tracks, turned on his heels and thrust out his chin. "Her Eyes Brown is valuable to me. Three horses with saddles then, but no more."

Lozen held back a rising chuckle. By the time the union was made, there were four horses, a Winchester, a fringed buckskin dress for Kinsee, and three wool Navajo blankets, one of which went to Lozen.

Now, returning to camp, she gave up the horse to Kayate, who was standing by his tipi. She told him what had happened. She didn't have to tell him what to do with the pony. That night, small pieces of roasted meat were piecemealed off to the tribe.

The next morning, she set out early. Near a stream, a young elk bounded through high willows, their catkins spinning after it, turning golden in a waking sky. She traveled onwards. Off to one side the high grass rustled, moved violently, quieted, and stirred again. Curious, cautious, Lozen walked in the direction of sound and movement, and spied the tip of a black-tailed rattler. Edging closer, she could see the serpent was being held between the crushing brown and white coils of a king snake. Body twisting, jaws spread wide, it was swallowing its victim headfirst.

She moved away. After crossing the low-flowing Gila River, found what she was looking for. There were six ponies in the corral, and a tall man wearing a straw hat was fitting a log between two upright posts. On his waist was a gunbelt, and a rifle leaned against one of the posts.

Hiding behind a creosote bush, Lozen studied the surroundings. There was no dog to catch her scent, no smoke coming from the white man's dwelling to indicate other humans. She estimated the distance from cover to target to be seventy strides. To make her shot even more difficult, the hard wind *Namode* was blowing. Attaching a hawk feather to one of the bush's branches, she stepped back several feet and studied its flow. The feather not only told her the direction of the wind, but the strength and steadiness of the gust, how far and high she would have to shoot off mark, so that the arrow would be carried back to target. It would take a full pull on her bowstring.

With a constant eye on the feather, she stepped from behind the cover, angled her bow upwards and aimed to the right of her prey, between the sun and flat horizon. The slanting winds took the twang of the bow and swoosh of the arrow, muffling the sounds in its own whistle. Lozen was so sure of her shot that she was on her way to the horses while the arrow was still plunging. The keen obsidian arrowhead struck the man through his wide-brimmed hat and he fell dead, cradling a fence post across his chest.

Mounting a gray mare, Lozen drove the herd out of the corral, each horse jumping the body that lay between the unfinished opening. Passing over the corpse, she was struck with sadness, an inexplicable sense of loss. Surprised by her feelings for a white man, she became angry, and as her mind groped to make sense of the conflict, a vision began to appear. At first, there were only swirling wisps of smoke traveling towards her over the ground. The apparition came closer, began to take human form, and when it stopped, suspended in space, Lozen's eyes went wide and she gasped—*"Shimaa!"*

Arms outstretched in front, white hair spiraling, Besh-a-taye's image fluttered in the wind. She looked the same as when she had died, but was unmarred. Her distant voice was clear as fresh water. "Each time you kill, you will feel farther away from Life Giver, daughter, for it is not only the spirit slain, but the one inside you that dies a little more each time."

"Is not our right to take what we need to live, to defend ourselves?" Lozen asked, puzzled.

"The need does not make it any less a waste."

Lozen raised her bow. "I am a warrior and should not feel softness for the enemy."

Besh-a-taye's arms spread wide. "You are also a woman, Lozen, and understand the meaning of death better than men, who seek power and glory, while women and children pay for their pride."

The wraith slowly started to dissipate, and Lozen was filled with an unquenchable yearning. "Do not leave, shimaa," she begged, her eyes watery.

"Now that you understand your sorrow, it is time for me to go back to that beautiful place underneath."

"Will you come back?"

"The entrance to the underworld is a big sand tipi. When I tried to climb it, the sand gave way underfoot, and I slipped back each time. I felt your pain, and your aching called to me. Little by little, I made my way to the top, and was able to roll down and out the other side. I must return the same way, and do not think I can get out again." Her last words dissolved with her.

Lozen looked into the sky. "Shimaa, I am still learning the way to the spirit world. Watch for me. I miss you, and someday will catch up."

The camp was stirring when she returned; shelters were

being taken down and possessions packed. Kinsee ran forward to meet her, an excited look in her eyes. "Your brother
met with General Hatch. That white *nantan* says if we stop
our raiding, we can return to the reservation at Ojo Caliente.
The council has agreed."

Two sunsets came and went. On the third, Lozen was atop
Sacred Mountain, her eyes dancing with her voice.

Again the sun kisses babies' foreheads
Again birds sing happy songs
Again the water we come from runs in our blood,
*   replenishes our souls*
Our children bloom like flowers and run with the eagles
Up into the mountains and forests
Along the streams, around the river bends
In our village, out in the meadows and plains
Once again, Apaches dance The Dance of Life
Here, between Father Sun and Mother Earth
Our hearts are held by the calling of our ancestors

Finishing her chant, she breathed deeply, and took in the
pungent smell of pine and juniper, the sweet nectar of jas-
mine and honeysuckle welling up from the slopes and valleys.
Night was falling, and instead of trying to return to the village
in the dark, she decided to stay on the mountain. There was
another reason as well—her spirit was full and she wanted to
hold the feeling as long as possible. The scooped-out log she
found was perfect for sleeping, and she lay down on the leaves
and pine needles inside. The night was awake with voices—a
nightingale's chirping skipped between the drawn-out hoots
of an owl, and the mellow "waaaaaa" of a whippoorwill
floated through the air.

Lozen thought about her mother, and her heart was struck

with the four arrows of loss, love, yearning and sadness. Like a tiny bubble, a tear came to one corner of her eye. She blinked it away and gazed into the sky. Besh-a-taye was there, smiling at her in a necklace of stars that sparkled across the throat of the night. Lozen could see her proud face, the eyes that could lance her with a look, but were more likely to twinkle in acceptance and understanding. Her thoughts roamed to the past.

A sudden cloudburst had sent her running to her mother, trembling in fear that the sky had broken.

"Not broken," Besh-a-taye explained in her soothing manner, as she wiped off her dripping child with a dry cloth. "The sky has split from old age. When the Great Spirit mends it, the sun will shine again."

Another time Lozen had complained fiercely about a playmate who did not want to share a doll.

"Do you remember the time you peed in your pants, and got a rash there the color of your red face, because you were ashamed to tell me?" asked Besh-a-taye.

Lozen nodded, wondering what possible meaning her mother could tie to her misfortune.

"Bad thoughts about others are like wetting yourself; they do not bother anyone but you." She touched her fingers to Lozen's lips, and stroked her daughter's arm. "Speak good words, and they will rub off on others."

CHAPTER TWENTY-TWO

NEVER TO RETURN

In the autumn frost, a colony of swallows created a moving mosaic of violet-green and white, swooping and banking in an ever-widening circle. Below, water roofed like mica pockmarked the brittle earth. The sun dribbled through a thin veil of clouds, turning from copper to brass to gold, warming the hills and valleys as the day wore on.

When Lozen came upon the fresh, partially hidden calf-kill that was covered with leaves and grass, she knew the mountain lion was holed up nearby—close enough to chase scavengers away, so it could return and feed until it had devoured the carcass. Maybe the puma was watching her now, even as she eyed its red, bald-faced prey.

The calf's chest was laid open at the shoulder, its heart and lungs torn out, the ground soaked in blood. Wide, four-toed tracks registered clearly in the soil, and by the size and depth of the imprints, Lozen judged the lion to be a large adult male.

A bellow from the underbrush startled her, and she moved quickly away as a wild-eyed cow rushed forward. The bawling mother stood over her baby, nudging it with her nose, trying to bring it back to life so that it could suckle on her swollen udder. Lozen headed in the opposite direction, and trotted along a stretch of ground walled on one side by a blunt-topped hill of boulders.

Rounding a covey of rocks, she stared into the face of a tawny cat, not forty paces away. The lion was sunning itself on a ledge and, when she approached, stopped licking its bloody paws and whiskers. Lozen knew it could close the distance between them in two bounds, and several thoughts quickly crossed her mind—none of them good.

Her quiver carried the arrows of war, their barbed heads fitted and secured flat to their shafts, so they would more easily penetrate between the ribs of the enemy. Animals' ribs ran the other way, and she did not have one hunting arrow notched with a straight up-and-down head. To further complicate matters, if the lion attacked it would be coming at her headlong, making a shot to the heart impossible. Even if she was lucky enough to inflict a mortal wound, an animal this size would take a while to die, and could cause a lot of damage until it did.

But there was no hint of panic from the *ndoicho,* its gaze calm, the black-tipped tail flicking leisurely. The puma yawned, gums curling back over its curved, white fangs. Then, it rolled over on its back and, with paws dangling and ears twitching, fell asleep on the warming rocks.

As Lozen moved past the heavily breathing cat, she wondered about its chances for survival. If the puma killed any more stock, the rancher and his dogs would hunt it down and slay it. She shook her head. It was the whites' invasion that had driven away the mule deer, forcing the lion to prey upon cattle.

It is not unlike what is happening to Apaches, for the Indaa *never want to look at their part, only to blame others,* she thought. She recalled the events of the not-so-distant past, and the ignorance of the Blue Coats, the betrayals that had sent the band on the warpath forever.

"The War Department has ordered that we are to be returned to San Carlos, even though we have been 'good Indians' and caused no trouble," a seething Victorio had told the shocked tribe.

Two weeks later, in the dead of winter, two hundred shivering women, children and elders were herded in mud and snow back to the reservation. Victorio, Lozen and eighty warriors watched from a forested rim, where they had bolted.

"When Juh came here with his son-in-law Geronimo and captured that wagon train, killed the whites, we took no part," Shinash-a-too said angrily. He held out his palms, then turned them over. "Not a drop of the *Indaa*'s blood is on our hands."

"Trusting White Eyes is like handing ammunition to the enemy," answered Tezye.

Victorio turned his horse into the whirling snow. "We will go to the San Andres, secure a camp where the mountains roll over on one another."

Huddled next to a dwindling fire, Lozen peered at the sleet falling outside of the small cave. "We have little meat or grain with which to feed ourselves. The storms hid our trail from the soldiers, but have also prevented us from hunting."

Victorio picked up a piece of wood. Realizing it was wet and useless, he cast it aside. "The Blue Coats say if we surrender, settle peacefully on the Bosque Redondo Reservation with the Mescaleros, that our families will be returned safely from San Carlos. I do not believe them."

"Our ammunition is scarce as the flesh on our ribs, and twenty-six of us now lie with the ice," came Lozen's teeth-chattering answer. She drew her blanket tighter around her shoulders. "Nana has gone to live with the Mescaleros. I think we must do the same, or we will all die."

Victorio bowed his head in thought. "When the snow melts from the passes, we will surrender once more."

In the spring, a dozen women and children were brought back from San Carlos. When Kayate saw Her Eyes Brown cradling a small bundle, he almost tripped over his feet running to her.

"You have a son," she said warmly, as her husband pulled back the flap of the blanket. Bright eyes twinkled back, and tiny fingers gripped his thumb.

"He is already strong, will be a fine warrior someday," Kayate replied proudly.

That afternoon Victorio went to the reservation office. When he returned and Lozen saw his face, her heart skipped. Eyes, where compassion once slept underneath, were now stone cold—they were the same merciless eyes she had seen in scalp hunters, and warriors that lived only for revenge. When he spoke, she thought his voice might send the snow crashing from the peaks of the Sierra Blancas.

"Because I did not carry the white man's paper, the whites deny us rations for thirty moons. The agent was there, and I spoke to him in a loud voice. I said, 'Russell, you did not wait to take our land and homes, but now want hungry Indians to wait a long time for the payment of food rightfully ours?' He was insolent and did not respond to my words. I became angry, and grabbed him by the fur on his chin, dragged him across the floor. I could see the fear in his eyes."

"The soldiers didn't stop you?" Lozen asked.

"Only Indians were there. I rode away quickly."

"Those whites talk pretty, think ugly thoughts. You can cut into one all day, never find a heart," came the testy reply.

"After leaving the agency, I met Magoosh, chief of the Lipans. He said a paper was made in Silver City, accusing us of murder and horse stealing."

Tezye tilted his head. "We can hear the Blue Coats' bugles blow from Soldier Canyon, and our scouts have sighted many troops moving through the valley of the Peñasco. They come to capture us, maybe hang us at Fort Stanton."

"It is easier to make war with the *Indaa* than peace," Victorio snarled.

Lozen ground her teeth together. "Whites say we should raise corn, not trouble. Is it not trouble if we defy the Great Spirit, plow the land, tear into our mother's bosom, dig under her flesh and expose her bones? If we cut grass to make hay, is it not the same as cutting our hair, so we can mourn our dead mother's spirit?" She gestured skywards. "*Usen* says nature rules; that animals, birds, plants and trees obey that law. Our ways will never be theirs."

Victorio's eyes blazed. "We will die before we accept scraps like dogs again, or flour the color of straw. Pack everything up. We leave at sunset. We will never live again within the lines the whites draw to keep Indians inside."

"The Pony Soldiers have orders to kill Indians found off the reservation," Tezye bitterly reminded him.

Victorio thrust his fist into the air. "They wish to kill Indians found off this reservation then? We will grab up the weapons Little Sister had us hide in the mountains, kill those who chase us, others who cross our path."

As Victorio's words rang in her ears, Lozen pulled a poisoned arrow from her quiver. Between thumb and forefinger, she rubbed the head that had been painted with the decayed liver of a badger. "Not for animals," she mouthed. "Saving these for you, white man."

The small war party had been patient about setting and springing their trap. Quite by chance they'd come across the trail of fifty Pony Soldiers traveling in the desert, and for five days stayed just ahead and out-of-sight of their enemy. After using the infrequent water holes along the way, they then poisoned them with the entrails of disemboweled coyotes. Between midnight and dawn, when soldiers and horses were known to sleep best, the Lozen-led band kept up a constant barrage of yelling, shot off their firearms and simulated screams of tortured prisoners.

"We should slay them now, in the darkness," a young brave told Lozen.

She looked sternly at the sixteen-year-old boy, who was chafing at the bit. "If we kill them during the night, we will forever walk in darkness through the Place of the Dead. It is the same reason Apaches do not scalp." She nodded past the campfire into the blackness. "The last watering place is a half-day's ride. It is a good place for an ambush."

Bow in hand, the boy leaped into the air. "I should leave now, poison it!"

"Leave it be. Already the soldiers' heads hang on their necks like dead birds, and their horses' noses touch their plodding knees. When they find clear water, they will forget all else, become unwary and off-guard. That is when we will attack."

With the sun at their backs, the warriors cached themselves among the high rocks that ringed the pool. They waited until the White Eyes' scout found the water, watched as he rode back and reported his find. They waited until the men stampeded their horses, until they jumped off their horses and began drinking. They waited until the soldiers ran into the water, splashing about like children out for their first swim. Then, they opened up with Winchesters and arrows, firing at a withering pace. To prevent any chance of escape, the horses were killed first. The soldiers hunkered down, but had only their dead mounts for cover. Pinned down by the fusillade, they had no chance. By sundown the bodies lay silent as the ground, the only sounds that of the wounded and dying. The band closed in, knives and lances finishing the job.

Standing in the center of the battlefield, Lozen looked at the sea of red, the cavalry blue covered with dirty white bandages like a wounded American flag. In front of her, a soldier hung from a wagon, pinned to the bed by three arrows through his chest. Another was sprawled over a boulder, brains oozing from his ears. A second wagon was on its side, one wheel turning slowly in the wind, the cargo of bacon, coffee, pots, pans and utensils strewn over the ground. Biscuits riddled with maggots spilled from a shattered crate of hardtack, boxes of .45 caliber cartridges littered the earth. The mules lay dead in their traces.

The band gathered up the weapons, and disappeared into a blood-red sun.

CHAPTER TWENTY-THREE

CORRER EL GALLO, CORRER EL RIO

Four ponies stood shoulder-to-shoulder, their riders eyeing the chicken buried up to its neck some fifty yards away. Three of the competitors were dressed in floppy peasant sombreros, loose fitting shirts, pants with waist sashes and sandals. They knew the game of *Correr El Gallo* well, but for the woman who challenged them, it would be her first time.

"Women cook chickens, they do not run them down," teased a tall boy of sixteen. His two *compañeros* laughed, and slapped their *amigos* on the back.

The sarcasm reminded Lozen of her first footrace, when her mother put mud on her feet for good luck, and the boys had mocked her. She had won that contest, and all those following.

"When you reach down for the chicken and fall from your *caballo*, we will be *gallantes* and not trample you," said the young man.

"I should race you on foot then," she answered playfully.

245

Lozen had a warm place in her heart for the simple Mexican village that lay between the *Rio Torreño* and *Rio Conchos*. The *campesinos,* the workers of the earth, who lived there had befriended the clan before, sharing their meager food, providing clothing and hiding them. The village headsman, Iturbe Molina, had been especially convincing in getting rid of General Geronimo Trevino, when he and his cavalry had come riding into the village.

"The Apache were here, eating their fill of our scant food, taking our clothing, doing as they wanted," the elder statesman told the officer. The color and texture of an earthen bowl, his face took on an even more severe look. He raised his bushy, white eyebrows, tweaked the ends of his mustache, and pointed towards the far-away peaks. "But when they heard *Mi General* and our most esteemed cavalry were after them, the fear shook them to their knees and they fled to the mountains."

Once the troops rode away, two hundred Apaches crept from the nearby hills. Victorio nodded after the troops. "Your cunning deceived the cavalry, kept us from harm. We are grateful, old one."

"*De nada,* but I want something in return," answered the elder, his eyes black stones. "We are farmers, and have no weapons or fighters. The *bandidos* come from the hills, rape our women and steal our children to be sold into slavery."

Victorio understood his meaning. "While we are here, we will protect you, as you have protected us." The two leaders clasped each other's arms in friendship.

Now, Molina strode to the center of the town's plaza. Flanked by adobe huts, he placed himself directly between the participants and the squawking chicken. Apaches and Mexicans formed a noisy gauntlet. Those wanting a better view of the contest stood on the wide rim of a fountain. With an eye out for the *padre,* a few of the braver boys climbed to the top of the small church roof.

The headsman motioned for Victorio, and when the chief stood next to him, put his arm around his muscular shoulders. "We welcome our friends the *Tchi-hénè,* and their brave chief, Victorio. We thank them for the food they have brought." He gestured towards the riders. "Today, his sister Lozen will try to out-duel three of our best players, and be the first to steal the chicken from the ground."

A stout woman with hair hanging to the back of her knees, yelled, *"Viva la mujer con la cabeza roja."* The throng laughed at the joke that made fun of Lozen's wide, red headband.

The headsman turned to face the contestants, who tensed on the bare backs of their ponies. "When I drop the bandana, the game will begin." He waved and twirled the kerchief, egging the noisy crowd on, teasing the players, enjoying the limelight. The bandana fell, the crowd screamed, and the horses jumped forward. Passing on both sides of Molina, they came together like water around a sandbar, and charged for the chicken.

The tall boy took a horse length's lead, and leaning down, swept his hand towards the hen's head. He shot past, ending up with only a feather in his hand. A second rider stretched too far, and fell off his horse. As the crowed clapped and laughed, Lozen sped past him. With her legs sandwiched around her horse's back and belly, she extended her torso parallel with the ground, and scooped up the chicken by the neck.

In one motion she righted herself, and pumped the wing-flailing bird over her head. Whoops and *oles* greeted her triumph.

"El pollo is ready for the pot!" the stout woman shouted. Several boys began unloading firewood from burros, and

soon steaming pans of tortillas, chile colorados, sweet-smelling onions, sauces and frijoles were simmering. From cowhide pouches, two girls unpacked figs and half-dried grapes, then placed them in clay bowls. A man took out a guitar and started strumming. Another dropped a sombrero and a couple began dancing around the straw hat. Holding a small drum in one hand and beating it with the other, Shinash-a-too joined them. Lozen and Her Eyes Brown followed, each shaking a gourd rattle. Eating, drinking, dancing and singing lasted late into the night.

Eyes at half-mast, his mustache red with salsa and his breath heavy with tequila, Iturbe Molina was the last to leave the party. Snoring loud enough to widen the cracked walls of his mud hut, he ignored the hand on his shoulder that was shaking him, and his son's pleas to get up. A ladle of water in his face finally aroused him, and he sat up in a sputtering stupor. The boy's urgent message sent him jumping from his cot and out the door. Blinking from the pain of the bright sunlight, he shaded his eyes with both hands. "Find Victorio and have him meet me at the fountain. *Rapido!*"

By the time Victorio and Lozen arrived, the old man had already scoured out dusty tracks in the sand. His words matched his nervous pace. "Those thirty slavers you killed and the twenty left wounded in the Candaleria Mountains were found by General Trevino. My son says one of our villagers was on his way back from Chihuahua, and saw him, that he hunts you with four hundred cavalry." He waved a liquor-stained arm. "He's on his way here now."

The elder stopped pacing and wiped the sweat from his brow. "I think maybe some of those were the general's men, that you killed some of his profits as well. He will not be fooled this time, and I am afraid he will play *Correr El Gallo* with me in the sand, maybe hang my people."

Victorio laid a hand on the man's shoulder. "We will put you in no more danger, and will leave right away."

"We will slay two of your pigs and goats, leave our arrows in them," Lozen said. "In that way Trevino will not question your word that we came here to raid."

"The silver we took from the *banditos*—I will leave it in payment," Victorio added.

Molino nodded his assent. *"Vaya con Dios, mis amigos."*

Under a sky spun with swirls of golden clouds, the band fled northeast, towards the Sierra De La Magdalena. They were careful to stay well below El Paso and Fort Hancock. Two hundred miles later, they crossed an easy-flowing Rio Grande into Texas. Riding up and down long stretches of rolling terrain, many slept on their horses, their bodies sagging and swaying with their animals' gait.

Passing through clouds that ringed the slopes of a mountain in a halo of gray, they emerged in a boulder-cached canyon. Climbing to the higher reaches, a clear brook and meadow awaited them. About to make camp, Lozen's warning stopped them in their tracks. "There is a wagon train heading for this place," she said, holding up a pair of blue hands. She could feel something else, something sinister. Eyes closed, she turned in the four directions. When she opened them, her palms had turned bright purple.

"More Blue Coats with many guns and fresh horses wait for us above. We do not have enough weapons or warriors to fight them."

"We must run back across the river," growled Victorio.

Unable to go back the way they'd come because of the wagon train, and hemmed in by the soldiers above, the band quickly made use of a rock sluice funneling off into a side canyon. It was slippery and narrow, and they had to be careful so that their horses didn't slip and fall.

Several children lagged towards the rear, and Lozen challenged them. "Are you white children, who whimper like puppies when their mother's milk goes dry? I think maybe you are Apaches, who tear enemies apart with their teeth!" A dozen little moccasined feet moved faster.

Hiding and marching, it took three days to reach the Rio Grande. Behind the rear of the column, a rising dust cloud was coming fast. Forty warriors wheeled to defend.

Riding to the front of the column, Lozen was surprised that no one had started down the banks. "The soldiers are close on our trail," she yelled. "Why do you wait? Jump your horses into the river!"

Kinsee gestured at the river. Lozen hadn't taken the time to look into the swirling waters of mud-brown whitecaps, but once she did, realized what was happening. The Thunder Gods in the mountains had chased the Water Monster down the slopes, flooding the wide channel. Horses and people were afraid.

She jumped off her black stallion, grabbed the reins of the pony behind and tied it to her mount's tail, yelling for the others to follow. When all were linked together, she remounted. "Tie those cradleboards tightly to your backs, or the babies will be swept away. Carry the small ones, the elderly and sick in front, shield them as we cross. Let the horses' tails and reins lead!"

As the women tapped their hands over their mouths in an ululating chant, Lozen prayed. "Creator, the water is deep and the current swift. Make us one with it so we may cross safely."

She raised her rifle over her head, kneed her horse and plunged into the churning water. With the others trailing, they plowed forward, the current tugging at the riders, trying to wrench them from their mounts. Women held onto their horses' manes, hunching over children that clung to the animals' necks. Elders gripped the waists of adolescents. Behind them, gunshots and men yelling could be heard. Just past the halfway mark, a massive undertow sucked the end of the chain downstream, threatening to break it apart. The tail-to-tether links held and the band forged across the border, their horses floundering up the slippery banks.

All during the crossing, Lozen had worried about Antelope Woman, whose belly was swollen with child. She hid the sixteen-year-old in the willows, then sent the women and children south. To provide cover fire for the braves crossing the river, she cached several older boys behind thick underbrush. Victorio came up beside her and she turned to him. "A child lays heavy in Antelope Woman's belly and she cannot travel. I will stay until it comes, then follow."

"We will leave two ponies, Little Sister."

"No. Their scouts have counted our tracks and will see two less took the trail. They will search for us in the willows."

"The Mexican's law says they cannot cross onto this soil," Tezye said hurriedly. He and the rest of the warriors had crossed the river. Lozen looked past him. "Tell it to the *Indaa*."

Following her gaze, the men saw a body of soldiers entering the turbulent water. The boys hidden in the thickets unleashed a volley, then burst from cover and jumped up behind the warriors onto the backs of their ponies. Before they galloped out of sight, Lozen was at Antelope Woman's side.

In full labor, the girl squatted, her hands gripping two horned stubs jutting from a log. Sweat poured from her brow and her face grimaced in pain. She bit down into the thick twig Lozen placed between her teeth. Thirty paces away, a scout yelled and pointed at the ground. Heading away from the women, he began to track. The cavalry trailed behind him.

Lozen could see the whitish waxy covering of the baby's head. She reached for the infant's shoulders. "Again," she whispered. The girl bore down harder and a pair of tiny, wet-red legs appeared. Lozen pulled the baby out. With her knife, she cut the umbilical cord and tied it off with a reed. "You have a fine girl-child," she said, handing the baby to its mother.

To safeguard against the possibility of the enemy coming back and spotting the afterbirth, she hid it under the log. On stomachs and elbows, and with Antelope Woman cradling her baby in the crook of her arms, they crawled away. In a small clearing surrounded by cottonwoods and clumps of billowing wild grass, they took refuge. A channel branched off from the river, and the women warmed the water in their mouths, dribbling it over the baby until it was clean.

Antelope Woman managed a weak smile. "I think my *shime'* will be called by the name River Child." Her smile reversed itself. "I have lost my sister to the Mexicans, my brother to the whites. I do not want to lose my daughter."

Lozen was focusing on the deepening stain drenching the girl's dress, and did not answer. She pulled off a greenish clump of mistletoe from a cottonwood and mashed it into powder. After mixing it with water, she applied the poultice to the girl's womb. "We will be safe here, wait until your flow stops, then escape." She glanced across the river, where the main body of soldiers were setting up camp.

Lozen scratched her chin. The only escape route was south and the open *brasada*—desolate gray brush country full of curling mesquite grass and javelina rooting among thorny thickets. Old White Lip, the *bandido* who sold Apaches into slavery for the mines at Zacatecas, was on the prowl. Then

252

too, there were the constant Mexican patrols. Their only hope was to reach the refuge of the far-away mountains and find Victorio. She shook her head—without horses, food or water, they would be inviting certain capture or death.

Lozen sank in a heap beside mother and child. How many moons had passed since she had slept? How many moons since there was peace? She closed her eyes, dreaming in overlapping flurries.

With Gray Wolf, she played hide-and-seek with the moon in the water until it turned into a raging river. Suddenly, she was White Painted Woman, running over the surface to the Sacred Basket. She fell, but instead of drowning, dropped from her mother's horse and crashed to the ground in her cradleboard. Something unseen attacked, crunching down on the hard wood.

She woke in the early dawn. Antelope Woman was sleeping, her baby tucked between her breasts. The grinding sound from the dream became louder. Quiet as the lifting mist, Lozen crawled forward. She parted the tall reeds. Chewing noisily on ripe river grass, three longhorns were feeding.

Lozen knew the beasts to be fierce defenders, having seen a pugnacious mother with arm-span horns drive away a mountain lion after its calf. Yet, they needed food and other necessities for the journey, and she stilled her heart not to be afraid. Lightly shaking a willow stalk, she watched its white catkins float in the air. The Wind God favored her; not a ribbon of scent would reach her prey.

Choosing a quarter-ton brindle cow, she clenched her knife between her teeth. Like a snake, she slithered forward. A spotted sandpiper, its tail nervously teetering, landed in front of her, then flew off on vibrating wings. The dim-sighted longhorn turned its heavy, angular head. Lozen's heart held a beat until it resumed feeding. She inched closer. Fifteen paces away. Ten.

Close enough to spring, Lozen hesitated. Even if she could get under the sharp curving horns, it would be impossible to slice through the cow's throat, the skin below its neck too thick. And, if it bellowed, and the other cattle came to its rescue or stampeded, the soldiers would be alerted. The kill would have to be quick—and quiet. Grasping a stone, she threw it, and when the steer's head shot up at the sound, pounced onto its back. Using a horn as a handgrip, she leaned to one side, reached around the neck and plunged her knife into the soft pad covering the jugular. The cow took two steps, faltered and toppled. Lozen jumped clear, and then glanced across the river. The sentries were walking their posts as before.

She skinned a section of cow, sliced strips of meat for drying and cut out the liver. Wrapping it all in the hide, she returned to Antelope Woman, who was nursing the baby. Lozen nodded at her lap. "Only a stain remains between your legs. When you are healed, we will leave this place."

"I do not feel like a strong Apache woman, do not think I can travel far."

"When your child takes milk you are like the Rio Conchos, the mother stream that nourishes the Great River, keeps it from dying in the desert. Do you understand me?"

Her face set, the girl looked down at her child. "I will do what I must for my baby."

Lozen rubbed the baby's soft cheek against her own, kissed its reddish-pink butt, and put the tiny body over her shoulder. River Child burped a sour thanks, stained her arm with warm liquid and began to squall. Its cry was hushed with a hug. Lozen spoke against the baby's ear. "We must be silent as shadows obeying clouds, River Child. There are sharp-eared scouts and soldiers across the water. Now sleep while I make you a safe place."

She gave the child back, took the hide to the river, washed it and returned. She scraped the inside smooth, cut a swath wide enough for the child, then a longer one in which she punched holes in the ends. Knotting strips of hide into them, she laid it in front of Antelope Woman.

"When we travel, put your baby in this sling and tie it around your chest. In that way, River Child will ride comfortably and your hands will be free." She scooped up some sand, jiggled it in her palm. "The Great River is dropping. Tonight I will steal horses."

When campfires burned low as the yellow moon sitting on a black horizon, Lozen swam the two hundred yards to the encampment. She crept up the bank and hugged it until the lookouts passed. Fading firelight outlined the bivouac—tents in rows, wagons squared, horses tethered at the far fringe. Melding with the darkness, she sneaked towards the rear of the camp. From the side of a tent, she lifted two hanging canteens and a water bag. Rounding the corner, she saw an Apache boy bound from neck to foot in a cord cocoon. Her heartstrings wound around him like the rope.

At the tether line, she worked quickly, searching for swift Indian ponies that the soldiers sometimes kept as second mounts. Finding none, she settled on a big, muscular black. Stroking its neck, she whispered, "You and I are of the same nature, running strong and fast with the wind. We are called by the same spirit of freedom."

The horse's ears perked and he shook his head. To keep him from whinnying, she looped a piece of hide around his nose and jaw, ran her hands slowly down his legs to calm him and cut the tether. She did the same with a dun, and with the two horses in tow, made her way back across the river.

By the time sunup came, the two women and girl-child were far away, heading into the Chihuahuan desert. They stopped briefly, after River Child's umbilical stub fell off. Lozen hacked gummy resin from a mesquite, ground it with stones, then mixed it with sand and placed it on the baby's navel. "To keep it from blistering," she told Antelope Woman.

The grateful mother smiled. "Because of you my daughter will live many harvests, cross lots more rivers."

Lozen touched the baby's nose. *Let's hope she survives long enough to speak her name,* she thought.

CHAPTER TWENTY-FOUR

>>>————————>

BROKEN CIRCLE

To catch up to the main body of Mexican cavalry that had been hunting the Apaches, the Tarahumara had run two hundred miles in two days. Barefoot and barelegged, they wore blousy shirts and poncho-type shells that fell past their knees, the cotton whiteness in stark contrast to their mahogany skin. Wrapped around their foreheads were bright headbands from which two long strips tailed down their backs. Each carried a ten-foot spear.

They began reading sign when light was low, and the casting shadows made tracks easier to see. There were two warriors among the band; the rest were women and children. A handprint on the bank of an arroyo told where a woman with a baby had leaned to rest. Wide and deep tracks pointed out a slow-moving elder who carried something heavier than a bow, much heavier than a carbine.

Along granite ground at the base of a steep slope, they scanned for a broken leaf or twig, a pebble wedged into a stone seam that could only have gotten there by the weight of a human foot. The lead tracker lay prone and carefully blew sand from a hollow in the rock, revealing a moccasin track. He motioned to the other two and they fanned out.

From a perch high above, Lozen lifted a spyglass. Aware of the trackers, she paid them little attention, focusing instead on the Mexican troops a mile away. Her only thought now was how to save Antelope Woman and the twenty Chiricahuas and Mescaleros waiting on the opposite side of the ridge.

She lowered the spyglass and squatted next to a thickset warrior with a flat, shovel-like nose and hair of melting silver. His lips barely moved as he spoke. "I told you when we met on the trail ten moons ago that Victorio was well. What I didn't tell you was that he raided the estate of the Governor of Chihuahua, killed his valuable breeding stallions and mares. A big bounty was placed on his head. Those troops out there are from the barracks at Carrizal to take revenge on any Apaches they can find."

Lozen gestured with the spyglass. "The trackers cutting for sign below?"

"The Tarahumara live in wide-mouthed rock shelters deep in the bowels of the *Barranca Del Cobre*. They have little choice but to help the *Nakaiyé,* or be taken into slavery with their families." He picked up a dark pebble, then a lighter one. "Those foot runners can spot a dab of birdshit in a field of black and white stones."

"Three are of no concern. We must stop the *Nakaiyé*."

It was hard to tell where the frown began and the deepset creases left off. "My eyes are still sharp like the hawk, yet I do not see how you and I alone can stop those soldiers."

Lozen tapped the barrel of his rifle. "The legend of He Shoots Eyes From Insects has been told many times around many campfires. It is not time for the stories to end."

"Ahh," answered the marksman, eyes narrowing under gray brows. "And a woman always knows how to pull forth a man's pride." He involuntarily raised his arm. "What do you want me to do?"

"Kill their leaders." Lozen stood and peered through the glass. "There is a Mexican chief shaped like a pear, another thinner one next to him. They are wearing . . ."

"I see only specks. In what position do they ride?"

"There are ten front-guard soldiers. Another carrying a cloth on a pole follows. Behind them, at the head of the column, are your targets. Shoot them both. When they are dead, the soldiers will not know what to do and scatter."

"Your plan is a good one. Maybe they will tell stories of two legends after this time."

"The foot runners?" Lozen asked.

"They'll turn back when the troops flee."

He Shoots Eyes From Insects picked up his rifle, took a handful of dirt and rubbed it over the thirty-four inch octagonal barrel. He was taking no chances that the sun's glint off the metal could catch an enemy's eye. "This here's a Sharps Long-Range Rifle," he said, without looking up. "Got in trade from an old trapper. Only cost me one wife for him to show me how to use it."

He pulled a .45-.70-caliber shell from a pouch and loaded the round into the single breech. Easing down on his stomach, he placed the end of the heavy barrel in a notched "V" between two rocks. He lifted the rear sight and peered through the pinhole-sized peep, adjusting for distance and his slow-moving targets. Looking down the tapered snout of the barrel, he aligned the front and rear sights, then cinched the rifle stock firmly into his shoulder. Drawing a bead on a pinhead figure, he took a deep breath, let it out slowly and squeezed back on the pistol-grip trigger.

The boom of the shot and the bullet hit at the same time, the three-inch round blowing apart the *commandante*'s head like a split pomegranate, spilling blood and brains over gold epaulets. Under the falling figure, the horse bolted, dragging the dead rider whose boot had caught in one of the stirrups. The confused troops stopped dead in their tracks. A second slug exploded the chest of the next officer in line.

He Shoots Eyes From Insects squinted. "I got them, eh?"

At first Lozen didn't answer, her eye transfixed to the spyglass like a staring statue. It was one thing to hear of someone's special power, another to see it. Two men were dead, each from a single shot fired from almost a mile away. The soldiers were turning, galloping away. Three figures with spears ran after them.

"Your legend lives on, my friend," she said, handing the glass back to him.

"And yours. Once again you have saved Apaches."

"Your people and mine are of the same spirit, born from women, from water."

They started down the ridge. "I will tell you a story," said He Shoots Eyes From Insects. "When I was a small boy living with my people in the Sierra Madre, a big race was called, many tribes invited. Our chief sent word to the leader of those foot runners, for he had heard of their swiftness and stamina and wanted to race them." The old warrior spit. "When their headman learned the race was only going to be fifty miles, he sent three women. My chief was offended and our men would not run against them, fearful that they might get beaten, lose face."

"Hah! Men are often cowards when truth fights with pride."

At the bottom of the slope, she said her good-byes, hugging River Child one last time. "Why do you not stay with us?" asked her teary-eyed mother.

"It is time for me to find my brother. Stay with these people. They will watch out for you."

She took a filled water pouch, then set out again. Caked mud from the river and dried blood from the longhorn stained her clothes. Late in the day, she came upon a party of Mexican civilians. Arms outstretched, a woman in a short-sleeved blouse held her dead baby. A bloody rock rested next to the child, another was embedded in its mother's skull. Lozen's face contorted in anguish and her heart dripped with sorrow. "*Usen,* these deaths are mean-spirited and a waste!" she cried.

The stout body of a Gila monster slithered from under the woman, its overlapping scales of shiny pink and black glistening next to the beaded images of birds and fish on her vest. "Men chew on women and children like that big lizard there, hold them in their jaws, poison and kill them," Lozen muttered. "It's not right."

Thirty feet away, two men lay dead in an arroyo, their bodies punctured with bullets and arrows. A fancy black carriage with gold trim was overturned on its side, its contents of baggage strewn over the ground. By their clothing and fine things—silver conchos running down black *pantalones* and gold jewelry, Lozen knew the travelers to be *ricos*, those of noble birth she had seen on prancing horses in México City and Sonora.

You were foolish to travel here, she thought. *Death does not care what rank you hold among your people. It is the same for everyone.*

She turned away. Careful to avoid rattlesnake holes, she threaded her way between towering pitahayas, sword-leafed agaves, sage and greasewood. The underbrush and cactus grew thicker, throwing up an impenetrable fence. She climbed a steep rise, dogtrotted along a hogback, then wound her way down into a ravine, its highest ridge crowned by a faint moon.

A shallow pool with a bed of polished stones welcomed her and she kneeled, cupping her hands to drink. The breeze brushed her skin in whispers, and flowers fell from a calico lantana, the orange and yellow blossoms settling in her tangled black hair. Closing her eyes, she listened to the creek that fed the pool. Her mother's voice seemed to be carried by the water, and Lozen was back in the village of her youth.

"Life exists in circles, daughter-of-mine. The beginning and end go around, meet again, start over. The dwellings in which we live are round, and we put them in circles so we can easily find our way home. An eagle's nest is the same. So is the Sacred Basket filled with life-healing pollen, and the mother's womb from which we are delivered. We build round pits for cooking; flames carry the energy of life." Besh-a-taye looked up into the sky. *"Father Sun lives in a circle, as does Grandfather Moon. I cannot see the shape of Mother Earth, but it must be the same as the others, for they are all connected."*

With her finger, she drew a ring in the air. "Inside each of us is a Sacred Circle. It lives here . . ." she put a closed hand on Lozen's chest, ". . . just above Animal Spirit, within the reaches of your heart. It extends out of your body and head, with a great light spreading into the sky and birds flying to each of the four directions." She pushed a finger into Lozen's navel. "From here a thousand spiritual cords flow down in a stream to the earth. White Painted Woman lives above in the stream, and below her, Child Of The Water."

"Where do the cords go?"

"Ahh. When you are in the Happy Place, filled with love and kindness, they spread as wide as the world itself, touch everyone. When you are afraid and angry, they knot up. Nothing can enter the Sacred Circle of your life forces."

"What happens then?"

"The path of peace trades places with hate and revenge, and you will live a life of illness, sorrow and evil deeds."

"It's not a good trade then," answered the ten-year-old.

Besh-a-taye rumpled her daughter's hair. "For one so young, you see clearly."

Lozen's memory was interrupted by tremors in her legs. When the muscles twitched on the inside, it was a good sign. These were on the outside, and she knew it was a warning. "That which informs one of the bad," Shinash-a-too had taught her.

She opened her eyes to see a shadow lengthening before her. Knife in hand, she leapt to her feet. Twenty paces away, stood Tezye. In arms like knotted wood, he cradled a rifle. Lozen breathed a sigh of relief. "It is good to see you, my friend." He averted her eyes, walking past her to the water.

"The distance and our enemies have separated us too long," Lozen called after him. "I have not seen my brother or my people for many moons."

Kneeling at the edge of the pond, he cupped a handful of water. Instead of drinking, he let it drip back though his fingers. Then, ever so slowly, he turned. "Your brother . . ."

Lozen's face became a mask of denial. "No. No, it cannot be!"

"He was my best friend, smarter than Mangas Coloradas, braver than Cochise, more fierce than Juh. He was Something Big." A tear escaped his eye, cut down a dusty cheek.

263

"Now, he rides the Ghost Pony."

Lozen shook the knife in her fist. "You are mistaken. Victorio lives. Hear me, I still say his name!"

Tezye's sad eyes did not flicker. "He Leaves Dead Enemies Stacked In Hills is gone, *dowaada*. We will speak his name no more, forever."

The knife stilled in her hand, Lozen stood as though she were a statue. Suddenly, her knees buckled and she sank to the sand. The air lay on top of her like a mountain. Anguish welled up in her throat and burst out her eyes. "Aye-yaaa, Aye. Aye-yaaa, Aye," she wailed, her voice rending the stillness. A black spot formed on her heart, and as she keened, became wider and deeper.

When the sun cast irregular shadows over the hills, she cut into her arm, and with the flat blade of the knife, smudged her face with blood. She continued the ceremony, honoring her brother by pointing Tezye's empty rifle to the sky. Cutting her hair, she placed it in a crevice far up the canyon—an appeasement to Victorio's ghost power so it would not persecute her. A prayer followed.

> *East, in your head, listen to me*
> *South, you listen as well*
> *West, North, do the same*
> *Restore my brother as he used to be in the Happy Place*
> *Show him the way on the path of life down below*
> *Let him see light, follow the trails of good hunting*
> *I appeal to you for this*

Tezye was seated by the water, and she turned to him. "Tell me what happened. I want to know everything. I want to know how my brother died."

"First, I will tell you that we had not seen you in a long

time, and thought you were dead. He ordered no one speak your name." He smiled thinly. "Those who escaped *Tres Castillos* will be happy to know Lozen lives. We could have used the Medicine Power of your blue hands there."

"*Tres Castillos?*"

"Three tall peaks in México. We had been raiding all over, owned the trails and hills between Socorro and Silver City far across the border. No settlers, wagons or supplies got through." He touched his nose. "Nana smells ammunition like a wolf catches elk scent, and we attacked the iron horse that smokes from its head, stole many guns and bullets. We made our way back across the Rio Grande to the mountains outside Chihuahua."

He picked up a stone and cast it into the pool, waiting until the ripples ended. "A council was held; we decided the Blue Mountains were safer for the women and children. In the time of the Indian Moon, we began the long journey. General Terraza's one thousand troops followed, but we out-distanced them. Hunger nipped our heels and we needed rest. By the time we reached the three peaks, our scouts had seen no dust cloud for two days. Your brother thought the *Nakaiyé* searched for us elsewhere, that we would be safe on the open meadow between the big sand hills and lake."

Tezye looked up at the fast-fading sky. "The sun was going to sleep as it is now. People drifted in, unsaddled their horses and led them to drink. Women bathed their babies, wood was gathered, cooking fires started."

At the mention of women and babies, Lozen stirred. Anxiety threaded its way between grief and anger. "What of Kinsee, Her Eyes Brown, the children?"

Tezye took the rifle from her lap, stood the stock in the sand. "Kinsee was captured. Her daughter's name cannot be spoken again."

Lozen's heart felt as though it had been pounded on rocks and wrung out to dry. "Agggh." It was a sucked-back gasp more than a cry, and she clutched her face in her hand. Tears formed like salt pools, staining her cheeks and neck. "Aye-yaaa, Aye," she wailed softly.

The sky turned from a ruddy glow into a light twilight. Somewhere in the hills that looked like the hides of old horses, a pack of coyotes yipped.

Tezye continued. "I was on the slopes of *Tres Castillos* when many gunshots rang out. There was lots of yelling and screaming. I ran down the slope with my rifle as others came running up past me. I saw the outline of a soldier against the moon with his long curved knife raised and shot him. He fell from his horse; another filled in where he had been. Moving torches burned across the plain and flashes of gunfire exploded in the darkness."

"Our people being hunted down," Lozen said, her voice breaking.

"We were being eaten away on all sides, yet no one cried out. I ran back up into the hills, hid in a cave. I could hear soldiers talking and laughing above me. Their horses snorted and I knew they smelled me. The riders paid no attention. I waited until dawn and crept from cover. I heard gunshots and yelling. On the top of the hill were your brother and four others, the last to be standing. They were bending their bows, shooting their guns. A hundred of the enemy surrounded them. A Tarahumara shot a warrior next to your brother, who in turn killed that foot runner with an arrow through his neck."

He raised the rifle above his head. "The rest of the warriors fell, but not before they took ten of the enemy with them. Your brother killed six more before they closed in on him. He did not want to be captured, and plunged a knife into his own chest."

266

As if in a trance, Lozen stared at a flock of birds that swept over the water, the reflection doubling their number. Unlike them, or the butterfly that flitted by, her once free spirit was mute and stilted.

"At nightfall the *Nakaiyé* built a big bonfire," Tezye said. "Fifteen young boys were lined up in front of the flames." At his words, Lozen came to life and grabbed his arm. "Little Tachita!"

Tezye's eyes looked like they'd been pummeled by a hundred horses. "The Mexicans made their own line of rifles and shot them down. A fat soldier in charge scalped them. The rest of the dead were brought there. Soldiers grabbed the arms and legs of Apaches and swung them into the fire. Many squaw dresses burned there, many cradleboards. All the elders were killed, for they could not be sold as slaves."

"No one escaped?"

The old warrior shrugged. "Some who were away hunting survived. Your uncle Nana lives, and I saw Kayate riding with him from *Tres Castillos*. I think maybe seventeen from our band got away."

"Only seventeen?"

"The Mexicans took lots of scalps, took prisoners. The next day they were driven like cattle to Chihuahua. Those who could not keep up were shot, even the children." Tezye rose from his cross-legged position. "When I found you here, I was headed for Juh in the Blue Mountains. Come with me now to the Sierra Madres. Some of our people are already on their way to safety there."

As she stood, Lozen's heart plummeted. Coldness crept through her like the rising, ice-blue moon. Her Sacred Circle shattered, and any thoughts of peace that she once had, died with desperation.

CHAPTER TWENTY-FIVE

SHORT TIME TO LIVE

Seated on an oblong rock under a lemon sky, Lozen took council with Nana. "My power has turned against me, uncle, for I was not able to save my brother," she said, head bowed. "I go to sleep at night not wanting to see the dawn, wake in the morning to darkness. The Ghost Face of Winter lives in my dead heart."

From a pouch at his side, Nana took tobacco and filled his pipe. Tall and frail, with a wide nose and gaunt face, his intense determination and strength belied his seventy harvests. Under his small-bowled white hat, long-chained watches dangled from craggy ears—gifts from timeless, dead enemies. His voice took on a sharp edge.

"Hear me, niece. I loved your brother as I do you. Yet self-pity never saved the life of one Apache." He swept his cane at the scene in front of them—children foot-racing, women cooking cattle heads in pits, girls serving food on pieces of bark to warriors who speared the hot meat with their knives.

"Is your name Trembling Squirrel, or Lozen? Our people respect and look up to you. If you must, mourn on the inside. Do not show your sorrow to others, or your dragging face will pull them down."

Lozen stared at the sprawling reaches, the eagles that challenged steep cliffs and dived into cavernous gorges. A line of clouds ran between the sweeps, cutting them in half with a strip of grayish-white gauze. "Apaches always end up downwind of bullets and death. It is impossible to win against so many White Eyes, so many *Nakaiyé.*"

"Listen to me now, I'm going to tell you a story. When I was a young boy, there was a woman who fell backwards into a cooking fire. From that time she was known as She Burnt Her Butt." He tapped his bad leg. "She was hurt badly, and limped as I do. It doesn't mean she never cooked again, or went near the fire."

Lozen shrugged.

Nana took a pull on his pipe, blew out the smoke in curls. "It is better to die a good death, as your brother did, than to surrender to your emotions." He gestured at a rider entering the camp. "Naiche, son of the great Cochise, comes. Geronimo is here with Dahteste, a woman who accompanies him on the warpath. He Hunts At Night, who has strong Jaguar Medicine, takes council with Loco, the fierce one Yanosha, with Juh. Your brother's old friend Crook Neck joined us yesterday with ten warriors. Chihenne, Chiricahua, Nednhi and Mescaleros band together. The impossible just takes a little longer."

"It is good so many come, yet my heart still screams in pain."

Nana touched the tip of his cane to Lozen's chest. "Your battle here is over; it is time for revenge. The dead demand it, the living seek it. War is how we live, weapons our best

269

friends. The *nohwik'edandiihi* does not expect us to trespass on their land again. We need your strong War Power to carry the fight."

A small boy with a dirty face and two fingers stuck in his mouth peered at them from the far corner of the rock, then scampered away. Lozen's eyes followed him to the encampment, where he joined his mother, who was suckling a baby. "We live our lives always on guard, yet freedom is seared into our bones and that of our children. It is worth any price; it is life." She paused, and when she spoke again, her voice was firm. "If only one Apache child breathes, there is hope."

"*That* is what I wanted to hear before I told you of the Mexicans. Crouched And Ready has spotted a small group of soldiers traveling south from Janos. One of them sits in your brother's saddle. If you go west to the Rio Chusvicar, you will cut them off before they reach Chihuahua."

Lozen's head snapped up. "I will take Kayate and ten braves."

Nana nodded with his chin at the strawberry-streaked heavens. "The sun already begins its journey to sleep. The *Nakaiyé* travel slowly. It will be easy to catch them after the moon passes. Tonight a ceremony will be made to honor the great leaders and chiefs. You must come down there."

"As you wish, uncle."

By nightfall, a throng of three hundred ringed a great bonfire. Fed by ocote, the pinewood whose centers contained black, quick-burning sap, the flames leapt high and bright. Four dead Mexican soldiers were dragged forth. The warriors chopped off the fingers and toes and dismembered the limbs. Lozen and the female relatives of slain Apaches took over. Howling and shrieking, they cut off the dead men's privates, spitting and urinating on them. For the final degradation, they roasted the parts, tossing them into the bushes for coyotes.

The people called out the names of chiefs, warriors and medicine men. Each took his turn according to importance; signaling his position, exploits and power. Faces daubed with red, white and black, they danced and chanted to thumping drumbeats around the fire. Some dressed in fringed buckskin shirts and leggings, their long feather bonnets trailing over spinning ankles. Others wore only clouts, bodies half-painted. They paraded and gyrated, casting sinuous shadows over the tops of custard-colored tipis. Children watched their fathers with prideful smiles; sagging elders with quivering voices trilled ancient songs of Apache triumphs.

At his own request, Nana came last. After dancing four times around the circle, he beckoned for Lozen to stand beside him. Dressed in a soft doeskin dress and moccasins inlaid with blue quillwork and purple beads, she walked slowly, humbly taking her place next to him. Standing straight as a ramrod, his eyes flicked to the chiefs, across the gathered horde.

"Lozen's brother, the chief of the *Tchi-hénè*, is gone forever, but his sister carries his blood!" The crowd cheered. Nana's hand slipped into hers and he raised them aloft. "She was his spirit arm and will continue to be ours, to let the Power Of The Blue Hands tell us when the enemy is near. She is courageous as any man, as good a fighter as any warrior here, more cunning than the fox." He affixed two tribute feathers in her hair. "No one deserves to be honored more." The throng responded with the loudest yips and howls of the night.

Lozen!

You are The One! You are The One!

We call your name again and again!

Nana spoke into her ear. "When the rocks stopped falling from the sky, the earth caught them and held them tight. The people do the same for you."

"Thank you, uncle," she said, then walked to where Kayate was seated.

Full of tequila and his own importance, Sergeant Vicente Gustavo Arroyo was a happy man. Underneath his hulking frame was the saddle of the dead chief, Victorio, and hanging from it, scalps from the fifteen Apache boys he'd ordered shot at *Tres Castillos*. Soon, he and his ten men would be back in Chihuahua, the City of Mules, and with the rest of the troops be honored by the governor for their great victory.

Between bulldog jowls covered in a scruffy beard, the sergeant took another swig from his bottle. The liquor ran over his lips and down his chin, dripping inside his uniform, mixing with sweat that ran under heavy folds of skin. With the back of his sleeve, he wiped his drooping black mustache, then looked up at the hoary cliffs where the wind had pumiced the tops into whitewashed stone. *"Compadres,"* he yelled. "There is nothing to fear now; the Apaches are all gone, dead or captured."

"We will get no more saddle sores from chasing those *cabrónes!"* shouted his corporal, taking off his tan cap with the black brim and waving it.

"Andale, amigos!" the sergeant shouted back. He grunted, thinking what his share of the estimated $27,000 for scalp and slave money would bring—a new sombrero, boots of the finest calfskin, a fancy black suit like the *ricos* wore. With a whore on each arm and a Cuban cigar in his mouth, he'd get prime seats for the bullfight where everyone could see him. "Look there," people would say. "It is the great Vicente Arroyo, elevated to the rank of lieu-

tenant for his bravery against the Apaches."

He would stand and sweep his sombrero in front of him, acknowledging the crowd. Instead of the Mariachis playing "Hail to the Matador," the song would be changed to "Hail Our Hero, Arroyo." It would be hard for the spectators to take their eyes from him and focus on the matadors, splendid in their tight suits of maroon and black, with discs of shimmering gold. After the bullfight, the rest of the day would be spent enjoying the carnal pleasures of his two *putas*. If he was well satisfied, he might even pay them.

Then again, maybe he wouldn't wait. There was always the hand-bound Apache girl at the tail of the column. If he and his men didn't mess her up too badly, she'd still be worth good slave money. He smiled wickedly, holding up the quarter-full bottle of tequila. "This first," he said, taking another gulp.

Neither he nor any of his men paid any attention to the "wheeerrrr" of the quail call, or saw the twelve-year-old slip from her burro and run into the rocks where the signal came from. "You did well," Lozen whispered, grabbing up the child and cutting her bonds.

"The *Nakaiyé* killed my mother and brother." Her forehead crinkled over inquisitive eyes, and small fingers touched the warrior woman's face. "You are Lozen?"

An affirmative head nod.

The girl wedged herself into a shadowed crevice. "They killed your brother too."

Crouched And Ready, whose face had the texture of a pebbled toad, thrust a lance in the direction of the canyon floor. "The walls are high; the ground is narrow with many bends."

Lozen's darting black eyes glanced at the back of a disappearing soldier, and she made an outward curving motion with her arm. "Once they have rounded a bend, the last one in line cannot be seen by any of the others. Starting from the back, kill them silently one-by-one and grab up their horses. Leave the one who squats in his own flesh for me."

"It will take many knife strikes to kill that fat pig," said Kayate.

"Short time to live, long time to die," Lozen snarled. The warriors moved through the rocks like dust on an angry wind.

Sergeant Arroyo finished his bottle and heaved it against a rock wall. Too bulky to turn in his saddle, he bellowed over his shoulder. "Corporal Diaz, bring the girl here!" No answer. He reined in his mount. "I order you to bring the *muchachita!*"

Suddenly, he realized there were no plodding hoofbeats behind him, the only sound the booming growl of his own voice. Turning his horse, his eyes took on the look of a man surrounded by rattlers. There were no men. No horses. Uneasiness mushroomed through him and beads of cold sweat broke out across his forehead. He had an intense urge to piss. *"Chingada madre,"* he said in a hoarse whisper.

An arrow struck, lodging deep in his beefy thigh. His body jerked and he yelled, clutching at his leg. Instinctively, he went for his pistol with his other hand. An arrow pierced his forearm; another struck his horse's hindquarters. It shot out from under him, and with a "thunk" he landed on his punctured arm, his weight snapping the arrow, the head carving a crimson wound in his side. He lay there, groaning. Finally, he managed to roll over on his good side. As he got to his knees, a rifle butt knocked him senseless.

He awoke, naked, on his back, arms and legs bound with rawhide strips that stretched him to four wood stakes in the blinding sun. Lifting his head, he tried to see what lay beyond his legs, but the bulging flesh of his belly blocked his sight.

Hacking with thirst, he wasn't sure which hurt more—his gashed and throbbing head, the shafts in his arm and leg or the wound in his side. The drone of blowflies feeding on the dried blood of open wounds filled his ears.

High-topped moccasins appeared by the side of his face. Under blistering eyelids, he squinted at the warrior who bent down next to him. His own scalping knife was held in front of his face, the blade glinting as it turned in the sun. "This *cuchillo* you used to take Apaches' hair," a voice said in Spanish. "Now it is time to smell your own death." He stiffened when the blade went into his nose, yowled like a beaten dog when his nostril was slit open.

Two days and a thousand screams later, Lozen abandoned the body to scavengers.

CHAPTER TWENTY-SIX

LAST CHANCE

Legs extended, Lozen sat by a lake, wiggling her toes in the dew of new grass. Across the water, a herd of elk drifted out of the pines. Thousand-pound bulls with massive antlers mingled with cows half their size, their spindly-legged offspring following them to drink. Hawks flew low, scooping up fish that broke the surface. A squirrel ventured too far from the trees, and a kite, its wings tucked in and swept back, dove for its first meal of the day.

It was good here at Turkey Creek in Arizona, and as Lozen watched, the gray dawn peeled away to a sky of pure blue. With green woods, abundant water and cool air, the country reminded her of her homeland. She picked up a smooth twig, held the ends between her fingers and began massaging her forehead, first from side to side, then in a circle. Eyes closed, she chanted the Morning Song.

Usen
My skin tastes the warmth of the morning sun
Cool blades of grass kiss my feet
Along the bank my footprints sleep in the earth
I am one with the water, animals, birds, trees, plants, rocks
You have answered my humble prayers
My people live in peace
Heartbeats and drumbeats join together in life's spirit

Her thoughts regressed to the past. It had been a long time since Victorio's death, not so long to the clan's surrender. It had been a difficult choice, the Big Chief Crook trying to convince Nana, Loco and Geronimo to stop the raiding and give up. Apache thoughts were divided. Geronimo and Loco were in favor of surrender, as was Cochise's son, Naiche. As many of the warriors, he still had family at San Carlos, and hadn't seen them in as many days as there were nights. Others wanted to stay and fight. While the decision weighed heavily on her own spirit as well, Lozen knew the women, children and elders were "war-worn." Councils were held; the last one in the highlands near Nacori. After two days, they voted to surrender.

They gathered up the people, a mixed clan of four hundred, and rode down from the mountains. Making their way out of the pines, warriors rode prancing horses, hugging naked children close to their chests. Women toted cradleboards, and carried the spoils of plunder in long conical baskets. They traversed over ribbed ranges and wound down steep and narrow paths, the cattle and horses clattering and slipping on loose shale that glittered with flakes of mica. Halfway to the valley floor, the slopes leveled to a gentler gradient, and they camped and rested among oak and cedar, then moved on.

With warriors riding ahead and behind, and flanking both sides, they traveled in a loosely knit wedge, cattle in the center of the formation. The hard-baked soil was soon churned into a whirling dust cloud that had children pawing at their eyes, and their parents spitting out teeth-chipping grit. They passed Sonora, crossed the border, and in a saucer-shaped depression four miles west of San Carlos, surrendered.

Lozen's thoughts focused on only one aspect of that day, and that was the dignity of her people. Not one bowed their head, or averted their eyes from the troopers. The whites could take their weapons, their cattle and horses—never their spirits.

Crook had welcomed them, the gray-bearded general in his funny-looking cork helmet sitting on a gray mule. He assigned another, younger chief by the name of Britton Davis, who would oversee them. He agreed to their requests to be treated fairly, to live their lives by their own customs. Otherwise, his terms were unconditional—they could stay at the desolate San Carlos, or go to the White Mountains and become farmers, not raid or try to escape. The council's decision was made before the next moon, and they were given the tools of their new trade.

Kayate's eyes blazed. He waved his arms, the rosary of his last victim dangling from his wrist. "We are fighters, not farmers," he said, spitting at a plow.

With a heavy heart, Lozen looked at her old friend. Since Her Eyes Brown's death, his face had been drenched in darkness; happiness and hope replaced by the single thought of revenge.

From a wagon bed filled with farm implements, Crouched And Ready held up a horse collar, peering through its center. "The White Eyes' horses carry these around their necks to pull their wagons. The small ponies they left us will run through them."

Lozen grabbed a hoe from the wagon. "Your whining is useless as a starving cow's behind. To survive, we must learn to use these tools, and the help given us."

That was a while back there, Lozen thought. Near the lake's fringes, amber-winged dragonflies skittered about, unaware of the golden-green trout waiting to ambush them. She sighed. Life was not as *Usen* had foreshadowed, yet it was good once again.

Below in the dirt, a bee was on its back, struggling to right itself. "That has been you there," she said to the insect, referring to herself. "Find the Great Spirit's path, and you will discover your wings again." She righted the bee with a stick, and it flew quickly away. She felt renewed, the dark spot on her heart now a faded memory.

The rest of the day was spent idly by the water, chanting and praying. At sunset, when the last flames of sunset turned the sky red, she went back to the village. Around her, the "whoit-whoit" of crimson cardinals rang in the air. Blue grosbeaks on buzzing wings zipped back and forth between aspens and spruce, and purple jays called harsh warnings. Somewhere, a mare whinnied and a stallion shrilled his reply. She passed the fertile fields where the clan had grown squash, corn, pinto beans and watermelon.

She approached the village, the brush dwellings that were built and covered with canvas left from the abandoned tents of soldiers. Overturned wagons provided protection against the wind for cooking fires. Together with a half-dozen dogs, a knot of laughing children scampered to meet her. The aroma of acorn stew and ash bread mingled with ritual burning sage and tobacco. A boisterous crowd was betting on the outcome of "Throw Rocks in a Hole." Each of three contestants took their turns, trying to cast stones into a shallow depression thirty paces away, and gain the twelve points needed to win.

She Cannot See Over Donkeys, a squat woman with a wide smile, was slicing meat from a skinned cow that hung from a tree, and invited Lozen to join in the evening meal. Lozen helped herself to an ear of roasted corn, a bowl of beans, meat and baked squash. Munching on a cookie made from mesquite meal, flour and honey, she patted her stomach. "May you and your family have a good life."

"It is a good place here," replied the woman. "The *Nantan* Davis sees that rations come on time; no soldiers or towns-people bother us. There are few biting insects or snakes, no scorpions or centipedes. We can bathe often to renew our spirits, worship in the ways of our ancestors." She tousled her daughter's ebony hair, and the girl proudly held up her buck-skin doll-baby. The woman continued. "My husband is happy playing hoop and pole, raising cattle, washing up at sweats. My children feel safe and run free, grow strong like the oak."

From the edge of a brush arbor a youngster appeared, struggling to carry a large watermelon. She Cannot See Over Donkeys laughed and called to her son. "You look like a green boulder with legs there." Arms sagging, the boy took two faltering steps, put the melon down and rolled it like a human wheelbarrow.

Lozen could hear drumbeats and chanting coming from Geronimo's dwelling, and knew he was performing a healing ceremony over an ailing elder. Geronimo began to sing, calling upon his Coyote Power to trick his patient's dog sick-ness and steal it away, so that the old one could be restored to health. He followed his chants with a series of coyote-like howls.

The night turned cold and Lozen started for her arbor.

Looking up, she saw the thin smile of a silver moon between two radiant stars. A maiden with a blanket draped over her shoulders brushed by, and Lozen could smell the sweetness of yucca suds in her hair. A young warrior waited by the trees, and the girl hurried to him.

Inside her shelter, Lozen dug through the ashes of a dead fire until she found a live ember buried deep in the pit. Placing a tuft of dry grass on top, she blew softly. A flame flicked out like a lizard's tongue, and she put twigs on top, and when they caught, small branches. The fire burned bright and she added some logs, then slid beneath a horsehair blanket and listened to the crackling wood, the embers falling, the wind whistling through the smoke hole. She could hear the horses outside stomping and snorting in their sleep. In the blue-black sky above, a falling star curved in a silver arc, disappearing swiftly into the earth's darkness.

With two toes on each foot planted forward and two back, a roadrunner stepped around an anthill, methodically searching for the horned toad it knew was somewhere nearby. Suddenly, the toad burst from an earthen hollow and skittered on bowed legs, then turned abruptly to face its attacker. From the pores of its eyelids the toad spewed blood in long, pointed streams, jabbing with stubby horns at the roadrunner. The bird easily dodged the defensive attempt, thrust its shaggy-crested head downwards, and spiked the toad's warty hide with its beak.

As they sat by a telegraph pole, Lozen and Dahteste watched the struggle. Since meeting her in Juh's stronghold, Lozen had been drawn to the wiry, brave and outspoken woman—a warrior with whom she had much in common. The band had fled Turkey Creek, and the two women scouted ahead, waiting for the rest of the Apaches to catch up.

Dahteste nodded at the impaled toad. "That's what we should have done to that coyote half-breed Mickey Free whose shit juts out."

Lozen's mind quickly ran through the events preceding their flight. Free was a half-breed scout, trusted and used by Davis as an interpreter. Free had convinced Davis that a moody warrior named Ka-ya-ten-nae was planning to kill the white *nantan,* and the brave was arrested. Anger and fear swept the village. If Davis believed Free, who would be next to stand trial in San Carlos, and be sent to the far-away prison the whites called Alcatraz? What other untruths lay hidden in ambush? In Geronimo's dwelling, warriors voiced their discontent.

"That one-eyed scout Free is of low birth, speaks lies that spill from his mouth like twisted rope."

"Davis has treated us well. Yet he is green as new grass and puts himself in places he does not belong. He says we have no right to beat our women, that we drink too much."

"When Mexican soldiers came, he let them take our captives, even though the women didn't want to go."

Geronimo spoke last. "The council sent word to our friend Crook about these things, reminding him we had kept our word not to raid or cause trouble. We told him that he had embraced our ways, to let us live by our own customs. Now we want to know what he is going to do about our problems." He threw a hand to the air. "We wait. No answer comes. More bad medicine will follow if we stay here."

Lozen stood and walked a few feet from the telegraph pole, staring at the roadrunner that was gulping down the last remnants of its meal. "The whites are always the same. They backtrack on their promises; steal our lives, hopes and dreams. I have it in for them."

Dahteste put her ear to the ground. "Our people come."

A scout appeared, followed by several boys of fighting age. "Climb to the tops of these poles here," Lozen ordered. "Cut the wires so the White Eyes' words cannot travel." She waited until the boys shimmied up. "Tie the broken ends with buckskin; bind it to the trees where you can to conceal the breaks." By the time they finished, one hundred fifty had come from Turkey Creek. Geronimo urged his horse among the people. "We will go south, back to the Sierra Madre," he ordered.

Kayate rode up next to Lozen. "It was smart to have those message wires cut, gives us more time to escape."

"They will fix them, tell lies about what happened here. Troops will come from Fort Apache, Huachuca, Grant and others. Their Indian scouts will track us, their posses will try and pick us off. Then, the Mexicans will box us in. It is no different than it was before."

"Then we'll kill them all, burn down their dwellings, hang their women and babies by the necks from meat hooks!"

Lozen's answer was a glare that could have turned a basket of sweet fruit sour.

Between the Teres Mountains and Bavispe River in México, the clan took council. They leaned against black lava boulders, sat between ocotillos with thorny whip-like branches, stood next to sword-leafed Spanish bayonets. From the surrounding hillocks, sentries kept watch.

Lozen held up her hand to the buckskin sky. "The sun hangs two fingers above the horizon, travels downwards and backwards, disappears quickly. It is the same with The People."

Geronimo sneered. "It has been more than a harvest since we escaped. The *nohwik'edandiihi* tires of the chase. The Mexicans cannot catch us. The Blue Coats cannot find us.

They will soon let us return to Turkey Creek, to live as we did before."

Lozen stared a bullet right through him. "Your other name, He Who Yawns, serves you well. Were you sleeping when we met with Crook at the Canyon of Tricksters, and after when their scouts came and told us of the Big Chief Miles who replaced him?" She put two fingers to her lips, then snapped her hand away. "Their chiefs are all of one voice, unmoving as mountains. We will not be returned."

"We must surrender, or fight until everyone is lost," added Dahteste. "Each trail we cross has rocks turned on their sides, showing Apaches need help."

A cloud grazed the sun, darkening half the council, then opening them again to sunshine. Lozen gestured at Dahteste. "What she says is true. Our women lie dead on twisting trails, brave boys are shot or hung in isolated canyons. Only six remain from our once-powerful clan." She tapped her skull. "Think, Goyolka. You have only twenty-four left, fourteen of which are women and children."

"The trusted Blue Coat Gatewood will ride with us, promises safe passage," said Naiche. "He says they will send us east, to a place called Florida where we will be reunited with our families. He says Miles is to be trusted."

Nana exploded. "Gatewood? Miles? Safe passage? Like the *Indaa* who betrayed your father and hung his brother? Trusted? Like the betrayal of those who cut off our Big Chief's head!"

In a continuing motion, Geronimo rotated one hand over the other. "Once, many horses, cattle, wives, children and slaves stood me in hand, made me wealthy." He scowled. "Now, I have nothing but my freedom. We must continue to fight."

The hair rose on the back of Lozen's neck like the bristles

of a cornered javelina, and she fastened him with a scathing look. "You are concerned only for yourself. You lead Apaches, but have never suffered like the women and children. Your headstrong ways will kill them, kill us all!" She stepped closer, her voice low and powerful. "Hear me. For the good of those who still live, our fight is over. Raise your rifle again and I will shoot you myself."

"When she runs out of bullets, I'll give her mine," Tezye said. A supportive groan went up from the council members.

Geronimo rubbed his chin. "I have no chance without you guarding my back. You have been fierce fighters and faced the enemy bravely." Taking a shell from his ammunition belt, he placed it in front of him. "If the promises are as the White Eyes say, I will swear to a treaty until the bullet breaks."

Nana tapped the ground with his rifle. "It is better we should die here, than be murdered." He abruptly strode away. Three men joined him. A while later, Lozen followed.

"Come with us," the old chief said. "Your spirit will die in captivity."

Lozen suddenly felt cold and she shuddered. The vision of a wolf, half its leg torn away, yet still struggling to free itself from the iron jaws of the white man's trap, crossed her mind. She shook the memory away, then took her uncle's leather palm and held it, looking into his broad, knotty face. "I know it will be as you say, yet I cannot abandon the women and children." Nana blinked his blessing and mounted his pony.

Kayate came forward, and for a brief moment, his features softened. "You have been a good friend to me since childhood, woman. I will miss you as I miss my wife."

"*Usen* goes with you, my dear friend. Someday, we will all meet in the Happy Place." As Lozen watched them ride away, tears filled her eyes, blurring the vanishing dots that melted into the horizon.

CHAPTER TWENTY-SEVEN

THROW-AWAY PEOPLE

The remaining few trekked north along the San Bernardino Valley, then through the narrow Guadalupes. Just over the border, Geronimo met with Miles in Skeleton Canyon. When he came back, he told of pledged horses, a reservation of their own, good land and farming tools in Florida. Warriors would be reunited with their families. In two years, all would be returned to San Carlos.

"Where do we go now?" Lozen asked.

"The soldiers will take us to Fort Bowie near Douglas."

Lozen's eyes were dull as dirt. "Another fort."

The time passed slowly. There was nothing to do other than eat, sleep and worry about the future. Seven moons later, the prisoners-of-war were loaded onto wagons. Lozen faced Geronimo. "Now where?"

"Gatewood says we are going to another place, the Bowie Station. A train will take us from there." The wagons rumbled forward. En route, two soldiers brought another captive.

"*Yada chindi?*" Lozen asked the elder, whose rawhide face looked like crows' tracks extending in a hundred directions.

He croaked his answer. "The news you ask about is bad. Right after you escaped, all *Tchi-héné* and Chiricahuas were removed from the White Mountains and San Carlos. Miles took away his own scouts' weapons and put everyone together, treacherous Indians and honorable ones. They were taken to Holbrook, sent by train to a place called Florida, never to return."

Whispered exchanges and gestures were accompanied by rapid eye movement. Lozen caught Geronimo's gaze. Their eyes spoke the same thought—*We should never have surrendered.* She felt as though her heart had fallen from a cliff and, with each bump of the wagon, it shattered more. Her mind talked to her. *No matter what side of the fence the whites put us on, it's always the wrong one.*

The wagons rumbled on to the station. Some of the women and children had never seen the white man's iron horse. Thinking it was a monster come to devour them, they shirked back. Its mouth was covered with gleaming black teeth, angry smoke poured from its head and it shrieked like Owl Giant when he swooped down to steal White Painted Woman's children. From its belly, fierce snakes hissed hot breaths on bare Apache legs.

They moved with clay feet, the soldiers pushing and shoving them along the trestle. Dahteste and another woman dropped to their knees and prayed. She Limps, a girl born with one foot shorter than the other, froze where she stood, eyes squeezed shut and small fists clenched. Lozen gently guided her up the steps and into the coach. When the train lurched forward, those not seated were thrown to the floor, or into each other. The train picked up steam. Rocks, mountains, cactus and desert shot by.

Lozen looked at the sorrowful faces of her people. In them, she saw her own dwindling spirit, the one Nana had spoken about. Animals, birds, trees and plants—the lands of Indian ancestors floated away in the curling smoke that rushed by. "Creator, do we ride the train to our deaths, just as the whites gallop away on the horses of broken promises?" she whispered. Only the clacking of speeding wheels on steel rails answered.

Two days passed, and the train came to halt, the nineteen survivors taken off. With the cars behind them, they were positioned on the bank of a river. Lozen sat just above and to the left of Geronimo. A white man with a box on legs stood in front of them, constantly adjusting a black cloth over his head. Behind him, a crowd stared with murder in their eyes. The man clicked something in his hand.

"What is that there?" Lozen asked.

"The white man captures the way we look in that box," explained Geronimo. "When we come out, everyone can see us on a piece of paper. It has happened to me before."

"Before you caused so much trouble, or after?" growled Tezye. They reboarded, the angry shouts of the crowd hurtling through the open windows.

Over the next few days, the landscape changed from brown to green and the air became cooler.

Lozen heard a soldier shout something like, "Misury!" She took She Limps on her lap, pointed out a great and swollen muddy river. To her, all the countrysides were the same now—endless and mysterious, full of unknown ways. Two days died. The climate changed again. Hot, humid air enveloped the car, turning it into a wet oven.

When a soldier yelled, "Florida!" Lozen's heart quickened and she turned to She Limps. "We will be able to bathe now, wash our dirty bodies and clothes." The train stopped and troopers hastened the men off the car. When the girl tried to follow, a tall soldier with a rifle across his chest barred the doorway. "Renegade men only," he said in Spanish.

Lozen stepped up next to She Limps. "One of the warriors is her father, and some of the others have husbands there."

The trooper's face corkscrewed into an evil grin. "They needn't worry about their bucks anymore." He threw a thumb over his shoulder. "They're gonna spend the rest of their days across the bay, at Fort Pickens on Santa Rosa Island."

The fury rose from deep inside her, and Lozen could feel the heat burning her neck and cheeks. "That's not what Miles promised. Families are not to be separated!"

The soldier bared his teeth and his eyes went wide. He swung the butt of his rifle around and rammed her in the pit of her stomach. Doubling over, Lozen hissed, "If I had a knife, I would kill you."

He laughed an ugly laugh and slammed the car door shut. Straightening, Lozen realized Tezye had been taken with the men. Heartbroken, she slumped into one of the seats. Everyone she had ever loved or cared about was gone.

Several more hours of tedium passed. They stopped at a big river, and after being ferried across, boarded another train. No one told them where they were going, or how long it would be.

In the depths of the night, the squealing of brakes woke Lozen's slumber. She looked out into the blackness, felt the train stop. The door was unlocked; bleary-eyed women and children stepped off. Lozen had kept a mental count since they'd left Fort Bowie. It had been nine moons. Three soldiers herded the remaining few along a deserted, cobblestone street. Yellow lights on long poles lit their way. Teeth bared and tails wagging, a pack of snarling dogs accosted them, biting at their legs and nipping at their heels. Lozen kicked one in the ribs and sent the mongrel flying. It turned tail and ran, the rest of the pack following.

"No matter how weary you are, each of you help the others," Lozen said to her lead-footed sisters. "We are in a strange land, but are not strangers to each other. We are still Apaches." She hoisted She Limps and carried her. A teenage girl held a frail woman's elbow, guiding her along.

The cubed shape of an ancient Spanish fortress loomed, and a bright moon lit four diamond-shaped bastions. Encircled with vines, old cannon barrels hung over the edge of a high gun deck, watchtowers peering down on them. Lozen nodded at a moat. "See there, a Sacred Circle of water greets us." She looked up at the massive walls of white coquina, shell rocks cemented by sand and time.

The prisoners trudged over a drawbridge, through massive carved doors and across a long courtyard. Inside the fort's recesses, they were led along a lantern-lit corridor, down a flight of stairs, then pushed into a foul-smelling cell. Women and children collapsed on the wood-slatted platforms that hung from chains embedded in the rock. The metal door banged shut behind them, the sound echoing their fears in the blackness. The air was as heavy and dank as the seeping walls. They could hear waves lapping, and the smell of salt impregnated their senses.

Just after mid-morning, a woman inmate dressed in an ill-fitting calico gown was let into the dungeon. "My name is Blunt-Worded One. I will show you around."

She led them to the roof. Housed upon a connecting square of flat rock channels that surrounded an open plaza below, hundreds of their people were squeezed into an area big enough for a quarter of that many. Surrounding them on three sides was the ocean; above, the relentless sun. Men smoked and gambled dispassionately. Women idly sewed. There was little room to walk, with any open spaces taken up by bodies escaping the tightly-packed sea of tents that acted like human broilers. Saddles, ropes and blankets were scattered about, as were scraps of dried meat and stale bread. The distinctive odor of human waste and sweat permeated the air.

Lozen's disbelieving eyes swept over the suffering. "What is this place?"

"Fort Marion. The village is called Saint Augustine," answered their guide. She pushed a hand through salt-caked hair, ran a finger over skin the color of burnt wood. "The White Eyes tell us the air is fresher outside the fort, but they do not live up here. I was the first to come from Holbrook, have been here many moons." She gestured towards several haphazardly-arranged tents. "There is a place for you at the far end. You are the last ones to come. There are no cots left, only blankets on hard stone. Come."

She walked as if weighted down by the sand that was everywhere, and her eyes were dead as the mullets being scooped up by screeching sea birds. Curled-up forms blocked their path, and they had to pick their way carefully so as not to step on anyone. Children whimpered from under shaking blankets and tortured moans came from all sides. A man on all fours vomited in front of them.

"What is wrong, why are they sick?" Lozen asked.

"It is called malaria . . ." she held up her forefinger, ". . . caused by mosquitoes this big that bite through the government's blankets. Their sting fires the skin, chills the insides." She clasped her hands to her temples. "Here, it feels like knives." Her hands dropped, fingers clutching her belly. "The stomach can't hold food."

"The White Eyes Medicine Man does not come?"

"There is only enough of their 'quinine' for soldiers, little for Indians. Twenty children have died; many are sick."

"You are not ill," Dahteste said.

The woman gestured in an offhanded manner. "*Usen* needs me, so he has spared me."

"We are all dirty, our clothes filthy," Lozen said. Suddenly, she realized how parched she felt.

Blunt-Worded One pointed to an unseen place below. "There are two tubs for five hundred. You have to wait in line all day. Sometimes longer."

Dahteste nodded towards the sea. "There is plenty of water there."

"Soldiers have to take you, so you can't go naked and bathe properly. They make fun of Apache women who wash up in their clothes, laugh and embarrass us." She touched her scalp. "When you go in the ocean, your hair becomes a salt rag; your skin dries like scales of dead fish."

Lozen picked up She Limps. "This one needs *ke'igans*."

"There are no skins here for moccasins." With bony fingers, she pulled playfully on the girl's dirty toes. "When those churchwomen dressed in black and white come, we will ask for shoes. Sometimes we get them, and clothes. Village women come to teach us English. No one here wants to learn."

She shuffled to a stairwell, the others following. They descended from blinding light into near-blackness. Along a narrow rock corridor illuminated by candles, their forms cast eerie shadows along the rough-hewn walls. They came to a room where rectangular windows with wrought iron grates let in streams of light, and the enticing smell of food. Blunt-Worded One answered the quizzical looks on the women's faces. "There are cooking fires outside where we make bread and tortillas. The whites give us plenty to eat, yet there is little fruit or vegetables and their rations taste like they have been swimming with fish."

Lozen grimaced. "We do not eat fish."

They moved on through a short passageway, out onto an open path where four girls were playing with seashells, and into a small courtyard with a well. Two squaws rushed forward and began pulling up the rope, raising the bucket along the fuzzy green-bearded walls. "Do not drink too much. The salt seeps in from the sea and will make you thirsty and sick," cautioned their attendant. Lozen gave She Limps a cupped handful before she took any herself. It smelled of fish.

In the days that followed, Lozen noticed the absence of novice-aged warriors. She questioned a woman who was seated upon a saddle, absentmindedly fingering the tin ornaments that hung from her belt. "The whites have taken my son, all others that have grown to the age of twelve harvests," she answered in a cracking voice. "They put them in a school far away called Carlisle, seek to strip them of Apache ways."

A form rose from behind the saddle. Stringy black hair speckled with grit spilled over hunched shoulders. "The white man takes everything from us," said the warrior, a pained expression on his face. He pulled at his army jacket. "Our clothes come from them. What they give us to eat is unhealthy; we are not used to it. We live in this place, yet nothing belongs to us—not even our children." He slumped back down.

"My husband was once strong and proud, full of manly ways. Now he barely eats, grows thin and sad. I am losing him in the cave of ambushed dreams."

Lozen was aware that with each passing day, she too had less of an appetite. When she moved, her bones ached, and she was constantly harangued by an annoying cough. While brushing her hair one afternoon, she noticed that for the first time it was more gray than black, and felt dry and hard in her hand. At fifty-six, she passed it off to her age.

In spite of her ailments, she formed prayer circles, leading the women in song, hoping to raise their spirits.

> *Warriors*
> *Ride the ocean, escape*
> *Return to the Southwest*
> *When you get there send for us, for your families*
> *We will come swiftly*
> *Ride the waves back to our homeland*

Nothing changed. The circles died and, with them, more Apaches. Days rolled over on top of one another like waves in the sea. The People wore the fort like a suit of armor, weighted down in apathy and depression. The men sang their own song.

> *A long time I have been a warrior*
> *It is over now*
> *I have a hard time with this life*

On a chilly fog-filled morning, Lozen and Dahteste watched two soldiers put a body into a small wooden casket and disappear with it into the enshrining mist. Lozen clutched a pair of nondescript shoes. "She Limps tried to wear these. They raised sores on her toes."

"Aya. It is a sad thing when one so young is no more."

"For a long time I prayed, blew smoke over her, rubbed water over her body. She had no fever, no chills. I could see nothing wrong, yet she became weaker. Last night she whispered in my ear that she missed her mother and father, that she would never see them again." Lozen held the shoes to her chest. "She died of a broken heart."

"Whites understand little about Apaches. They put her in a box where her spirit has no chance to breathe, bury her in the sand," Dahteste lamented.

At day's end, Lozen went to the edge of the roof. Squeezed between a black thunderhead and watery horizon, the sun threw a shaft of fiery flame across a rolling sea, catching the eagle-spread sail of a passing ship and turning it into a reddish-gold. Still holding the shoes, she threw them over the wall. They floated, bobbled on the waves, then sank. Lozen's hopes went with them.

CHAPTER TWENTY-EIGHT

WEEP NO MORE

Mount Vernon Military Barracks, Ninety Miles West of Mobile

My eyes are closed, yet I can see the sparkling sky beads that are Grandfather Moon's children. With no voice, they say, "Go ahead, touch us; we are very close." I reach out with my fingers and the glitter is in my grasp. Then, a black robe wraps around them. My smile and sleep are no more.

In the sweet, cool air of an Alabama morning, Lozen slowly opened her heavy-lidded eyes. Sleep came in tangents now, constantly interrupted by the hacking, painful cough that had gotten worse since Florida. "One of their big war chiefs in Washington has ordered Apaches to a new reservation," Blunt-Worded Woman had told her. "You are the first to go. Other tribes live there as well."

From her bed of pine needles and sand, Lozen picked up a cone and absentmindedly turned it over in her hand, the sharp prickles reminding her of her stinging throat. She stood on wobbly legs and leaned against the orange-brown bark of a pine. Interspersed between the trees, she could see the peaked roofs of sharecroppers' log cabins. High on a sand ridge behind them stood the barracks that housed the Second U.S. Artillery, guardians of the sprawling marshlands and the six tribes who lived there. White families were filtering in to picnic near the barracks at Cider Creek, where they would trade goods with the Indians and purchase their handiwork.

Lozen despised the prying eyes of the fancy-dressed men who stared at bare-breasted maidens, their stupid women giggling and gawking from under floppy bonnets at loin-clad braves. She wanted to choke the children who squawked like frightened chickens, and fed on fat drumsticks in front of starving Indians.

She usually didn't come in this close, preferring the privacy afforded by the deep reaches of the woods. But her condition had driven her to seek the White Eye's medicine. Like the scant rations, there was never enough, and she was turned away. In the time she'd been here, two men and five women had already died from what the whites called "consumption." *The germs of disease and hopelessness make formidable enemies,* she thought.

Darkness ringed her eyes like the mask of a raccoon, and she was pale as the anemic soil underfoot. Her wasted frame had dropped thirty pounds, her bones clearly visible. She could smell her own stench in the Mother-Hubbard dress the whites had given her, felt more dead than alive. If she could only muster the energy to wash up, she knew she'd feel better. Determined to renew her spirit, she dragged herself to the edge of the nearby tidal swamp. On the other side, a freshwater pool lured.

Panting like an afternoon dog, her back against a maple tree, she slid to a sitting position. The ducks foraging on the forest floor paid her no more attention than the lily pads that floated like lime-green spiders. Deeper in, beyond the flowering pink petals of dogwood trees, wild grapes and plums grew about the mosquito-plagued bayous. Had the fruit been placed in front of her, she couldn't have taken a single bite.

A movement caught her eye, and she turned to see a dark brown snake with yellow bands glide by the half-submerged trunk of a cypress, its wide menacing head raised above the water. The cottonmouth disappeared into the rushes, her thoughts going with it. *This is a slow death like that swamp-killer's poison.*

Darkness came early in the tangled woods with its shrouded canopies, and she pushed on, hoping to reach the pool before the light had gone. The trail wound through high grass and pickerelweeds, their stalks topped by heart-shaped purple flowers. She moved with turtle steps, willing her feet to carry her.

The surface of the pool reflected the sunset, but any pleasure she felt at the sight ended abruptly. Driven to all fours by the hacking cough, she retched, spitting up bloody phlegm. Her fingers dug into the ground, tips becoming raw with her pain. Spittle ran down her chin and she wept, praying for the agony to stop, wishing she had a knife to plunge into her chest. Body racked and mind empty, she was unaware of the drizzle that began to fall. Raindrops mingled with teardrops, with sweat. Huddled on the bank, exhaustion forced her to sleep.

When she awoke, the dusky form of a great cat was sitting not ten paces away. It could easily have killed her, but instead spoke through slitted eyes of greenish-gold.

You and I are one. We belong to these forests, the trees that shade us, the water that quenches our thirst. We hunt

*the animals that are our friends, who give up their lives so
we may survive. We hear sounds others cannot, see things
they do not see, smell things of which they know nothing.
We are Spirit Sisters, and I will carry yours wherever I go.*

The panther blinked, turned and was swallowed up into a
blackness as dark as itself.

Lozen sat a long time, and feeling a return of strength em-
bodied by the panther, crawled on hands and knees to the
water. The pond was shaped like a long-necked gourd, and
she slid into its throat, scaring away a darting shoal of small
fish. Although the night was sultry, the water was fresh and
cool, and she ducked under and resurfaced, brushing back
her hair from her face. It had been so long since she was clean,
since she'd tasted the sweetness of water! She ducked under
again and again, each time moving farther away from the
bank.

Suddenly, there was no bottom. Arms flailing, she began
to paddle, feeling with her feet for mud and sand. She had
never felt close to death before, but she did now. She tried to
swim, but her body was a rock and she went under, sinking
into emptiness. The voice in her head was a whimper more
than a prayer. *I do not want to die here, alone in the mud of a
strange place where no one knows my name.*

Then, without even realizing what was happening, she was
pushed upwards. Her head broke the surface and she gasped,
sucking air in short, wheezing breaths. From the back, a
man's strong arms gripped her at the waist, holding her out of
the water. She went limp and he slung her across his broad
shoulder. She hung there—a wet doll with arms dangling on
one side of him, legs on the other. He carried her out of the
water and began walking.

"You are not the smartest one ever born, woman. Alone,

299

far from others, bathing in the dark," he said, the words rumbling in his chest. "You are fortunate I came upon your Apache medicine bag that you left on the bank, or you would be dead now."

The sound of his voice haunted her. Who was he? Who? Threads of memory spun through her head, but she could not catch them, had no strength to try. She began to shiver uncontrollably. With her head facing down she couldn't see the smoke, yet smelled its sweetness, and in the next instant was put down next to a campfire. The flames reflected off a knife blade aimed at her chest, and terrified, she shrank back. Had this man saved her only to kill her?

"Do not be afraid, I will not harm you," he said kindly. "You are cold, and I must cut off your dress." *Better to die,* Lozen thought, hiding her face in her hands from shame. He wrapped her in a warm fur robe and she curled up next to the fire, trying to control her quivering body.

Her rescuer removed his moccasins and hickory shirt, then took a tin cup from his pack, pouring in water and herbs. "I saw your blood signs on the ground. I have seen many suffer in the same way."

"I owe you my life," she rasped, and her words triggered memory, as if one or both had uttered them before.

"Thank the panther. I was hunting her and had to stop when the light went. She and the God *He'-No* led me to you."

He'-No? Not *Usen?* He wasn't Apache, but spoke her language. Lozen coughed convulsively and sat up, holding the robe around her. Who was he? The uneven light of the fire allowed her only shadowed glimpses of a sculpted nose, the tightly braided iron-gray hair that hung past angular cheekbones. "This will make you feel better." He leaned toward her, offering the handle of the steaming cup. She saw the amulet with the two clasped hands of peace, and then, she knew.

300

Her voice, barely audible, skipped with her heart. "Gray Wolf."

"You are like all women. You would rather talk than do as you're told." He put his hands over hers to steady them. "You cannot get well by staring at me. Drink."

She took a sip, then another. The warm, herb-scented liquid helped dissolve the knotted ball in her throat. Finding her voice, she reached out and touched his arm. "Gray Wolf," she whispered.

"How is it you know my name?" He searched her face. Thirty years ago, he would have known her in a crowd of a hundred women. Now, eyes that once sparkled brighter than stars were dead pools, the smiling mouth pinched down with pain. Smooth, robust skin the color of red clay had turned gaunt and pallid, etched with wrinkles. Lustrous, ebony hair that held the glow of moonlight was now white and brittle, a nest of dry twigs.

She reached up, took the amulet, clasped it in the palm of her hand. "You gave me one of these on our last night together. Before you returned to your Senecas, your people."

Gray Wolf straightened. Their eyes locked, his turning from astonishment to a gentle compassion, hers from dark torment to the afterglow of a sunset.

"Is it you? Can it be?"

To her, he was still the same warrior she had loved and never forgotten. She lifted a hand and touched his cheek. "Other than my people, you have been my one and only love." It was a whisper, scarcely more than a falling leaf.

He put his hand on his heart and then placed it over hers. "I have thought of you often and yearned to be with you. You are the blood that runs in the rivers of my heart."

She smiled, blinked a doe's soft blink, coughed and slumped against him. He wrapped her in his arms, cradled her against his chest. She buried herself in the never-forgotten smell of him—wood fires and smoking pipes, salty sweat of the warrior-hunter, the sweetness of a man who had always been hers. They nestled into one another, sitting in silence, watching the lull of the fire. Lozen eased deeper into his chest, and as the dying embers flickered, closed her eyes for the last time.

From the heart of the woods, a panther screamed.

ABOUT THE AUTHOR

A former thirty-year advertising and marketing veteran, Stan Gordon has written and produced award-winning campaigns for radio, television and print. Among his many credits are a series of radio commercials he wrote and produced with the late Rod Serling of "Twilight Zone" fame. Following a short stint as a reporter for *Women's Wear Daily*, Gordon went on to become a staff writer for "Hollywood Squares," and a story analyst for Paramount Studios. He later joined an advertising agency and soon became the creative director, then went on to open his own shop. Today he divides his time between writing and acting as Director of A Lighter Path, an educational adventure program for at-risk youth. An avid outdoorsman and runner, he and his wife Linda live in Tucson, Arizona.